Demon Born
MAGIC

Demon Born
MAGIC

Ella Grey Book Three

JAYNE FAITH

Demon born magic / a novel by Jayne Faith

Paperback Edition ISBN: 978-1-952156-05-2

Andara Publishers

Edited by: Mary Novak
Proofread by: Tia Silverthorne Bach of Indie Books Gone Wild
Cover by: Deranged Doctor Design
Interior Design and Formatting by

www.emtippettsbookdesigns.com

Published in the United States of America

Books by
JAYNE FAITH

Ella Grey Series - *urban fantasy*
Stone Cold Magic
Dark Harvest Magic
Demon Born Magic
Blood Storm Magic

Tara Knightley Series - *urban fantasy*
Oath of Blood (prequel)
Edge of Magic
Echo of Bone
Trace of Fate
more to come

Stone Blood Series - *urban fantasy*
Blood of Stone
Stone Blood Legacy
Rise of the Stone Court
Reign of the Stone Queen
War of the Fae Gods
The Oldest Changeling in Faerie

Sapient Salvation Series - *dystopian sci-fi romance*
The Selection
The Awakening
The Divining
The Claiming

I t had been over a month since I was cut off from my magic. Every morning when I woke up, my power's absence barged into my consciousness. It was like a boulder that came crashing through the roof and landed squarely in the middle of my existence.

It was like my own personal circle of hell. I couldn't work because magical aptitude was a requirement for Demon Patrol officers. According to the department, without my powers I was a hazard to myself, my partner, and the public. I couldn't practice any of the drills my Patrol partner Damien had assigned me. And by far the worst of all, as a powerless normal I couldn't go into the Nevada desert to bust my brother Evan out of the vampire den.

Worrying over Evan was just about the only thing to distract me from the void of powerlessness. The memory of touching magic, but feeling only dead nothing where my magical senses and awareness used to be, was a permanent ache that had settled across my shoulders. It was funny how you took a thing for granted, even hated it a little for being so inferior, but then when it was gone all you could think of was its absence.

I'd used up my sick days and was now whittling away at my vacation time. Once that was gone, I'd have to go on medical leave, but I was determined not to let it get to that point because I was fairly certain I would lose my marbles long before then.

Unable to use my own necromancy while I had no magic, I'd begged Rogan to send his demon pets to Nevada to see what he could find out about the compound where Evan was being held. The former reaper had done me one better by also volunteering to go out there himself and poke around.

Keeping to my exercise routine, I'd risen early for my morning jog, and by the time I got home, Deb was gone for the day. She'd been living with me since she decided to divorce her husband, and her job as a teacher at a school in a neighboring city meant her alarm went off early on weekdays.

I began running through my calisthenics in the middle of my living room while my hellhound-labradoodle Loki watched from the sofa. I had one eye on my phone, hoping for news from Rogan.

I was desperate for a glimpse of my brother, any sign he was still there. I'd been searching for so long, and my worst fear was that he would once again slip through my fingers like a wisp of smoke on the wind.

Rogan had also promised to thoroughly scope the place out and get us some recon, and I appreciated his assumption that he and I would soon be able to go after Evan as originally planned.

But first, I had to get my magic back.

I was so fixated on my phone I nearly jumped out of my skin when the front door unlatched. Spinning around and lowering myself into a defensive crouch, I was greeted with Damien's wry grin and a spark of amusement in his sky-blue eyes.

"Sorry," he said, nudging the door closed with his elbow. "Didn't mean to scare you."

I straightened and shook out my shoulders, trying to look casual. "I wasn't scared. Just working on keeping my reflexes sharp."

He stretched out a hand to pass me one of the two Starbucks cups he held. "Dark roast with cream, no sugar?"

I accepted the cup gratefully, my fingertips still throbbing a little with the biting chill from my run.

"Thanks," I said, and took a sip. "What are you doing up so early?"

He shrugged a shoulder. "Thought I'd stop by and say hi before I head to work."

I narrowed my eyes at him. Since the battle against the horde of Baelmen, he'd been popping by a lot more than usual. I had a feeling it was something he and Deb had arranged. In the fight, I'd pulled too much *in-between* magic and nearly killed myself. After, Damien and Deb had devised a spell that saved me but cut me off from magic. The spell was contained in two charmed rings I wore, and I think Deb and Damien were worried I'd get fed up and yank them off. I appreciated the sentiment, but not the implication that I needed a babysitter.

"So what do you have planned today?" he asked.

I snorted a laugh, seeing straight through his attempt to make sure I wasn't up to anything he'd disapprove of. Like, oh, I don't know—pulling off the damn rings and hightailing it to Nevada after Rogan to get my brother.

"Going to see Jennifer Kane this morning," I said, opting for honesty. Deb would find out anyway, seeing as how she, Jen, and I were in the same coven and news traveled fast among the witches.

"Oh, really?" He cocked his head.

"We're going to talk strange magic," I said. "She's apparently got some skills with spells involving magic beyond the four elemental powers." I couldn't help gripping one of my rings and turning it around my finger.

His eyes flicked down to my hands. He shook his head and drew a breath to argue.

Before he could say anything, I quickly continued, "Don't worry, I'm not going to do anything rash. We're just going to talk about it. You know, discuss theories." I gave a little smile, hoping he'd like my use one of his favorite nerdy words.

I could tell he wasn't quite buying it and still wanted to protest, but he finally nodded.

If Jen had a spell that worked, it would solve one of my problems. The other one being the reaper that had nearly gnawed through my soul. But that was the catch. Damien and Deb feared that putting me back in touch with magic would also reawaken the reaper, and then it would make short work of what was left of me. If the reaper consumed the rest of my soul, it would take over my body and mind, and Ella Grey would cease to exist.

"I guess I'd better get to work," he said, rising from the sofa arm where he'd perched. "Just . . . be careful, Ella."

I saluted and made a little deferential inclination of my head. "Of course."

He left, and I stood staring at the door for a moment.

Careful, my ass. I'd waited around long enough, and I was willing to try just about anything. Damien was incredibly skilled and knowledgeable, but in spite of his extensive studies, he'd been unable to conjure up something that would give me my magic back without killing me. It was time to figure out a solution so I could get on with my life and go after my brother.

I chugged the rest of my coffee and went to get cleaned up so I could head out to Jennifer's.

I felt a sense of kinship with Jennifer Kane because she was undead, and I'd been, well, temporarily dead. As a docile vamp, she could walk in sunlight unharmed and didn't suffer from the raging bloodlust that made wild vampires the creatures of nightmares.

Her front door swung wide as I went up the driveway, stepping through her wards without triggering them. She must have been watching from the window.

"What's up, witchy bitch!" She greeted me with a broad smile lighting up her full-cheeked, heart-shaped face.

I cracked a grin. She was just about the only person I knew who could successfully pull off "bitch" as a term of endearment.

My affinity for Jen probably also sprang from something else we had in common: she was a vampire who could use magic, which was a rarity, and I was a necromancer who could use magic, also an unusual combo. But that was pretty much where our commonalities ended. Beyond the basic four elements, we commanded different types of magic, and we were technically two separate species.

Nobody would ever guess it looking around her little bachelorette house, though. With her balls of yarn piled in the knitting basket next to an easy chair, a couple of Hollywood gossip mags on the coffee table, and orchids on a stand near a sunny window, she seemed as human as anyone I knew. Probably more normal in some ways than I was, come to think of it.

She glanced at the rings on my fingers. "How are you holding up?"

I lifted a shoulder and let it drop. "I'm still here," I said flatly.

Planting one fist on her hip and stroking her chin with the other hand, she scanned me up and down for a moment.

"Yeah. Well, let's get to work." She flipped her fingers at me, indicating I should follow her, and turned toward a short hallway off the living room.

One end of the hall led to her bedroom and bathroom. The other dead-ended at a room that I'd visited before. It held her altar, and it was the place where she'd used her special brand of magic to identify my reaper. At the time, I hadn't known what had followed me back from my brush with the grave.

I was grateful for her help, but recently the scrying mirror she'd used to discover what had attached itself to my soul had fallen into my uncle Jacob Gregori's hands. That meant he knew exactly what I was. I'd been on edge for weeks waiting for him to make a move on that information, but so far he'd remained quiet. I hoped he was too busy fighting the murder and attempted-murder charges Supernatural Crimes was trying to pin on him for sending the Baelmen to kill Lynnette Leblanc's coven. Regardless, I knew eventually he'd circle back to what he'd learned about me from the scrying mirror.

"Alrighty." Jen turned on the overhead lights, dimming them to a bit above candlelight strength, and plopped down on one of the two oversized round cushions on the floor. I took the other one.

She reached for the tablet that rested on top of a stack of books piled next to her and powered on the device.

"So . . ." she said, looking up at me. "Unique magic. Mine isn't quite like yours."

"Well, yeah. Yours is hot pink."

She peered at me more intensely. "Do you know what it means? The neon pink?"

I frowned, tilting my head. "If I had to guess, I'd say it's a mix of fire and . . . something else."

"It's a combination of the four elemental powers plus what the mages call ethereal magic."

My brows lifted. "Ethereal? But only mages can touch ethereal power."

In my mind's eye, I recalled the bursts of white light in the sky during the battle against the Baelmen, when mages had projected themselves here to help. Their pure-white magic had shot up like fireworks and then expanded into huge net-like formations to trap dozens of Baelmen with each sweep. I'd obviously been distracted at the time, but it dawned on me that it was the only time I'd seen mage power in action.

She spread her hands. "I can't command mage levels of it, obviously. I'm still just mid-range on the Magical Aptitude Scale.

But I am able to access it. The odd thing is, I can't pull ethereal magic alone. I can only access it along with the four elements."

An icy little point slid down my spine as my thoughts flicked to Damien. If he knew that a non-mage crafter could pull ethereal power, he'd be extremely interested in understanding the phenomenon. When I'd first met Damien, I'd thought his curiosity about finding ways to boost magical aptitude was mostly academic. It was certainly that for him, but I'd come to realize it drove the majority of his decisions. An interest that tipped into obsession.

"Okay, so we can both access unusual magic," I said. "But it's not even the same type, so I'm not sure what one has to do with the other."

She leaned in and gave me a conspiratorial look. "My experience with mage power was similar to what happened to you."

I turned my head to the side and looked at her out of the corners of my eyes, not sure where she was headed.

"The first time I touched it, after my transition to vampire, it flooded into me in such huge amounts it nearly killed me. I had to figure out how to slow it to a trickle. It was either that or keep myself permanently cut off from magic. Sound familiar?"

My mouth dropped open, and I blinked a couple of times. "You figured out how to control the flow."

"Yep. It's a damned complicated spell, but it worked."

"You know my dilemma, though, right?" I asked. I lifted my hands. "These rings are holding off the reaper, too."

"Yep, and that's where I'm less certain." She held up the tablet. "I've been reading up on reapers."

I'd been doing my own research over the past several days, too. But I wasn't sure how much of the information I found was trustworthy. Truth and lore tended to intermingle when it came to supernatural phenomena and creatures that couldn't be easily studied by the living. Plus, different cultures had vastly different takes on the personification of Death, which also muddied things.

From my own experience, I knew for a fact that Death wasn't just a single entity. There were multiple reapers. I'd begun to think of them as their own class of supernatural beings. In the Hindu tradition, there was one king of death who used several agents. Death's minions were charged with the responsibility of carrying souls into the *beyond*. This rang truest to me, according to what little I knew to be fact about reapers and the *in-between*.

Jennifer talked through her notes on the various regional and religious beliefs about angels of death, and they mostly matched what I'd discovered.

I waited until she was done. "Okay, so where does all of this leave us?"

She shook her head. "We don't know enough. So I think we need to go to the source. What do you say about a little ritual to contact your reaper?"

"Like we did before with the scrying mirror?"

"This will be different. More like rituals to contact spirits of the dead. No mirrors this time. Don't worry. I do this kind of thing a lot. Connecting the living with their dearly departed was one of the supernatural services I provided before I was infected. I used to go the whole nine yards, dressing up as a fortune teller and everything. I think I can do the same kind of thing with your reaper."

I rubbed the back of my neck and looked down at the floor between us for a moment. Something was prickling at the back of my mind. "That makes sense. But I need to ask you something. What's your motivation for helping me with this?"

Her brows drew together. "What do you mean?"

I peered at her, trying to discern whether she was deliberately playing dumb.

"Don't get me wrong, I really appreciate your effort here." I gestured at the tablet. "But why are you so invested in this?"

She let out her throaty laugh. "Suspicious much?" When my expression didn't change, she sobered. "For one, you're my coven sister. We treat each other like family and try to help each other however we can."

I gave her a brief stretch of my lips but waited for her to continue.

"And in that spirit, Lynnette has charged me with the responsibility of trying to resolve your . . . challenges," she said. "For obvious reasons, I was the logical choice. I would have volunteered anyway, though."

So this was all under Lynnette's direction, and Jen would be reporting back to her. I wasn't really surprised, but it didn't mean I was entirely easy with the situation, either. At various times I'd sensed that Jen might be an ally in the coven, but I couldn't be sure. I wasn't going to settle on that assumption without more proof.

I gave her the most direct look I could summon. "You know Lynnette forced me into the coven, right? She used verbal magic. I literally didn't have a choice. Did she coerce you, too?"

"No," Jen said quickly. She licked her lips and shifted her weight on the cushion. "Look. It's no secret that Lynnette isn't all rainbows and sunshine. She's as controversial a witch as you'll find this side of black practices. Using verbal magic on you certainly isn't the approach I would have taken. But it demonstrates that she didn't think she could convince you otherwise, and that's saying something. She can be incredibly persuasive even without the verbal magic."

My ire flared. "So, what, you think I should be *flattered*?"

"No, that's not what I'm saying. She just really, really values what you have to offer. I mean, she wanted you *bad*." She paused for a moment with her lips pressed together. "If she hadn't roped you into the coven, she would have coerced you into doing something else for her. Maybe something that would have been much worse. At least this way you get the benefits of the coven."

I felt my face twist into disbelief, and I barely held myself back from demanding how she could be so unsympathetic. More than once, I'd thought she'd understood my stance against Lynnette and even agreed with it but just didn't want to speak out against the coven leader. Apparently, I'd overestimated Jen.

I blew out a slow breath, trying to calm down. Jennifer wasn't truly the one I was pissed at, and picking a fight with her wasn't in my best interest.

"While you're stuck with us, you can at least let me try to do something to help you. Or is that too much togetherness for you?" she asked with a wry arch of one brow.

"No, please." I inclined my head and made an open-palmed motion for her to continue.

She brought up one knee and leveraged her hand on it, pushing herself up to her feet. "It'll take me just a minute to get set up."

I watched as she gathered a few items from around the room: a round glass tray, a tall pewter candlestick into which she fitted a white candle, and some other smaller things, which she set on the floor in front of me. When she had what she needed, she sat down again and arranged everything. The candle went in the middle of the tray with four crystals spaced around it. From a small ceramic bowl, she took pinches of dried herbs and then sprinkled them around the other items.

She rose again and turned off the overhead light, and I felt the electric breeze of magic prickle across my skin as she drew power. She quickly moved around me in a clockwise circle, chanting under her breath as magenta magic streamed from her finger and formed a circle on the floor. The third time around, the circle expanded to form a half-dome over me, Jen, and the ceremonial items.

It was a relief to be able to sense and see magic, even if it was someone else's. When I'd first awakened with the charmed rings on my fingers, I was so numb from the magical trauma I couldn't sense any magic at all, and it had nearly sent me into full-fledged panic.

When she sat down again, I caught the glow of power in her irises—a curious quirk of a vampire-witch, as I'd never seen another crafter's eyes illuminate this way.

The temperature in the room began to fall. She reached for a small box of matches and struck one. The acrid sulfurous smell of a burning match head wafted between us as she lit the candle.

As I watched her eyes lose focus while she sank deeper into the trance, I thought about the irony of a vampire witch being able to draw the ethereal magic of mages—power considered to be celestial and superior to the more common elemental magics. And yet somehow, when she was drawing her unique mix of power, the chill of the grave filled the room. Before when she'd read my reaper soul in the scrying mirror, she'd warned me beforehand of the cold of her grave magic, as she'd called it. It was a curious, contradictory phenomenon—an undead witch pulling heavenly power to connect with the world of the dead.

"Gaze into the flame. Let it fill up your awareness completely," she intoned. Her voice had taken on a strange timbre. It was pitched lower and reverberated as if there were two Jens speaking in unison.

I fixed my eyes on the small flicker of fire atop the candle and slowed my breathing. The room was growing colder, but the deeper I moved into a meditative state, the less it seemed to bother me.

Jen was speaking at a near-whisper, inviting the reaper into our circle.

"We do not know the name to call you, but we do know you," she said. "We ask you to grace us with your presence and to speak through your host."

Host? That must be me. I had my doubts that this would work because the charmed rings had essentially cut me off from the reaper. I couldn't sense its presence, and it couldn't influence me.

"Are you with us?" she asked. Her gaze sharpened and flitted around the room, as if looking for something in the air.

My lower jaw dropped, opening my mouth as if someone had grasped my chin and yanked it downward. My heart skipped a beat as a moaning sound emitted from my throat. The candle flame swelled and began to flicker like mad.

"I am here."

Each syllable was like the low strike of a giant gong. The words came from my mouth, but my lips didn't move to form them. The voice welled up through me, as if using me as a ventriloquist dummy.

My eyes widened as I stared at Jen across the flame.

"We thank you for joining us," she said, as if this were the most mundane thing in the world. Her voice still held an almost-echo. "If you're willing, we have questions for you."

"I am willing." My teeth vibrated with the low force of the words coming from the reaper. My jaw was forcefully propped open. I couldn't have pulled my top and bottom teeth together if someone put a Strike Team blaster to my temple and demanded it.

"What do we call you?" Jen asked.

"Xaphan."

My heart thumped. My reaper had a name.

"How can we release you from your host Ella Grey so that she may survive and you may return to your own realm?"

"I will not allow myself to be extinguished."

"Are you saying that separating you from your host would kill you?"

"I will not allow myself to be extinguished."

Gee, helpful.

Jen inclined her head in a little nod of concession. "We understand. You must protect yourself. Is there something you desire that we could offer in return for you allowing the preservation of your host's soul and her survival?"

I didn't have much hope of that, even if by some slim chance Xaphan was agreeable. Rogan had said he had no choice when it came to the consumption of his human's soul. He didn't want to take over a human body, but he'd been unable to stop what happened.

"I will not allow myself to be extinguished."

Seriously? Come on, we got that the first time.

There was a pop of pressure against my eardrums, and the candle extinguished and plunged the room into darkness except for Jen's eyes and the faint trace of the magic circle she'd cast around us.

I snapped my jaw closed, and realizing the reaper was no longer using my throat as its personal PA system, I reached up to press at my strained jaw muscles.

Jen huffed a sigh, clearly exasperated, and the pink glow faded from her irises. "Uncooperative little prick," she muttered.

I snorted a laugh.

"But at least we were able to contact him. If we could do it once, we can do it again," she said. She stood and walked around me to open the circle and then flipped on the lights.

I knew she was trying to give me some hope, but I didn't have the patience to sit through a dozen séances trying to coax information from a reaper who obviously wasn't too excited about helping us out. There had to be a faster way.

I pushed slowly to my feet and pulled my hands down my face as she put her things away.

She caught sight of my expression and paused. "Hey, chin up. We'll figure out something."

I made an apathetic sound.

"I'll see you at Lynnette's tonight, right?" She forced a cheery smile.

My apathy transformed into an undisguised groan. Could this day get any more awesome? "Ugh, I forgot about the coven meeting. Yeah, I guess I'll be there."

She walked me to the door, and I trudged out to my pickup. Just as I reached for the rust-dotted metal handle, my phone gave a jangle that pulled me from my thoughts of the coven. A glance at the caller ID indicated it was a call from the Demon Patrol station. Maybe Damien had lost his phone or something.

"Hello?" I answered.

"Officer Grey," came my sergeant's southern drawl. "This is Sergeant Devereux."

Every part of my body seized a little at the sound of his voice. I was pretty sure he wasn't calling to see if he could bring me chicken soup while I was on medical leave. In fact, Sergeant Devereux rarely spoke to me unless it was to deliver bad news.

"Did something happen to Damien?"

"I'm sure Officer Stein is fine. I need you to come to the station. Report to my office by eleven."

"Today?" I asked, confused.

"Yes, Officer. *Today.*"

He hung up.

I stared at my phone for a moment and then dialed Damien as I got into my pickup and started the engine. I was about a half hour away from the station downtown, and it was already ten fifteen. Devereux hadn't given me much of a cushion.

I let it ring, but Damien didn't pick up. I disconnected before his voicemail greeting started to play and tried again. Still no answer.

My reaper was an obstinate crank, my partner wasn't answering, and my boss was demanding that I appear in his office within the hour. An already so-so day was clearly about to take an even shittier turn.

The station was fairly quiet, with most of the Demon Patrol officers out on their beats and the Strike Team personnel either gone on assignments or keeping to their own wing of the facility.

The familiar smell of the place—a mix of stale coffee, sweat, and the sulfurous brimstone of the demon traps—was like coming home. I'd gone straight into the Demon Patrol Academy after high school, and this was the only place of work I'd known since. But today the station didn't feel homey. I was torn between the urge to drag my feet in a vain attempt to avoid whatever awaited me in Devereux's office and the urge to hurry and just get it over with.

The first thing I noticed when I stood in the open doorway of my sergeant's cramped little space was that he wasn't alone. A short-haired woman dressed in slacks, a black turtleneck sweater, and gray pumps sat across from him. It took me a second to place her, and when I did, my stomach dipped. She was high up in Human Resources. A visit from HR never boded well.

"Officer Grey, come in and close the door," Devereux said, flipping his fingers in a little beckoning motion. He pointed at the foldout chair that had obviously been brought in just for me. "Take a seat."

A muscle in my cheek twitched as I looked back and forth between the two of them. The woman gave me a brief, tight stretch of her lips that didn't quite qualify as a smile and then peered at me with a practiced expression of neutrality, which did nothing to put me at ease.

"If this is about my leave, I'd be happy to return to work," I said. I looked at the woman. "Trust me, I'd much rather be working. And my magic really wouldn't be an issue. My partner Damien has enough supernatural power for the both of us."

She and Devereux glanced at each other, and then she turned back to me. "As accounts of the recent events have come in, concerns within the organization have arisen."

I stared at her, trying to discern what she was referring to. "You mean the battle with the Baelmen?"

She folded her hands on the tablet that lay across her thighs. "Yes."

My brows lowered in the start of a frown. "What concerns?"

"Your role in the matter, and the power you used against the creatures."

I set my jaw, steeling myself. "You're going to need to elaborate if you want me to understand what you're saying."

"The magic you used was an unknown type of power, and you used enormous uncontrolled amounts of it," she said in a lecturing tone that made me clench my teeth. "To be blunt, saying that you wielded it would be generous. It was clear that you were not in control of the magic you were using. And in fact, it nearly killed you."

My face twitched. "How do you know any of this?"

Sure, there had been a bazillion people around for the Baelman battle, but I'd somehow thought that from my spot in Lynnette's back yard I'd been hidden. Or maybe that in the chaos my strange magic might have gone undetected.

"I can't discuss those details with you. But multiple agencies were on scene, utilizing many different monitoring technologies," she said, as if that should have been obvious.

She glanced down pointedly at the rings on my index fingers. Then her eyes skirted over to my sergeant. He seemed to take that as a signal that she was tagging out of the conversation.

"We can't have out-of-control crafters on the Patrol. It's as simple as that," Devereux said. "And currently you're completely cut off from your magic, which makes you ineligible for service."

"It's *temporary*," I said. "I'm not going to be cut off forever. In fact, I've already found someone who believes she has a fix."

He looked back at the HR lady, whose name I still couldn't remember.

"We're letting you go, Ms. Grey," she said.

I stared at her, certain I must have heard wrong. "Excuse me?"

"We regret that we have to let you go," she repeated. "Your severance includes a month's salary plus payout of any sick days and vacation you've accrued."

Heat prickled up my neck and face and over my scalp. "You're *firing* me?"

She powered on her tablet and began reading from it.

"Your termination is effective today. Before you leave the station you are required to turn in all service items and uniforms that have been assigned to you, including one service belt, a stun gun . . ." She continued listing things.

My gaze swung to Devereux, and I must have looked murderous because he shifted back in his chair.

"So you're firing me from Patrol for having too much power? Or because I'm cut off from my magic?" I demanded.

He opened his mouth to respond, but she cut in. "Don't answer that, Sergeant."

Then she went back to reading from her stupid script.

Ignoring her, I stood and unhooked my whip from my service belt and then unlatched the belt from my waist. I dropped it on Devereux's desk, and the belt flopped open like a big fish, splaying across the papers, tablets, and other things scattered across the surface. He scrambled to catch his pen cup before it toppled over the edge.

"I'll send my uniforms," I spat.

I wheeled around on my heel, yanked the door open, and stalked down the hallway and out to the parking lot, gripping my coiled whip so tightly my arm shook.

When I got in my truck, I slammed the door shut hard enough to leave my ears ringing. My chest heaved as I sat there staring through the windshield at nothing, so incensed I was nearly blinded by it.

Vengeful thoughts streamed through my mind. I imagined stomping back in there and punching Devereux in the face.

Grabbing the HR lady's tablet and smashing it. Threatening to sue for wrongful termination.

My entire body thrummed with anger. Where did the department get off treating me this way after years of service? I'd *died* for this job. And this was the appreciation I got? In the end I was just an inconvenience because of the power I'd drawn to protect Deb and the others.

Discarded, cut loose because of the *in-between* magic. Because I'd channeled too much of it. I let out a bitter croak of a laugh. Me, whose magical aptitude barely registered on the scale, fired because my power made them uneasy.

I had no education. No other experience. At that moment I didn't even have any magic.

What the *hell* was I going to do now?

I didn't know how long I sat there with my fists wrapped around the steering wheel, steeped in my indignant, angry inner monologue, but when motion in the corner of my eye drew my attention, I snapped out of my thoughts to find Damien standing next to the truck.

I lowered the window.

He stood with his hands braced on the roof of the truck and peered down at me.

"I heard," he said, his sky-blue eyes intent and sincere.

I slouched and looked straight ahead so I wouldn't have to see the sympathy on his face.

"This place always was a fricking bee hive of gossip," I said sourly.

A little ache of loss seeped through my anger, and it just pissed me off more. Demon Patrol was what I did. Frying minor demons wasn't glamorous, but it was satisfying work, and I loved walking my beat. Even when I had to kick through half a foot of slush piled on the sidewalks or when the sun beat down on a hundred-degree day. I couldn't imagine ever chaining myself to a desk or staring at a computer all day. I couldn't picture myself doing anything else at all.

"Hey, at least you've got the coven for support." He managed to say it with no irony.

I tilted my head back and let out a sharp peal of laughter. "Gee, thanks for the reminder."

"It'll be okay, Ella. You'll land on your feet. Maybe this is even a good thing."

I let my hands slide to my lap. "This is all I know how to do."

"That may have been the case a couple of years ago, but you're not the same person you were then. Literally, you're not the same. It might be hard to see it right now, but I think the universe is telling you it's time to level up. You don't need Demon Patrol anymore."

A lump formed in my throat, and for a moment, I couldn't respond. I didn't quite believe that I didn't need Demon Patrol, but it helped a lot to hear him say it.

We hadn't talked about attempting to increase my magical aptitude in a while, but I got the sense that was one of the things he might be insinuating. And speaking of not needing Demon Patrol, if anyone was too powerful for this job, it was Damien. He wouldn't get fired, though. His control of his magic was near perfection. The department didn't have to worry about Damien Stein becoming a loose cannon.

"You'd better get back to your beat," I said, glancing in the rearview mirror. "I don't want to get you in trouble."

He scoffed. "Devereux can kiss my ass," he said loudly.

He almost pulled off the bravado, and I managed a snicker.

"Besides, I've got lunch break in five minutes anyway," he added, completely destroying his rebellious façade.

I reached to start the ignition. "I should probably get out of here before they try to cite me for trespassing."

He straightened. "Okay, we'll talk later."

I nodded, and then for the final time, I pulled out of the spot in the officer parking lot that had been mine for the past several years.

My anger fled abruptly, and I was left with a forlorn, empty feeling. I found myself clinging to Damien's words, even though I'd brushed them off in the moment. Sudden, unexpected gratitude swelled in my chest, adding to the chaos of emotions that were having their way with me. Damien was the last good thing Demon Patrol had done for me. When my old partner Terrence retired, I'd never imagined that anyone could take his place. Damien and I had only known each other a few months, but from the start, he'd jumped to the forefront of my life. Next to Deb, he was the person I relied on the most.

I grumbled and swiped my fingertips under my damp eyes. Fed up with my mushy feelings, I grabbed my phone. I called Johnny Beemer so I wouldn't have to sit in the silence of my thoughts.

Johnny and I had been seeing each other since August. There was an obvious mutual attraction, but lately I'd started to wonder whether the relationship really had any legs.

Lately, it seemed like we'd been arguing more and more. Our fights usually had something to do with a decision of mine that he disapproved of. He seemed to have fallen into a pattern of accusing me of impulsiveness and taking risks that made him nervous. Still, he'd been there for me through more than one tough moment.

He answered on the third ring. "Hey sugar, what's up?"

"I just got fired from Demon Patrol," I said, my voice thick with indignation.

I recounted the whole thing, and he was suitably outraged on my behalf. It made me feel a little better.

As I went into my apartment, I called Deb. It was still the middle of the school day, so I didn't expect her to answer, and she didn't. I left her a long, outraged message.

Realizing I still hadn't heard anything from Rogan, I called him next. He didn't pick up either, so I left him a voicemail.

"Guess what," I said. "I know the name of my reaper. It's Xaphan. Oh also, I just got canned from my job. Call me."

I knocked around my apartment for a while, unable to focus on anything for more than a minute or two. Finally giving up, I changed into sweats and a parka and went out into the back yard to practice with my whip. It was a lot less fun to go through maneuvers without magic to enhance my movements and control, and in some ways it was like learning to use it all over again. But I figured some practice was better than nothing.

Damien and I had created a target dummy out of a thrift-store snowsuit stuffed full of wadded newspaper and plastic soda bottles weighted with water. Brice, as we'd named the dummy, hung suspended from a limb of the maple tree that reached over into my yard. Brice's head was a man's mannequin head secured to the neck of the suit with tacks and a lot of superglue. The dummy's name was courtesy of Damien, and he'd picked it in honor of an old boyfriend who'd dumped him by moving to Paris one weekend and then texting him from overseas to tell Damien it was over.

I took out my frustrations on Brice for the next couple of hours. By the time I was done, sweat dripped down my temples and my right arm ached.

Deb called just as I got out of the shower.

"Ella, I can't believe they did that!" she said vehemently. "Are you okay? Do you want me to come home?"

I knew she'd planned to stay after school and grade papers for a couple of hours.

I wiped condensation off the mirror with the heel of my hand. "Nah, that's all right. I'll see you when you're done at school."

She demanded I tell her again how it went down, so I did. After we hung up, I dressed and went out to grab a sandwich at Blossom's Deli downtown.

I didn't have to be at Lynnette's meeting until later, but I wanted to talk to her alone beforehand. Several of the witches in the coven still didn't know that she'd been opening small interdimensional rips in order to harvest the powerful rip magic around them, and that was what led to the death of one witch and the Baelman horde being sent to kill the rest of them. Even Deb still didn't know about the rips.

I was going to force Lynnette to confess. She might have bound me to the coven against my will, but I had no intention of making life easy for her. And Deb needed to see Lynnette's true colors. My best friend was committed to the coven, but there was too much she didn't know. I couldn't force her to quit, but I sure as hell could help her understand what was really going on.

I didn't have my magic, but I was determined to try to accomplish something. One of those things on my to-do list was to get myself and Deb out of Lynnette's clutches. If I could find the silver bullet to do this, I'd gladly use it, but I suspected it was going to be a process.

No better time than the present to get started on it. I tossed my sandwich wrapper and headed to Lynnette's house.

With no small sense of irony, I realized that my forced membership in Lynnette Leblanc's coven was one of the few things I had to focus on these days. I was still pissed about how she'd manipulated me, but the coven was a distraction from my other troubles.

When I'd first awakened from the battle with Jacob Gregori's horde of Baelmen assassins and realized I couldn't draw magic or feel the reaper soul within me, I'd thought for sure Lynnette would release me from my magically binding agreement. At the time, I'd thought getting kicked out of the coven might actually be the only good outcome of nearly dying after pulling too much magic from the *in-between*.

But Lynnette refused to let me go, even though I was basically dead weight to the coven. None of the witches held it against me. On the contrary, they'd spent the first week after the Baelman attack bringing me casseroles, homemade teas and tinctures, and other gifts. I'd almost sacrificed myself to save them, and they weren't shy about showing their gratitude.

The shower of offerings and teary hugs was more than I could take, though, and I demanded that Lynnette call them off. They didn't quit entirely. They just got sneakier about it. The day before, for instance, I'd opened the front door to get the mail and nearly stumbled over a wicker basket with a six-pack of my favorite locally brewed lager, a box of salted caramels, a bag of organic dog treats for Loki, and a gift card for pizza delivery, all wrapped up in cellophane and tied at the top in a big purple bow.

Most of the women in the group did seem to be good people as Deb had claimed. It was their leader who posed the problem. As much as I wanted out, I had enough sense to see it would be easier to help Deb understand she needed to distance herself from Lynnette if I did it from the inside.

Just as I eased my pickup to a stop in front of Lynnette's modern Victorian two-story, a light dusting of snow began to fall from the overcast sky. It was early December, and winter had firmly set in with daytime temperatures dipping into the thirties.

Soft light glowed invitingly from Lynnette's windows. I stepped onto her property and crossed a series of wards on the way to the front door, but none of them resonated to register my presence—a quirk of the reaper soul I carried. Good. If I could take her by surprise, all the better for me.

I pressed the doorbell with my thumb. I saw movement at a side window, and then the door opened.

Her usually sleek ebony hair was twisted up in a messy bun, but it was the only thing that betrayed she wasn't expecting anyone yet. Her eyes narrowed briefly before she composed her expression.

"Hi, Ella," she said. She stood in the doorway with one hand holding the door close, so her body took up the open space. Not exactly inviting.

"Hello, Lynnette. I need to speak to you before the others arrive."

I moved forward a step, and with some reluctance, she stepped aside so I could go in. She closed the door, turned to me, and crossed her arms. She stayed near the door, leaving several feet between us, as if she expected to let me right back outside.

"I still have preparations for the meeting," she said.

"Okay, I can make this quick. You need to tell the entire coven exactly why Jacob sent the Baelmen after all of you. Tonight. It's time to come clean."

Her mouth flattened into a tense line as she regarded me silently.

"Or?" she asked, drawing the word out a little.

I raised my brows innocently. "What, you don't think honesty among coven sisters is important? What about all that no-secrets-in-a-coven talk I keep hearing?"

Her arms dropped to her sides, and her eyes took on an intensity. At first I thought she was gearing up to argue, but then it hit me. She was pulling magic. I couldn't feel it, though. It was too subtle. I had no idea if she was going to try to slip in some verbal magic or do something more overt.

I curled my fingers into loose fists, my right hand ready to snatch the whip that was attached to my belt loop.

When I saw the index finger of her right hand twitch, the handle of my whip was in my hand, and in the next split second, I'd flicked my wrist and caught her arm in a neat, tight coil. I twisted and yanked, jerking her arm hard. She started grabbing at the end of the whip at the same time, distracting her enough that when I pulled her off balance she fell to one knee to catch herself.

It all happened in a blink. I gazed down at her with a satisfied smile tugging at the corners of my mouth. If somebody took a quick picture right then, it would look as if Lynnette were bowing before me.

She sprang to her feet, red-faced and cursing. She unwound the end of the whip from her arm and threw it at me.

"Don't ever do that again," she hissed through clenched teeth, fury flashing in her eyes.

I rotated my wrist, making the end of the whip dance across the tiles.

"Then don't ever use your magic against me again," I said. I slowly coiled up my whip. "Tonight, you tell the others about the rips you've been opening and how they put you in Jacob Gregori's crosshairs. If you don't do it, I will."

I could have told the witches about it myself, but I feared it would be too easy to brush off, the way Jen and Deb had found ways to dismiss how Lynnette had manipulated me into the coven. I needed to try a different tactic. If I stood up and started slinging accusations, I'd look like the enemy. The women appreciated me, but they were deeply loyal to their leader. They needed to start hearing about the deceptions straight from the horse's mouth.

I snapped my whip back onto my belt loop and gave her a steady, unblinking look. She was still rubbing her arm where the whip had left a reddened band of skin. In the silence, I started to wonder how long our staring contest was going to continue. After a few seconds I realized she was still trying to compose herself. The rage in her eyes surprised even me.

"Get out," she said through clenched teeth.

"Which is it going to be?" I pressed.

"I'll tell them about the rips," she finally said, her face twisting as if the words tasted like spoiled milk.

I nodded once, turned, and let myself out. I wasn't stupid enough to stand around and gloat.

My phone buzzed as I pulled away from Lynnette's. It was Deb. I knew she was worried about how I was taking my loss of employment. She was probably at home, and seeing that I wasn't there, felt the need to check in.

"Ella, that place is just shit for letting you go. Obviously! How are you doing?"

"Still pissed," I said heatedly, fueled by my confrontation with Lynnette, on top of my simmering anger about losing my job.

"Is there anything you can do about it?"

"I guess I could try to fight it, but I really can't afford to," I said.

She huffed a loud sigh. "It's too bad Demon Patrol isn't unionized like teachers are. You'd have someone to go to. Maybe it wouldn't have even happened in the first place."

There was a group of officers pushing to unionize, and we'd actually had a couple of votes in my years on the job, but there was never a big enough majority to get the union going.

"I'm just going to have to figure out something else." I forced my voice to brighten. The last thing I wanted to do was stress her out more. Deb had enough weighing on her mind. "It's an opportunity to pursue something new, right?"

She snorted a laugh, and I knew what she was thinking because I was thinking it too. I didn't say sunny things like that. Not with a straight face, anyway.

"Hey, I'm heading home," I said. "The truck's warmed up, so I'll swing by to get you, and we can stop at the yogurt place before the meeting."

One of Deb's current pregnancy cravings was pomegranate frozen yogurt, so just about every night we went to Cherri Berri to get her some.

"Okay, I'll be ready. See you soon."

Daily fro-yo wasn't really in her budget these days, what with the pending divorce, baby on the way, and her miniscule teacher's salary, but for how happy it made her it was worth it. I hoped her next craving would be something cheaper, maybe along the lines of deep breaths of fresh air or rays of sunshine, because my sudden and untimely exit from Demon Patrol and its regular paycheck certainly wasn't going to help with the financial strain.

"How're you doing *really*?" Deb asked after she settled in the passenger seat with the lap belt tucked below the small swell of her belly.

My jaw muscles clenched as if reflexively resisting any talk about my feelings.

"I really am pissed," I said. "Now I feel even more cut off from everything. Magic. My job. An income."

The ability to gallop away to Nevada and bust Evan out.

Useless. That was how I really felt.

"As soon as the coven charter goes through, you'll have that income, at least," she said. "I mean after we're profitable."

Right. I'd almost forgotten that coven members were required to pool their respective incomes to the group. The money would then be distributed equally between everyone, after operating expenses. But the coven was brand new and likely wouldn't be in the black right away. I had no interest in mooching off the group, anyway. Plus, I intended to make my exit before I got too entrenched in the business dealings of the coven.

We both went silent as I drove through downtown, and the gravity of the situation hung heavy in the air. Deb had moved in with me to save money and so I could help her out. When my severance money ran out, she would be the one supporting me. I couldn't allow that.

"It'll all work out," she said after a while, but she sounded tired.

"It always does." It came out sounding more grim than I intended.

I pulled into the lot of the strip mall that housed Cherri Berri FroYo. Inside, I got a small cup of pom yogurt, too. The older couple who owned the yogurt place greeted us both by name, and they gave Deb's Cherri Club punch card a few extra punches. I didn't usually partake, but it always worked so well to cheer up Deb I figured it was worth a shot. We sat at one of the tables for a few minutes.

"Yummm," Deb crooned around a mouthful. "I just want to live in a swimming pool filled with this stuff. Can we open a shop?"

"Bad idea," I said. "You'd spend the whole day dispensing it straight into your mouth."

She gave me a mock-hurt look. I quickly downed the rest of mine and tossed the cup so I could pull on my gloves. It was too cold out for frozen treats. I had to admit my mood was a little lighter, though. Or maybe I was just anticipating Lynnette's confession to the coven.

I slid Deb a sideways look when we idled at a stoplight. She was a decent person with a good heart. But her allegiance to Lynnette had nearly gotten her killed and the coven charter wasn't even sealed yet. I just really wanted her out of Lynnette's clutches.

At Lynnette's we all piled into the living room, a space with faux leather sofas and heavy velvet drapes. It was the place where we'd carried the limp bodies of the unconscious witches after the first Baelman attack. Then, it had looked like a disaster triage, but Lynnette had put the place back together, and there was no sign of that violent night.

I shivered, remembering the sigils illuminating over my skeletal arms in the *in-between* and the torrent of silver magic that had rushed through me from that realm to this one.

I caught Lynnette's eye, and the coven leader gave me a beatific smile that I didn't like at all. It wasn't the face of a woman who was about to confess something that could possibly do irreparable damage to her reputation. My mood turned darker as I scrutinized her expression.

She raised her hands and spoke over the chatter. "Okay, let's settle. We've got a lot of things to talk about tonight, and I want to get right to the agenda."

The energy and anticipation in her voice caught everyone's attention. I chose a spot at the far end of the room, sitting on the floor where I could watch her as well as everyone else.

"First, I have something unexpected, and really quite . . . remarkable." She blinked rapidly and shook her head as if still trying to process something. She drew out a pause and then spoke in a hushed voice. "We have an anonymous benefactor."

She beamed at us.

"Like some long-lost miser uncle who wants to leave us his fortune?" Jen called out.

"Just about," Lynnette said. She held up a few pieces of paper with typed text on them. "I received this last week, and it took me some time to verify its authenticity. Someone is offering to fund our coven as an angel investor. The only thing they want is to ensure that we get our charter and seal our membership immediately."

She paused, and her eyes found mine. "As long as we can lock in our current membership, our mystery angel will grant us sixty thousand dollars a month for the first six months of our charter. So as long as none of you are planning on jumping ship, we're going to be light years ahead of other new covens."

She swept the room with her gaze as some of the women gasped.

I ground my teeth against the growing pressure in my head.

She was not only locking me in, she'd managed to reveal something that would make it all too easy for the witches to overlook the transgression with the rip magic. I could already picture it. Before the glow of the announcement wore off, she would grow somber and penitent and present her rip magic dabblings as a terrible but innocent mistake on her part.

While the women turned to each other and all began to talk at once, Lynnette gave me a triumphant grin the clearly said: *checkmate.*

Just as I expected, Lynnette didn't wait long before turning serious and making her confession. She managed to look sincerely remorseful, even scared at times. As I watched her, I wondered if she'd practiced in the mirror before the meeting.

"There are many others harvesting rip magic, too, but that's no excuse for the recklessness that brought such terrible consequences," she said, her voice trembling. A tear slid from one eye, and she reached up to delicately wipe it away with one navy-painted nail. "If I'd had any idea how dangerous it would turn out to be, I wouldn't have done it. I'd do anything to take it back."

My eyes flicked from one face to the next while Lynnette continued her tearful speech. I was waiting for at least one of them to circle back to the angel investor. Seriously, not one of them questioned the mysterious money that seemed to have appeared from nowhere?

As I watched their reactions, something hit me like a splash of cold water. These witches were truly under Lynnette's influence. I didn't know if it was her charisma, if she'd used verbal magic on all of them, or both, but there was no doubt in my mind. It wasn't that she'd flat-out brainwashed them cult-leader style. I'd have noticed that kind of change in Deb. No, it was subtler and more insidious.

She'd found ways to use the women's deepest desires to tie them to her. The strings were firmly in place, and Lynnette knew just how and when to tug on them.

Jennifer's words came back to me, and another piece of it slipped into place. She'd said that Lynnette had wanted me, and whatever talents of mine she perceived, very badly. If Amanda's death hadn't opened up a spot in the coven, Lynnette would have found another way to rope me in. To obligate me to her. Jen understood perfectly Lynnette's designs on me and knew that I'd been forced here against my will. Yet she'd seemed oddly at ease with it all. Deb, too, I realized, seeing it with more clarity. I'd chalked up her reaction to the fact that she was so thrilled we were both in the same coven she preferred not to dwell on how it had happened.

I could have tried to snap the women into the reality I was seeing. I could have stood up and bashed Lynnette for going behind their backs and doing something so stupid and dangerous it got one of them killed and nearly wiped out the rest. But I knew it wouldn't be that simple. She was playing a long game with them.

As I sat there, I knew I'd have to do something about Lynnette. I couldn't allow her to continue leading this coven. Not just for my own sake, but for all the women involved. It might take time, but I would find a way to outmaneuver her.

I spent the rest of the meeting observing. Watching the subtle ways Lynnette manipulated the mood and energy of the group. I didn't have the magical aptitude to sense some of her subtler forms of magic, but I suspected that most of the time she didn't have to rely on her powers. The other witches would notice if she were using significant amounts of magic. Maybe at first she had used whispers of verbal magic as she had on me, but these women had been with her for months. She'd already laid the groundwork for her control. Now, it was more a matter of keeping them distracted, fostering their loyalty, and maintaining her dominance.

I might have been the powerless one in the room magic-wise, but I was pretty sure I was the only one who completely saw through Lynnette's bullshit.

With a sort of detached incredulity, I watched her little act play out.

When we finally took a break, she excused herself to the kitchen, and I was hot on her heels. She turned to the fridge and stiffened when she realized I was right behind her.

I gave her a few slow claps.

"Great performance," I said sarcastically. "I'm surprised you can even move your hands, with all those witches wrapped so tightly around your fingers."

She looked off-guard for the tiniest moment and then gave me a cool smile. "Loyalty. It's the foundation of a strong coven."

"I'm not like them," I said. "You may have powered me into this, but I see you for what you are."

She shrugged a shoulder and began pulling out a platter with sliced fruit and cheese on it. "Twelve against one, Ella. Not very good odds."

She set the plate on the counter and peeled back the plastic wrap.

"I don't need odds. I've got the truth in my corner. Once Deb sees it, we'll get the rest to see too."

"Deb is as committed as any of them. It's because I can give her what no one else ever has, including you." She paused and placed her palms wide on the marble countertop. "Stability. Belonging. Family."

My blood pressure spiked.

"We don't need you," I said though clenched teeth.

But I remembered what Deb had said, that this, the coven, was the solution to her problems. This was her plan. Her future.

Lynnette looked past me as someone else came into the kitchen.

"Can I give you a hand?" Elena asked, swinging her long curtain of brown hair back over her shoulder.

"If you could take this platter, it'd be a huge help," Lynnette said. "Ella, could you grab the champagne from the fridge? I'll get the flutes out."

"Champagne!" Jennifer said, poking her head in. "Damn, pre-VAMP2 Jen loved champagne."

Elena gave a voluptuous laugh. "You can still drink some."

"Yeah, but it's just bubbles without the buzz," Jen lamented.

I woodenly moved to the refrigerator and pulled out the two bottles of Veuve Cliquot inside.

If Lynnette had a fricking toast planned, I might lose my shit. She'd just confessed that her greed was indirectly responsible for Amanda's death, and, what, we were going to sit around and sip champagne? If I weren't there to witness it, I would have said it was unbelievable.

By the time the meeting broke up and Deb and I headed out, my head was pounding with the effort of holding it together. She asked me twice in the truck if something was wrong, and I told her I was just still upset about losing my job.

She went to bed not long after we got home, but I was too keyed up to sleep. I went online, trying to dig up anything I could find on Lynnette Leblanc. I knew she'd been in a coven prior to the one she was now leading. I wanted to know why she left. I found the charter number for her old coven, which had become inactive. I had no idea if she got out before the coven dissolved, and I wanted details.

But when I kept hitting dead ends on dirt specifically about Lynnette, I switched gears and started reading about coven law. Apparently you couldn't simply up and decide you wanted out. It wasn't just a matter of handing in your coven card. There was a lengthy process, and you had to prove extenuating circumstances. Dissolving a coven was actually easier to do than to exit as an individual. If the coven wasn't profitable during a period of four consecutive years, the members could vote to dissolve the charter. They could also vote to change the type of organization and lose the charter but still maintain the group as a sort of social club. From what I could gather, social club status was a mark of failure and most failed covens preferred to disband instead.

Four years. Damn.

Even if I was forced to wait it out, that rule wouldn't help me since our mysterious angel benefactor was gracing us with huge loads of cash that all but ensured our profitability from the outset. I rubbed my brow with my fingertips. Who the hell would just do a thing like that, anyway? Had Lynnette used her magic words on someone who had a bunch of money to throw around?

When my phone lit up with a call, I was happy for the distraction. It was Damien.

"Hey, what's up?" I answered.

"I quit Demon Patrol."

I sat up straighter. "What?"

"After my shift ended, I went home. I thought about it for two hours. Then I typed up my resignation letter, printed it out, and took it to the station."

"I . . . don't understand."

"I'm free!" he crowed.

"Free of a regular paycheck?" I said. "Maybe that's okay for you, what with your trust fund and all, but for us normal folk, that's not a good thing."

I couldn't imagine why he was so damn cheerful, and in my current mood, it kind of ticked me off. If he didn't want to work Demon Patrol, he didn't have to wait for me to get canned so he could leave. He had plenty of education and skills to pursue something else. I, on the other hand, was royally screwed.

"No, free to do something more interesting with you," he said, only a bit more subdued. "We're going to start our own firm."

I puffed my cheeks, blowing out a noisy breath. "I honestly don't know what you're talking about. Did you really quit Demon Patrol? Have you been drinking, Damien?"

"I assure you I'm completely sober," he said. "And yes, I quit. C'mon, this will be fun, Ella!"

My mood began to soften. He'd just *quit his job* in an effort to cheer me up. If that wasn't a gesture for the ages, I didn't know what was. Not that it was purely altruistic—he was always playing his own angle—but still, it was a sweet thing to do.

"Okay, explain your plan to me in really simple words, preferably one-syllable ones if possible, because I've had a hell of a day and I'm clearly missing something."

"I was just thinking earlier about how I could pursue more interesting work. Something with more variety. You know, to contribute to my studies and observations."

"Right, your scribblings in your nerd notebook," I said. It was immature, but I was tired and cranky.

"We've got contacts at Supernatural Crimes now," he said, ignoring my little jab. "We could probably wrangle some contract work while we figure out our niche market."

"Back up. Niche market for *what*?"

"Our own supernatural investigation and magical services firm," he said, as if it should have been obvious all along.

"You mean freelance, like Johnny does?"

"Yes, essentially."

"Huh," I said, still trying to process.

"C'mon, what else do you have to do?" he cajoled.

"Oh, I don't know, figure out how to escape Lynnette's clutches, stop a reaper from eating my soul, and get my magic back. You know, just a few little things."

"But you need a job regardless."

I chewed my lip. I honestly couldn't think of what I might contribute to Damien's venture. He was the most powerful crafter I knew. If there was a job he couldn't handle, I couldn't imagine what good I'd be.

But really, what did I have to lose?

"I'm in," I said.

"Dude, we are *not* calling our business Systematic Supernatural Solutions," I said, a little breathless as I jumped out of the way of Damien's staff, which he'd just tried to use to sweep my feet out from under me.

I knew he'd minored in charmed weapons, but I hadn't discovered until recently that he was also pretty damn skilled in the actual use of a variety of traditional weapons. He'd spent his youth earning black belts in a several martial arts disciplines, too. An outlet for his frustrations as the family black sheep, he'd said.

I blocked his staff as he slashed it diagonally at me, and then I quickly whipped mine around and jabbed the end of it forward toward his midsection. I stopped short of actually jamming it into him, but he still contracted in anticipation.

"Good," he said. "Your reflexes are improving."

I set the end of my staff on the floor and planted my other hand on my hip.

"That's a completely unappealing name, plus it sounds like some kind of bio-magic start-up company," I said.

We were at his place, a spacious open-plan residential loft in one of the downtown high rises. I had no idea what the rent was and didn't really want to know. The number would probably make

me puke. I could just about fit my entire apartment in the area
Damien had set up for sparring.

He held his staff across his thighs, his hands loose. He looked
like a giant letter A, as if he were posing as a human compass, the
point-and-pencil kind used to draw arcs and circles in geometry
class.

"Fine, what do you think we should call it?" he challenged.

I shifted my weight back and forth, thinking. "Perfect Circle
Supernatural Services," I said.

He raised his brows. "That's not terrible. We can keep that one
on the table."

"I still don't understand what market niche we're going for,"
I said. "I have no specialties, and you can do just about anything
sub-mage."

"You *do* have specialties," he said.

I leaned my staff against the wall while he went to the kitchen
island, slid open a drawer, and pulled two bottles of water out of
the refrigerated compartment. He tossed me one, and I caught it in
one hand and cracked open the lid.

"Well, yeah, the necromancy," I said. "But I'm like a preschooler
in that department."

"But you can learn." He took a long pull from his bottle. "You
can also reap souls. That's a skill. You can de-haunt places."

I recapped my bottle and shoved my bangs back from my
forehead. "I can't do shit with my magic blocked, though."

"That *is* a problem," he said. "But you could solve that if you
know how to hold back the reaper, right?"

"I think so." I glanced out the floor-to-ceiling windows, catching a glimpse of the pale pink morning sky on the east-most end of the view. "Jen seems to believe she can help me hold back the tsunami of magic from the ley line."

"Okay, so you just have to find a way to make a deal with the reaper," Damien said. "And there's one person who might be able to help."

I nodded. "Rogan."

Aside from a quick text the day before to let me know he was still in Nevada, I hadn't heard much from him. I drew a slow breath. Damien was right. It was time to get Rogan to take me fully into his world. I needed my magic back for too many reasons to count.

"Ready to go again?" Damien asked.

I set my bottle on the counter next to my phone and went to grab my staff. We faced off, both in identical knees-bent positions. Then I straightened and took a step as if to leave the mat.

"Was that my phone?" I said.

When he looked, I lunged and swept my staff around to the backs of his legs, tapping hard enough to make his knees buckle.

He narrowed his eyes at me, and I gave him an evil grin. He wordlessly pushed to his feet. "Oh, it's *on*."

I gave him a villainous cackle.

For the next half hour, I lost myself in the rhythm of our sparring and the sharp clacks of the long wooden dowels hitting together. Then we practiced with pairs of plastic daggers.

When we stopped again, I checked my phone.

"Speak of the devil," I said. "I've got a message from Rogan."

I'll be back in town in a couple of hours. I'm coming straight to your place.

He'd sent the text over an hour ago.

I looked up at Damien. "I've gotta run. He's on his way back."

At home, I went into my bedroom to grab clean clothes. Deb had been sleeping in my bed, and I'd taken the fold-out in the living room. Her clothes were stuffed alongside mine in the closet and piled in plastic crates in one corner. There was space for another dresser, but we hadn't gotten around to second-hand stores to buy one.

In the corner, I noticed some plastic shopping bags. Wondering if they held infant things, I poked one of them. It shifted, revealing something glittery. I leaned down for a closer look and tugged on it. It was some sort of banner.

"Oh, no," I muttered, when I realized what it said.

HAPPY BIRTHDAY!

I rummaged through the other bags. Dollar store party hats, a bag of balloons, and colorful paper plates and napkins. Lots of them.

"Nooo," I moaned, sitting back on my heels.

My birthday was coming up, and it looked like Deb was planning a party. I wasn't a fan of big parties. Even less so of surprise parties.

I shoved everything back in place and grabbed my clothes. I had bigger things to worry about than how my best friend intended to torment me in celebration of my twenty-fifth birthday.

When Rogan arrived, I forgot all about the party supplies. As usual, he wore his duster and just a t-shirt, navy this time, underneath. It was barely above freezing outside, but he seemed oblivious to the cold. I did a double take. One of his cheeks looked like it had skated across the sidewalk.

"What happened to your face?" I blurted as I let him in.

Loki started circling him, sniffing as if Rogan had rolled around in roast beef sandwiches right before he came over. Rogan started to lift his hand to pet my dog but then seemed to think better of it.

"Last night I tried to get onto the compound property through a drainage tunnel." He reached up to touch the scrapes. "I misjudged what would happen if I had to get out quickly and ass-backward. My face took the punishment for my mistake."

I cracked a small grin at his wry explanation. "No one saw you, did they?"

Loki stopped his frantic snuffling, backed off a few feet, and sat. With his pupils pulsing hellfire red, he went stone-still, watching Rogan.

He shook his head. "I made it out in time."

He glanced at Loki and then scanned the room. I watched Rogan look around, and I suddenly remembered it was his first time inside my apartment.

"I'm dying here," I said, making rolling motions with my hands. "What did you find out?"

"Evan is definitely still there," he said. "That's the good news."

"And the bad?"

"There are a lot of vamps there. More than a dozen. And the lead vamp appears stronger than I expected," he said. He planted his hands loosely on his hips and blew out a breath.

A hint of a shiver ran over my scalp and down my spine. My hands curled into fists, and I crossed my arms, tucking my hands under my elbows.

"All rogue vamps are dangerous," he said. "But this one is really strong. He must be one of the older VAMP2 rogues, one of the first created at the Manhattan Rip. Honestly, I'd hoped the vamps would all be weak, and thought maybe I could just bust in there and make off with your brother. They could mess me up, but they can't kill me. I figured I'd heal."

I couldn't help a tiny smile in reaction to his side plan to be the hero. And I wasn't sure I'd ever heard him say so many words at once.

"But then when I caught sight of the head honcho and how many there were total," Rogan continued. "I figured it wasn't the best idea to go in there alone."

"Evan is okay, though?" I asked. "Relatively speaking, I mean."

"He's alive. He's drugged and emaciated but in decent shape all things considered."

My breath seemed to leave me, and I sank down to the cracked leather cushion of the only chair in the room. Propping my elbows on my knees, I held my head for a moment. Evan was alive, and I knew where he was. I had actual confirmation.

I heard the rustle of Rogan's coat as he moved closer.

"Ella?" The concern in his voice was clear.

"Sorry, it's just been a really long road to this moment," I said, finally looking up. "Thank you for doing that. For going clear out there. I owe you."

"I'm sure you'll be able to return the favor someday," he said.

I squinted up at him as a vague unease swept through me like a cold sweep of winter air. The word "favor" triggered the ugly memory of trying to resist as Lynnette forced me to join her coven. But I didn't think Rogan had anything that nefarious in mind. He wasn't a manipulator like Lynnette.

"Why did you do it, anyway?" I asked.

He ran his hand over his short, dark hair, ruffling the already random spikes that seemed to point every which way of their own accord. His hand hooked around the back of his neck, settling there, and his eyes flitted off to the side.

"I'm still hoping you'll be the solution to my . . . problem," he finally said.

"Your   I-want-to-kill-off-this-body-and-return   to-the-*in-between* problem?"

He nodded, looking even more ill at ease. "I think you're going to be the only one who can help me."

"Why?" I asked. "Why me?"

He pulled in his bottom lip, biting down on it for a second. "I was told to look for someone, a person who would be the key to what I want, and you fit the description. You're not exactly what I . . . expected. But I still think you're the one."

"Well, that's fricking morbid." I slapped my hands against my thighs and then stood. For some reason it pissed me off that he was bringing this up. And I hated that he still thought I was going to figure out how to kill him, or somehow help him do it.

"Topic change," I said. "I need to find a way to hold off my reaper. I've got to get these damned rings off my fingers so I can use my magic and rescue Evan. And I think *you're* the solution to *my* problem."

His brows rose the tiniest bit, and I could tell he was interested in the challenge. Or maybe interested in my belief that he was the key to getting my magic back. I was relieved to move on from the topic of Rogan's death—or rebirth to his own world, as he probably saw it—and the pinch of worry in my gut lessened a little.

He stood a little taller and pursed his lips for a moment. "I have a friend we should talk to. A very powerful friend. Are you up for a little trip?"

"My schedule's pretty open these days, so the timing is definitely right." I gave a wry laugh. "Where do we find this almighty contact of yours?"

I noticed Loki still sitting like a big, dark, furry statue and snapped my fingers. He trotted over to me, sat again, and resumed his unblinking observation of Rogan.

"Just north of here, it turns out," he said. "Want to take a trip with me tomorrow?"

Before Rogan finished speaking, the front door swung open. I was expecting Deb, but Johnny Beemer stood in the doorway instead.

He looked back and forth between me and Rogan. I stared wide-eyed at Johnny, off-balance at his sudden appearance and the way he'd just walked right in. Why hadn't he knocked?

"Johnny, I wasn't expecting you," I said. I moved toward him, not really liking the sour turn of his expressive mouth. I took his hand, pulling him into the center of the room. "Rogan, this is Johnny Beemer. Johnny, Rogan."

"Hi." Johnny offered his hand, but I thought I saw his eyes narrow.

Rogan nodded and shook Johnny's hand.

"Did we have plans?" I asked. "I'm sorry if it slipped my mind. It's been a hell of a couple of days."

"I thought you might be able to use a distraction and wanted to take you to dinner," Johnny said. His jaw muscles flexed. "Unless you have other plans?"

I frowned at his implication.

"Sure, dinner sounds good," I said. Actually, it didn't sound all that great. Not unless Johnny's mood chilled out. But anything was better than the awkwardness of standing there with the two of them.

"I'll be in touch." Rogan gave us a nod, strode to the door, and let himself out.

As soon as we were alone, I turned to Johnny, my hands on my hips. "You could have been a little friendlier."

"Whoa, I just met the guy." He lifted his hands and gave me a look of wide-eyed innocence.

Maybe I was overreacting. I shoved my fingers into my hair. "Sorry. You just surprised me, busting in here without any warning."

"Why would you need a warning?" Johnny's voice was mild, but his eyes glinted. "Because you're planning to go somewhere with that guy?"

I folded my arms. So he'd heard what Rogan said and was already jumping to some conclusion.

"Yes, as a matter of fact. He's trying to *help* me."

Johnny made an irritated growl deep in his throat and looked at the ceiling before meeting my eyes again.

"Ella, if you'd just let someone exorcise the reaper in the first place like I suggested, you wouldn't be in this position," he said. "You wouldn't have to rely on someone you don't know. What makes you so sure you can trust him, anyway?"

I threw my hands up in the air as anger surged through me. "We don't even know if it's possible to exorcise a reaper! It might kill me to try it. And as a matter of fact, Rogan is helping me with Evan. Rogan just got back from Nevada, where he confirmed my brother's location. Rogan has never given me a reason to not trust him. I'm not a complete idiot, you know. I'm capable of judging someone's character and intentions."

That really seemed to piss him off.

"You don't seem to see that *I've* been trying to help you all along," he said, not really angry but almost pleading. "But you never listen. You always go off and do whatever impulsive thing pops into your mind. It's only gotten you in deeper trouble."

His tone was softer, and I knew he was trying to make me see his side, but his words just came off like a thinly veiled I-told-you-so. And worse, this felt like a continuation of the same push and pull that had been going on for weeks. Maybe since the start. His disapproval of my choices and the patronizing tone he often took, however well meaning he was, just grated more and more.

I crossed my arms again, giving him a cool stare even as resentment simmered in my veins. "Maybe your help just isn't the type of help I need."

As soon as I said it, I knew I'd gone a little too far. But I didn't entirely regret it.

His eyes widened and then narrowed. "Point taken."

He turned on his heel and marched out the front door, pushing it shut behind him. It closed hard. Not a slam, but with enough force to rattle the front bay window.

I shoved my fingers into my hair and pulled. I turned to Loki, who was cowering around the side of the sofa, peeking at me.

"Why does he have to be so disapproving?" I asked my dog.

He blinked at me and then lay down, resting his head on his paws.

The door opened again, and I just about jumped out of my skin.

"Oh, it's you," I said with a rush of relief when I realized it was Deb.

She gave me an alarmed look. "I saw Johnny drive away. He looked like a walking frowny emoji."

"We just had a fight," I said dully. My adrenaline was starting to fade, and my head felt thick with the threat of a headache.

"Oh, no. How bad?"

"Not bad enough to end it," I said. "But pretty bad. He walked in right as Rogan asked me to take a day trip with him. But it was weird. Johnny just came on in without ringing the bell or anything. It was like he was already primed to be ticked off."

"I missed Rogan?" Deb asked, looking back at the front door as if he might reappear for her benefit. She snapped her fingers. "Damn. He's such a mystery man. Wait, what trip?"

I quickly recounted my conversation with Rogan for her and then gave her the play-by-play of my argument with Johnny.

"Johnny's probably just mad 'cause Rogan's encroaching on the hero role," she said. "Johnny wants to be the hero in your life."

I wrinkled my nose and started to protest but then remembered my internal reaction when Rogan had told me he'd hoped to gallop away from the vampire den with Evan. Maybe there was something to Deb's theory.

"Oh also, Damien and I are starting a company," I said.

She giggled and flopped down on the sofa, her hands automatically moving to rest on her lower belly. "This had to be his idea."

"How'd you know?" I gave her a wry arch of one brow.

"Um, because it would never occur to you," she said.

I laughed. "That was kind of a rhetorical question. But now that I think about it, Damien isn't usually so impulsive."

"What do you mean?"

"He quit Demon Patrol last night. As he told it, he went home after his shift and started thinking about it, and a couple of hours later handed in his notice."

She tilted her head and stared off to the side. "That is a little odd. If he weren't gay, I'd say he has a fixation with you." She focused on me. "Although a fixation doesn't have to be romantic."

"There's no *fixation*," I said, rolling my eyes. "Don't make this weird, Deb. He's a trust fund baby, and he can afford to walk away from a steady paycheck. He was bored with Demon Patrol, and this was an excuse to move on."

She gave a little shrug of one shoulder. "Maybe . . . I guess."

I shook my head, dismissing the doubtful look on her face. "The only thing that really matters right now is that we start bringing in clients," I said.

"Clients? What business are you guys in, exactly?"

"Magical services," I said, waving my hands around to indicate I fully realized how vague that sounded. "He said he wants to get the business off the ground with some Supernatural Crimes contracts."

"You do know people there, but . . ." She looked pointedly at the charmed ring on my left index finger.

I curled my hands into loose fists and folded my arms, tucking my hands under my elbows. "Yeah, exactly. I'm not much use without my magic. Don't worry. I'll get it figured out soon. And in the meantime Damien and I will get things up and running, and with any luck we'll have a contract before the end of the month."

Before my last Demon Patrol paycheck ran out, I hoped.

"Hey, doesn't Johnny contract with SC all the time? Is he going to see you and Damien as competition?" Deb asked.

"Nah, he shouldn't. We'll be offering completely different services, since he doesn't do magic and we don't have his fancy gadgets."

"The services actually might complement each other really nicely," she said. "You might suggest it to him, see if he can help you get some jobs."

I heaved a sigh. "At this point, Damien would probably have a better chance sweet-talking him into that than I would."

She gave me a sly smile. "Aw, come on. Use your feminine wiles."

"So, pushup bra and bat my eyelashes a lot?" I asked sarcastically.

"No, you're way too flat-chested for a pushup bra to be any help. You'll just have to flutter those eyelashes *really* hard," she said, her face perfectly serious.

I picked up a sofa pillow and chucked it at her, and she punched it away with a giggle.

Before I went to bed, I texted Rogan.

Sorry about what happened earlier. Johnny acted like kind of an ass.

A moment later, he responded.

Don't give it a second thought. Still up for a journey north tomorrow? We'll make it back tomorrow night.

It was probably going to piss off Johnny even more, but I certainly wasn't going to let him stop me from going with Rogan.

Yep, I'm game.

I'll come for you at 7. Bring hiking boots and a warm coat.

My pulse bumped in anticipation.

I'll be ready.

When I went out to Rogan's Jeep the next morning, it was still dark enough for the streetlights to be illuminated.

"I think we should bring your dog," he said when I opened the passenger door.

"Loki? Why's that?"

"I think Switchboard will find him interesting."

I shot him a skeptical look out of the corners of my eyes. His face had healed already, leaving no sign of the scrapes he'd sustained when he went through the drainage tunnel at the vampire compound.

He gave a short laugh. "Trust me. Bring the hellhound."

I went back in and put Loki on his leash. Probably expecting a walk, he started wagging so hard his entire backside swayed from side to side. He looked up at me with tongue-out doggy joy as I took him out the front door to the Jeep.

With Loki standing in the back seat poking his head forward between us, we were off. He didn't seem bothered by Rogan this morning, but maybe his excitement about getting out of the apartment was enough to overcome his former caution.

"So where are we headed, exactly?" I asked.

"Not far from McCall," he said, naming a small mountain town situated on a natural glacial lake about a two-hour drive from Boise.

"And this Switchboard guy? Tell me about him."

"He's kind of a strange old coot. Lives alone in a cabin in the woods," he said.

"What kind of name is Switchboard?"

Rogan glanced at me and grinned. "It's kind of a joke, really. He has powers of telepathy. I think it's part of the reason he has to isolate himself. In a populated area it's too overwhelming to be surrounded by thousands of minds."

I watched him as he spoke. He seemed more and more at ease with me as time went on.

"I just hope he has some answers for me," I said. "Or knows someone who will. It's driving me bat-shit crazy to be this way." I held my hands up, looking at the charmed rings on my fingers.

I hated to feel useless almost as much as I hated being obligated to other people.

"Oh, I'm sure he'll have some sort of insight," Rogan said. He eased to a stop at a red light and looked over at me. "It may not be exactly what you want to hear, though, so don't let your expectations run wild. And sometimes he likes to test people, make them jump through some hoops for his amusement."

"Sounds a little sociopathic," I said.

"He's not a bad person, just eccentric."

We were silent for a few minutes as he navigated the morning commute traffic on State Street, heading toward the turnoff for

Highway 55. Loki had abandoned his excited vigil and lay curled up on the backseat.

Realizing that I had Rogan captive for the next couple of hours, I began queuing up questions in my mind.

"You once mentioned that Rogan, the original Rogan I mean, was a mage," I said. "I haven't seen you do mage-level magic, though."

His jaw tightened before he answered. "I don't use high-level magic often. It draws too much attention. I'm wearing someone else's face, and if anyone were to recognize it, there would be questions I couldn't answer. Like why I haven't aged in the past several decades."

"Odds are pretty slim that anyone would recognize you at this point, though, right?"

"Probably," he conceded. "But I'm also cautious with the magic because I have power but very little skill. Only what I was able to glean before I, uh, assumed complete control of this body. Mage-level magic in the hands of a novice is like a revolver in the hands of a child. He might know it's dangerous and have rudimentary understanding of how to use the thing, but he could accidentally kill himself or someone else."

I nodded. "Good analogy."

Something dawned on me, and I shifted in my seat so I could partially face him. "You're the most powerful crafter I know. It just hit me. I always think of Damien, but he's not a mage. Technically, you are. You're also a necromancer. And a reaper."

His eyes shifted to me and then away. "Yes, all of that is true."

"You're a valuable commodity," I said. "Deb explained it to me before. People with rare configurations of powers are sought after. She made it sound like I'd be headhunted or something. That hasn't happened yet, but probably only because my skills are pretty meager and also aren't widely known."

"Another reason to stay under the radar."

"Yeah, but seriously, you're like . . . a really powerful version of *me*." I chewed my lip for a few seconds, trying to wrap my mind around that thought. "Can you channel the ley line magic from the *in-between*, too?"

He shook his head. "That's one area where we're different. How'd that come about, anyway?"

I lifted my hands, looking down at my arms. I was wearing long sleeves, so the faint silvery sigils weren't visible. "I don't know. It's something to do with the markings on my arms. They appeared after I, uh, resurrected."

I winced. *Resurrected*? I didn't intend to sound so self-important, but I still wasn't completely sure how to describe my returned-from-death experience without using words that seemed loaded with drama.

"How did it happen?" he asked. "The first time. How did you start channeling the ley line magic?"

"I brought my arms together in the *in-between*, and the sigils were glowing. I read them, somehow. It was almost like something else took over. Something that understood the language of the sigils. My voice didn't sound like mine." My brows pinched as I recalled how disconnected I'd felt. "You said reapers don't wield magic. So it wasn't my reaper taking control?"

"I wouldn't have thought so," he said, but he sounded hesitant.

"What?" I watched him.

"The name your reaper gave," he said. "I've been thinking about it a lot since you told me. When you said it, I assumed it was a lie, that your reaper was trying to protect himself."

Trepidation crept through me. "What do you mean? Do you—did you—know Xaphan?" I asked.

"Xaphan is kind of a legend among reapers," he said. "He was a fallen angel, cast out of heaven to become one of the first high-ranking demons. But he had a reputation for stirring up chaos, and he pissed off the other fallen angels so much they killed him, supposedly."

My chest felt too tight all of a sudden. "*Demons*? I thought reapers were angels of death."

Rogan took one hand off the wheel, leveled it, and then tilted it from side to side. "Six of one, half dozen of the other."

"What the hell does that mean?" I demanded. "Am I possessed by a reaper or a demon?"

He glanced at me with a bemused expression. "Humans. So bent on labeling and categorizing." He gave a little chuckle.

"I'm serious," I said. "I'm freaking out here, in case you haven't noticed."

"What do you think a demon is?"

I blinked a few times. "I *know* what demons are. They're the things that I used to trap when I was on Patrol."

"That's just the name humans gave the creatures that come through the Rips," he said. "Those winged creatures didn't fly out with nametags on them that read: Hello, I'm a demon. A demon in the old sense, the context I'm talking about, is the same thing as a fallen angel."

I stared out the windshield, my eyes glazed. We'd made it to the highway, but not yet reached the altitude where the high desert turned to mountains and evergreens. It was overcast, and miniscule particles of snow had begun to dust the pavement and further gray out the scenery.

"Okay. So clear this up for me. Are the winged creatures, the ones that come through rips, related at all to angels of death?"

"Yes," he said. "But only in the sense that a housecat is related to a lion of the Serengeti. For the sake of semantics and the preservation of your sanity, let's just stick with 'reaper' or 'angel of death' when we're talking about—you know." He pointed back and forth between us a couple of times.

I felt a little sick. I gave my head a shake, but that only made the reeling sensation worse. "Back to Xaphan. You think my reaper could be the real Xaphan?"

"I'm starting to think it's possible. It would explain your ability to use the magic of the *in-between*. Satan and the other originals have abilities beyond the run-of-the-mill reapers like me."

"I didn't realize there were different categories of reapers. Classes? Levels?" I puffed my cheeks, blowing out a long breath. "I think you'd better start at the beginning. School me on reapers, Rogan. I want to know everything."

"Hmm . . . Well, to start, new reapers rarely come into being. Most of us have existed for a very long time, by your standards."

"Who creates them?" I interrupted before he could really get rolling.

"Like I said, the original fallen angels—Satan and crew—have the power to reap, among other things. But that's not what they wanted to do all day apparently, so they gifted lower demons with the ability to do this work."

"So you started your existence as a lower demon?" I asked.

"Presumably, but I don't remember anything from that time."

"Okay, some demons received reaper powers to do the dirty work for fallen angels, got it," I said. "What else?"

"Well, becoming a reaper means getting permanently housed in the *in-between*, as you call it. Lowly reapers can't move between realms like the angels of death, or like you and I can go from here to the *in-between*. Reapers are stuck in one realm."

"But Xaphan was a fallen angel turned angel of death, so he could move between realms, right? Because he was one of the big alpha angels?"

"Exactly. Now you're getting the distinction."

"I'm not so sure about that, but please go on."

"Reapers, the ones who are worker bees like I was, are solitary creatures. It's almost as if we repel each other. I think it has something to do with distributing us in a way that's most efficient for reaping souls."

"Did you ever keep a soul instead of setting it free?" I asked.

He cocked his head and frowned. "I don't think I'd be able to, even if I wanted to. I don't recall ever having the desire to try."

A shiver trickled over my back. I wasn't entirely sure what to make of that.

"So you just wander around in the gray mist alone for eternity, cutting souls loose every so often?"

He let up on the gas to slow down as the highway began to make tighter curves, snaking through a steep canyon alongside the North Fork of the Payette River.

"I know it sounds strange to a human, but it's what reapers are made to do, and it's the only thing we desire," he said. "In fact, reapers don't really *have* desires."

I peered at him, trying to imagine living that way. Not longing for people or love or money or power or peace, or any of the other things that seemed to drive humans.

"This must be incredibly strange for you, then," I said. "Living in this human world."

He sighed heavily. "You can't even imagine. But remember, I had time to learn while Rogan and I still shared this body, and I've had decades here to adjust since then."

"It all probably seems very messy and busy, and—" I waved a hand around, searching for the right word. "I don't know, emotional."

"Yes," he said. "This is an extremely physical world, as well as a very spiritually tumultuous one. So many longings and struggles."

I sank into my seat a little farther and watched the snow drift down in slow motion. This was some heavy shit.

"I guess that explains why you're not much of a people person," I said.

He gave a short laugh. "What makes you say that?"

"You don't seem interested in creating actual bonds with others. I know there's a practical reason for it, that you're trying to avoid notice, but it goes beyond that. You don't *need* it the way most humans do. I'm sure the few people you interact with pick up on that lack of interest, even if they can't quite put their finger on it."

"I've had relationships," he said. His slight emphasis on the last word suggested he meant the romantic variety.

"You have?" That little revelation bumped me off balance.

He snorted. "Are you really so surprised? I've been in a human body for over half a century."

"I just . . . I don't know, *assumed* that you wouldn't have any interest in that aspect of the human experience," I said, trying not to sound ruffled.

"They were brief, I admit," he said.

My pulse thumped as I contemplated that in silence for a few seconds. Rogan suddenly seemed a whole lot more human, for lack of a better word. There was a heart beating in that chest. A handsome face with watchful eyes. A well-built body that felt the pull of mortal desires. I blinked hard, cutting off that train of thought.

"Back to topic of the passionless lives of reapers." I paused, afraid I already knew the answer to the question I wanted to ask.

"Is there anything, I mean *anything*, that I could offer my reaper in return for not eating the last little nugget of my soul?"

It was hard not to hunch forward and curl around myself whenever I remembered that only a very small amount of my soul remained. The fragility of the situation felt like balancing on the edge of a cliff that fell away into nothing. So naturally I avoided the thought as much as possible.

"Normally, I would say no," Rogan said. "Because as I said, reapers don't really have desires. But if your reaper is indeed Xaphan, it may be different. I don't know for sure."

"There is something my reaper covets," I said. I peered at him closely, watching for any reaction as I spoke. I hadn't really talked about the cloud of souls that appeared in my left hand whenever I reaped. Even though I hadn't created it, and so far had resisted adding to it, I somehow felt ashamed of it. "The few times I've reaped souls, I've had to fight the temptation to add them to Xaphan's collection instead of freeing them."

His hands tightened slightly on the wheel.

"Collection?" he asked. He kept his voice carefully neutral.

"It's a black cloud that appears in my left hand, with tiny lights in it," I said, feeling slightly sick just talking about it. "The lights are trapped souls."

His eyes on the road, he grunted a noncommittal sound.

"Does that give you any better idea about whether this reaper is the real Xaphan?"

He finally glanced at me. "I'd say the possibility is very good."

The snow had started coming down thicker, and Rogan switched on the windshield wipers. The sky was completely overcast, the clouds so dense there wasn't even a faint disc of light to indicate where the sun was. For a few minutes, the rubbery swish of the wiper blades and Loki's soft snoring in the back seat were the only sounds in the Jeep.

The road was empty ahead of us and behind, and we'd passed few vehicles since we'd hit the mountains. I knew the stretch of highway between Boise and McCall well, and we were a few miles from the halfway point. The road curved tightly along the river in this section, at times so close to the edge of the drop-off there was little more than a metal guardrail and a couple of feet of dirt to keep cars from plunging into the river below.

Rogan slowed as we approached a short arched concrete bridge that would take us to the other side of the canyon.

Something moved off to the side of the bridge. A huge, mottled face came into view.

Rogan slammed on the brakes.

"Oh damn, I was afraid of this," he ground out as the back of the Jeep fishtailed.

"What the hell is that?" My voice rose in alarm as I watched the thick, lumpy form of a creature climb up from the river and lumber over to the road, blocking entry to the bridge.

Loki started barking like a maniac.

The creature had rheumy eyes as big as dinner plates, and its legs were like two solid columns of greenish-brown flesh. It lifted a foot, brought it down in a stomp that shook the ground, and then turned its face to the sky and roared.

"Bridge troll," Rogan said grimly, throwing the Jeep into park.

I felt the prickle of magic as Rogan gathered his power.

"Trolls are slow and dim-witted but strong and extremely determined," he said, his words hurried and clipped. "They draw their strength from eating people with magical ability, and they can only be defeated by magical means. Stay here."

He jumped out of the Jeep and slammed the door just as the troll raised his fists and then smashed them down onto the road like a giant angry toddler throwing a tantrum. Spittle flew from his mouth as he hollered again.

Like hell I was going to stay in the car.

I reached for my whip and got out, letting the weapon unfurl onto the snow-dusted asphalt. I rolled my wrist around, warming it up, as I watched Rogan.

My mother had taught me about the dangers of various supernatural creatures when I was young, but damned if I could remember anything about trolls beyond their likely habitats—which obviously included the undersides of bridges—and the fact that they were nearly impossible to kill even with the strongest magic. You could defeat them by sneaking past their post, which was easy if they were sleeping. Or you had to get them to back down. Once they retreated to their hidey-holes, you were safe to pass.

But they were so vanishingly rare, I'd never been totally convinced of their existence.

Rogan had his hands up, and he was moving them in patterns in the air, weaving strands of magic. Power zipped outward, smacking into the troll's nose. He balked as if he'd been punched in the face. He shook his massive shaggy head but stayed on his feet.

The creature took a lumbering step forward and swiped out a hand, trying to grab for Rogan. The troll wouldn't move far from where he stood—his deepest instinct was to block our passage because if we made it onto the bridge we were almost as good as home free and he wouldn't be able to pursue us.

Rogan was being careful to stay clear of the troll's long arms, but pummeling the creature with magic from several yards away didn't seem to be having much effect.

"Get closer," I yelled. I flicked my whip, and it popped loudly. "I'll cover you if he tries that again."

Rogan kept his eyes on the troll. "Get back in the car, Ella!"

"C'mon, I've got you!"

I could feel that Rogan was powering up, reaching for everything he had. He inched forward. I tensed, ready to strike out at the troll's thick arms, and stayed even with Rogan.

The troll didn't seem to be paying any attention to me. Maybe being cut off from my magic kept me off his radar. Normals were usually of little interest to trolls.

"On three," Rogan called. "One, two, three!"

He sprinted forward, and I was right there with him. He planted his feet and hurled magic. The troll started to reach out with one thick arm, but I snapped my whip hard enough to draw a line of dark green blood across the creature's wrist. Rogan launched another face blast at the troll. The creature threw his head back and jammed his fists into his closed eyes and started pitching blindly.

"Back to the Jeep!" Rogan yelled. "We need to get past before his eyes recover!"

I wheeled around to run, but mid-stride something clipped one of my ankles. I went sprawling onto the pavement, scraping up my hands. My whip slipped from my grip as I scrambled to right myself.

I looked up and saw Rogan already at the car. His eyes went huge, and he started racing back toward me just as an enormous hand closed around my legs and yanked me up off the ground.

I dangled upside-down, twisting and clawing at the troll's hide.

I heard Rogan yelling and swearing and felt the troll buffeting under the magical attack, but the creature's grip on me was firm. I had a knife strapped to my ankle, but it was trapped under the troll's fingers.

The giant moved to the side of the bridge, aiming to take me down the bank. Once under the cover of the bridge, he'd eat me.

I pummeled and scratched his fingers, but to no effect. When he turned to back down the steep incline leading to the river below, I swung and the side of my head cracked against concrete.

I groaned into the blinding pain radiating over my skull as blackness crowded into my vision.

No, no, don't pass out.

I wasn't going to win a physical fight against the troll, even if I could get to my knife. The creature was too strong.

Defeat with magic, defeat with magic.

My head pounded with pain and panic.

When the stars cleared from my vision, the troll had me under the bridge. The world swung dizzyingly as he flipped me upright and squeezed me in one big fist. I swung my arms wildly, trying to keep him from clamping them against my body with his other hand.

When one fist grazed his shoulder, he let out a high-pitched screech. My swing had left a smoking track across his skin.

My ring. That had to be what had caused the wound.

His big stinking mouth stretched wide, revealing sharp front teeth and crushing molars the size of my head.

I pulled off one of my charmed rings and hurled it into the smelly maw. It hit the back of his throat and he grunted. His grip loosened and I wiggled free, dropping to the rocky river bank below.

Scrambling up the bank, I threw one last glance over my shoulder and saw the troll with both hands at his throat, eyes bulging, and making strangled noises. The charmed ring wasn't big enough to choke him, but the magic in it must have been doing something in my favor.

A tingling trickle began to pour into me. At first it felt delicious, like warm rays of sun after a long, dark winter. The sigils on my arms began to illuminate so intensely they shone through my sleeves. But the trickle rapidly swelled into a storm. The ley line magic.

"Ella!" Rogan reached down for me.

I tossed my arm up. He caught my hand and wrist and hauled me up over the lip of the bank.

"My ring," I ground out. "I threw one of my rings into the troll's mouth. The magic is flooding in."

I gripped my head as the agonizing pressure began to take over every sense. The ley line magic was going to gut me or make me explode. Either way, I couldn't survive its force.

"Help me!" I don't know if I said the words aloud or only screamed them in my mind.

White light filled my eyes, and then the world dissolved away in a flash of exquisite pain.

When consciousness returned, it was filled by a man's grizzled face looming over me. He had a scraggly beard that looked like a tangle of steel wool and eyes of a blue so light they bordered on gray. A galaxy of stars seemed to swirl in his pupils, and my heart bumped at the sight as I realized what it signified.

This man was a mage.

"She'll live," he said, blowing beef-jerky scented breath over my face.

I pushed slowly up to my elbows to discover I was on a cot in a one-room rustic log cabin. Rogan was hunched under an army blanket near the fireplace. He was half-turned toward me, and the look of relief on his face was evident, but he appeared haggard and exhausted.

"This is Switchboard," Rogan said, his voice hoarse. He tipped his head toward the bearded man, who'd moved to the potbellied stove where he sipped something from a steaming tin cup and regarded me with his pale eyes. "He saved your life."

I wanted to stand, but I was already shaking with the effort of holding up my own head. My temples throbbed, and my entire body ached as if I'd spent the day inside a rock tumbler. Even my skin hurt.

"Pleased to meet you, Switchboard. I'm indebted to you," I said. "How did you do it?"

Switchboard jerked his thumb toward Rogan. "He did mosta the work. Blocked off the magic himself, holding it all the way here."

My eyes lingered on Rogan again. No wonder he looked so awful. Magical exhaustion.

Thank you, I mouthed.

He lowered his eyelids and nodded once.

"I managed to tie off what he did," Switchboard continued. "But if you lose *that* ring, you're up shit creek, young lady."

I rubbed my thumb over the charm on my right index finger. Switchboard looked like a caricature of an Old West gold prospector. Not at all like my mental image of a mage. Not that I'd ever been in the presence of one, but every so often a mage appeared in news footage. They were usually polished and stately looking. Dignified.

"So which one of us is going to fish the other ring out of a pile of troll crap?" I asked Rogan lightly.

A smile cracked through his exhaustion.

There was a scratching noise and a yip at the door, and Switchboard went to open it. Loki trotted in. Seeing me awake, he bounded over and started bathing my face with his smelly tongue.

"Glad to see you too, boy," I said, petting his head and at the same time trying to fend off his slobbery affection.

I sat up and turned so I was sitting with my back against the wall, and that small movement just about did me in. I closed my eyes briefly and let my full weight sag against the support of the rough-cut logs.

"Drink this, you'll feel better." Switchboard held out a second dented tin mug. When I brought it to my face and inhaled the aroma of strong coffee, my head seemed to clear.

He moved away to perch on a stool that was basically just a two-foot-high cut chunk of log. Loki went to lie on the dirty, faded rag rug spread in front of the fireplace. He curled up and rested his head on his paws, his eyes trained on me.

"Atriul tells me he wants ta be called Rogan now," Switch said, propping one fist on the top of his thigh. "Says you're the only other person he's found walking around with a reaper in this world."

I nodded. "Lucky me, I died and came back, and now I've got a reaper. It's trying to take over, and I need to stop it."

There was no reason to keep anything secret from Switch. I was desperate to reclaim my magic, so I had no reason to hold anything back. Besides, if he was really a telepath, he could probably see inside my head, anyway.

He barked a rough laugh. "Doesn't quite work that way, young lady. I can only see the thoughts you leave open for me to see."

"Oh," I said sheepishly.

I held up my right hand and wiggled my fingers. "Mostly I was hoping you'd be able to tell me how to get rid of this thing and start crafting again. You know, without either the magic or the reaper killing me immediately." I gave him a droll look.

He let out another grunt of a laugh. "Tall order."

I waited for more.

"I suggest you go see the dragon," Switchboard finally said.

I started to glance at Rogan in question, but then a memory jolted through me. The huge creature that had loomed behind Lynnette during one of the coven rituals. At the time, I had assumed it was a giant demon. My mouth went dry.

"I think he already paid me a visit," I said. "Scales, hellfire eyes, leaking rip magic? And he called me by name."

Switch's bushy brows shot up. "Well, now, look at you. You're a step ahead."

"What is he, exactly?" I asked.

"He's an oracle. He likes to think he's *the* oracle," Switchboard said with a snort.

"He can tell me what to do about the reaper?"

"Eh, maybe. If he feels like it. Gotta bring three for backup. Two darks and a light."

I looked at Rogan for a translation.

"The dragon is indeed an oracle," he said, hitching the blanket higher around his shoulders. "You ask the oracle a question, but it can't be any old question."

"Nope, gotta be something from the heart," Switch chimed in. "Don't screw it up, or you'll get fire-roasted like rabbits on a spit."

I looked at Rogan in alarm.

He brushed a hand through the air. "It's only happened a few times, and they deserved it. Don't worry, you'll be fine."

I didn't feel terribly reassured.

"The bigger worry is getting in. An audience with the oracle isn't guaranteed," Rogan continued. "For some reason he likes it when you bring three others with you, and this ups your odds of his cooperation. Two people who are death-touched, and one who isn't. Some people say the dark-light thing is symbolic, that even though you may be death-touched, there's a part of you that remains light. Or, at least it *should*."

"You've paid a visit to the oracle, I take it?" I asked.

"Decades ago, yes." He peered at me, his eyes seeming to glow in the firelight. "I didn't know the dragon had already sought you out. That's . . . unusual. Normally Switch here has to go and make an offering before the dragon will even acknowledge a person."

"Oracle must be curious about you, young lady," Switch said. He almost seemed a little insulted, as if I'd somehow undercut his authority because I hadn't required his intervention. "That means you ain't gettin' out of a visit to him."

This was all interesting in its own way, but I didn't really have time for dancing through a bunch of ceremony.

I turned to Switchboard. "I don't mean to sound ungrateful for what you've already done for me, but Rogan seemed to believe that you'd know how I could—"

"Get yer magic back and turn off the reaper," Switch cut in. "Yeah, yeah, I know you're eager, girlie. *Everybody* knows you're chomping at the bit." He spread his arms wide, his coffee sloshing, as if to indicate a room full of people.

I bit back a smart-ass response, trying to keep my edginess from spiraling out of control.

I took a quiet breath before opening my mouth. "I'm impatient, I know that. I apologize." I clamped my teeth together, fighting the urge to plead my case.

Switch wagged a finger at me. "And that's going to get you killed, if you're not careful."

"Is there anything else I can do, or someone else I should talk to?" I asked with as much humility as I could possibly muster.

"Dragon," Switch said shortly.

He stood and went over to the kitchen area. From a few feet away, he tossed his tin cup into the sink, where it rattled against other dishes and flatware already piled there. He shambled to the pegs near the door and reached for a worn knee-length leather coat lined with sheepskin.

"I expect you to be gone by the time I get back," he said. He grabbed the shotgun leaning against the wall and opened the door but then turned to me as if remembering something. "Bring your hellhound mongrel along with your crew. The dragon'll like him."

He disappeared outside as a billow of winter air swept into the cabin.

I turned to Rogan, my brows lifted. We both laughed at the same time.

He shook his head. "I know. He's a lot to deal with."

"Did he heal you?" I asked. "Are you okay to leave?"

The color had returned to Rogan's face, but fatigue was still settled deep in his eyes.

"Yeah," he said, but I wasn't completely convinced.

He pushed the blanket off his shoulders, wincing as if it hurt to move. He must have been in very bad shape to still look so pained after a mage's healing.

I steeled myself, scooted to the edge of the cot, and dropped my feet to the floor. My head swam. I gripped my hands into fists, waiting for the swaying sensation to clear.

Rogan moved to my side and offered his hand. I took it and hauled with all my strength to try to get myself up onto my shaky legs. Still unsteady himself, I nearly pulled him over. He found his balance and caught me around the back with his free hand, pulling me against him to get me upright.

Suddenly I was practically nose-to-nose with him, our chests pressed together and his arm around my waist. For one crazy moment, it almost felt as if we were slow dancing to some unheard tune. His gaze seared into mine, sending my pulse jolting.

I turned my face to the side, focusing on Loki who stood expectantly near the door.

"Thanks," I said. I shifted back, opening some space between me and Rogan. "Look at us. A couple of invalids."

I could still feel his eyes trained on me. He let go of me slowly, his hand trailing around my back and side before dropping away. Last, he released my other hand.

I wasn't sure if his lingering gaze and touch actually meant something, or if I was imagining things. Either way, I wasn't looking for anything to happen between us and hadn't sent any inviting signals. Things were rocky with Johnny, but that didn't mean I was going to do him wrong.

"I'm good to drive," he said. "But we're going to have to hike to the Jeep. Are you up for it?"

I nodded and called to Loki, unnecessarily, but it was an excuse to avoid the intensity in Rogan's eyes.

The three of us went out into the dingy winter cold. I had no idea where we were. Aside from Switchboard's cabin, there was no other sign of humanity within sight. It was too gloomy to see much beyond the immediate grouping of tall evergreens surrounding the cabin. Not pitch black yet, but if the sun wasn't down yet, it would be soon.

Rogan took the lead, aiming us to a barely-visible path through the trees. He turned on his phone's camera flash, using it to light our way. We passed a very old pickup truck with cinderblocks where the wheels should have been. I was grateful to find the ground was level. I didn't think my legs could handle any inclines yet. It took all of my focus to stay on my feet, and it seemed Rogan was absorbed in his own trek, too.

When we finally reached the Jeep, I turned to him. "You hauled me all that way while you were holding some kind of magical barrier together to keep me from frying?"

Not only that, but he had to have already been fairly drained from slinging magic at the troll.

He shrugged modestly, and I just kept staring at him.

"Let's just say it's a good thing someone like Switch was waiting for us at the end of the path," he said. "Otherwise we'd both be in trouble."

I shook my head in awe, and he got in the driver's seat.

I let Loki in the back. I retrieved my phone from the foot well below the passenger seat and then got in. With my arms clamped to my sides, I tried in vain to stop my shivering. I was feeling something similar to magical exhaustion, though it was obviously not due to crafting. Maybe Switchboard had rigged my new charm to draw energy from my own vitality, the life force that even non-crafters emit. Rogan started the car and then reached behind him and dragged a thick wool blanket into the front.

"I keep this in here for emergencies," he said, pushing it toward me. "Sorry it's a little grimy."

I settled part of the blanket over my lap and reached to spread the other end across his. He started to protest, but I pushed his hands away.

"I've never seen you react to the cold, except back there," I said. "You're still drained. I don't want you going into shock."

I checked my phone, but there was no service so I turned it off to preserve the little bit of juice left in the battery. Once we were back on the highway, I powered it up. It pinged repeatedly as text messages piled in.

Most of them were from Damien, with a couple from Deb. One from Johnny was an apology, ending with, *Can we meet up tonight when you get back?*

I paused but then scrolled on without replying.

The last text from Damien caught my eye. It started with three shocked-face emojis.

We have our first prospective client, but it has to be a joke. Claims he's Phillip Zarella.

I called Damien.

"How did he contact you? How did he even know we're hanging out our shingle? What did he say exactly?" I fired off questions as soon as he picked up, bypassing any pleasantries.

"Hello to you, too," Damien said. He sucked in a breath and paused dramatically. "I'd just started setting up a website and barely had an email account established when the message came through. It said, 'I have a job for you. P Zarella.'"

Well, that was a little anticlimactic.

"You really think it could be him?" Damien asked.

"Did you put my name on the website or associate my name with the business in any way?"

"Well, yeah," he said. "Both our names are on the website."

"It's him."

There was a moment of silence. "We're going to say no . . . right? I mean, with his history as a murderous psychopath and all, we couldn't possibly take him as a client."

I bit back a grin. Damien was dying to find out more. So was I.

"We should at least ask him what the job is," I said. I adopted an airy tone. "For the sake of professional courtesy and whatnot."

"Right, right," Damien said. "Professional courtesy. Because we're professionals, and professionals should always be courteous."

I snorted a laugh. "Seriously, he wants *us* for a reason. I have no intention of helping him, but I do want to know what the hell he's up to."

Even as I said the words, I felt a tiny cold pebble of uncertainty rattle through me. It wasn't that I wanted to help Phillip Zarella— no moral person would *want* to do anything for the man. I'd once read an article about Zarella that labeled him the figurative unholy demon child of Hannibal Lecter and Angel of Death Nazi doctor Josef Mengele. His was a rare and atrocious brand of evil. But even locked up on the Gregori Industries campus, Zarella had reach.

"We're headed back home," I said. "Let's talk first thing in the morning."

We ended the call, and I turned to Rogan.

"Phillip Zarella," I said.

I watched Rogan's face. His gaze skittered a little, dodging over to me and then returning to the road.

"What about him?" he asked apprehensively.

"I know he's alive. I've seen him in person twice, so there's no need to pretend he was killed trying to escape max security. What kind of sway does he have in your so-called underworld network?" It was a bit of a shot in the dark, but from what little Rogan had mentioned about the "underworld," I figured Zarella was probably connected to it in some way.

Rogan's jaw tightened.

"More than you want to admit, I'm guessing," I said.

His shoulders shifted under his duster. "I don't want to give the impression that underworlders are bad. *Some* are bad, sure. Some are downright evil. But the majority isn't. Most of us are like you and me, when it comes to a moral compass. It's a mixed bag like any slice of humanity. But Zarella is one of the world's most powerful necromancers, so because of that he has . . . influence."

"So there's some kind of hierarchy in the club of the underworld?" I asked.

"Of course. Every organized subset of human society has a hierarchy." He wanted me to drop the subject, that was clear enough. "And it's officially the Society of the Underworld."

"What's Zarella's position?" I pressed.

He glanced at me again, pausing. "There's a council. Zarella is on it."

I stared out the windshield at what little the headlamps allowed me to see on the dark highway. "You all must be a loyal bunch to not rat out someone like Zarella to the public and the press. You wouldn't even have to murder him. If it got out that he was still alive and living in comfort on the Gregori Campus, someone would do it for you. How did he get on the council? Did you all vote him there?"

"The three most powerful necromancers have automatic placement on the council," he said stiffly. "But rest assured that most underworlders have no reverence for Zarella."

The conversation was obviously making Rogan uncomfortable, but if he had any relevant info on Zarella, I wanted it.

I drew a long breath in through my nose. How did I keep getting mixed up in crazy shit? Fending off a reaper soul, getting coerced into Lynnette's coven against my will, and now a mad man who was supposed to be dead wanted to hire me.

I just wanted to get Evan back. Maybe then I'd find a little cabin in the middle of nowhere like Switchboard and live out my hermitage in peace.

I tried to ease the tension from my shoulders.

"How does he attend council meetings if he's stuck on the Gregori campus?" I asked, forcing a lighter tone. "Wait, don't tell me. He sends a demon in his place."

"Close," Rogan said. "He uses a zombie."

I whipped around to see if he was kidding. "What?"

"He uses necromancy to drive a zombie. Watches through its eyes, listens through its ears, and speaks through its mouth."

I recoiled. "That's just . . . ew. You underworlders and your creature pets. For the love of the universe, can't you just use cell phones or set up some video conferencing or something? Maybe Skype like normal people?"

He snickered at that. "Just wait. Soon you'll be one of us, and you'll send out demons with notes instead of texting."

"Highly doubtful," I said. But his comment sobered me up again.

One of us.

With a shiver I tried to imagine controlling the mind of a zombie, a victim of the NECR2 virus. It was a mutation of VAMP2, but unlike the vampire virus, there was no second life for anyone struck with NECR2. It was said the bodies of zombies were nothing but living shells, empty houses where a person used to reside. The virus wouldn't allow the body to die naturally, even after the soul had fled. It took a high degree of skill to control a zombie with necromancy. It wasn't something I saw myself pursuing. But then, lately I'd done a lot of things I'd never expected.

I scrolled through my text messages again, stopping at the one from Johnny.

It seemed apologetic. No, scratch that. An apology would actually contain the words "I'm sorry" or "I apologize," and his message didn't say either. He wanted to meet up. I guess I could take that to mean he was in a conciliatory mood. But was I?

I stared at the screen, trying to think of what to write back. The fact was, I didn't really want to see him. I was still pissed about the way he'd acted. And I was exhausted. I typed a reply.

We're still an hour from Boise. It took a lot longer than planned, and long story short, I lost one of my rings and the ley line magic nearly fried me. I'm not up for anything tonight. I'll catch up with you tomorrow.

I read it over a couple of times. It sounded cold. I knew it and found I didn't much care. I hit send.

"Got troubles?" Rogan asked.

I flipped my phone face-down on my lap and gave a humorless little laugh. "You mean besides the obvious?"

I twirled my ring around my finger, letting the silence stretch out.

"I'm an idiot when it comes to relationships," I said. "If there were a relationship I.Q. scale, I'd be in the moron range."

"Oh, I don't know about that. You seem to have pretty tight bonds with people in your life," he said mildly.

He was playing dumb, talking about platonic friendships when he had to know I meant romantic relationships.

"Friends are different," I said, taking his bait. "But the men I pick usually turn out to be . . . not the greatest matches."

I'd almost said, "turn out to be jerks," but realized that wasn't totally true. Sure, it was the case for some of the guys before Johnny, but Johnny wasn't an asshole. We just seemed to push each other's buttons in irritating ways.

"Maybe you pick poor matches on purpose."

I scowled at him, but his attention was on the road. I slumped a little lower in my seat.

"Why would I do that?" I asked.

"So you have an easy way out later. Maybe you just don't want a quality relationship with a man." He said it so matter-of-factly, I kind of wanted to punch him.

My scowl deepened. "Who the hell are you to make such an assumption?"

"If you truly desire something in life, regardless of what it is, you have to make decisions that demonstrate your desire. Decisions that make sense along the path that leads to what you want. Otherwise, you're just going to keep sabotaging yourself, and you're going to become more and more unhappy. When you realize the gap between your desires and the choices you make is too wide, that's when you know you're ready to make a change."

My entire being prickled with irritation at his sage observation. I wanted badly to argue, but I knew he was right. I folded my arms.

"Ugh, you sound like Deb. How'd you learn all this wise junk, anyway?" I groused. "You're a loner."

He chuckled. "Nobody's *that* much of an island."

I squirmed in my seat, hating that I felt so exposed and unable to escape, and that he seemed to see right through me. I wanted to change the subject, but by doing so I would somehow make my discomfort even more obvious, and that would just piss me off even more.

I groaned internally, finally cracking. "Let's talk about something else. *Anything.*"

"Who are you bringing with you to try to get in with the dragon?" he asked, humoring me.

My mind seemed to grind as I mentally switched gears. I tried to remember what Switchboard had said. "Two death-touched and one not, right?"

Rogan nodded.

"Well, the only other death-touched people I know well enough to ask are you and Jennifer Kane. And Phillip Zarella, too, I guess, but that's not happening." I looked at him. "Are you up for it?"

"Absolutely." He drew out the word as if relishing it.

"For the one not death-touched, I'd like Damien." It might upset Deb that I wasn't choosing her, but I didn't want her going on any crazy adventures while she was pregnant. I straightened. "Hey, where will we go for this dragon meeting, anyway?"

"I don't know," Rogan said. "Switchboard will tell us."

"What do you mean you don't know? You've seen it. It? Him? Whatever. Where did you go?"

"The dragon doesn't really live . . . here." Rogan was getting that squirmy look again, the one that meant he was about to reveal something unsettling. "We'll have to go through a rip."

My head dropped, and I gaped at him from under my brows. "We're going to walk *through* a rip?"

"Don't worry. It's not as weird as it sounds."

Right.

We'd reached Boise city limits, and fatigue had settled so deeply into my bones I could barely hold my head steady under my own power.

When Rogan turned onto my block, my stomach dropped. Johnny's Mustang was parked on the curb in front of my building. My mood immediately clouded.

Rogan parked and reached to unbuckle his seat belt. "Let me help you inside."

I held up a hand. "Not a good idea. Johnny's here. But thank you."

"To the door, then."

"Nuh uh."

Moving slowly and wincing the entire time, I maneuvered myself out of the Jeep.

"I know you don't usually go for this, but you need a healer. Promise me you'll see one?" I said to Rogan.

He nodded. Loki jumped out and trotted next to me up to the front porch. I waited until Rogan pulled away before opening the door.

Johnny was sitting in the living room with his phone in his hand. He set it down as I came in, and he rose to his feet. A furtive glance to the side showed the bedroom door was closed, and the strip of space under it was dark. Deb was probably already asleep.

"Don't be mad at her for letting me in," he said. "I told her you were expecting me."

That admission didn't do a thing to lighten my mood. But it made what I needed to say next even easier.

"This seems to be a theme between us," I said. "You trying to manage me by way of your disapproval of my decisions, and then getting pissed when I don't go for it. I specifically said I didn't want to talk tonight."

He propped one hand loosely on his hip and lifted the other. "I'm not trying to control you, Ella. I'm just trying to help. I don't want to see you hurt."

I ran a hand over my hair, my exasperation building. "I don't know why you're even trying to do this. You've never been a one-woman guy. At least not for long stretches."

"C'mon, that's unfair," he said. Then his face darkened. "You've changed since Rogan came into the picture. Is that what this is really about? Is there something going on between the two of you?"

My anger flared, and my pulse surged with it.

"Seriously?" I hissed, trying to keep from shouting. "I don't know what it is about him that you don't like, but *that* was uncalled for."

He blew out a breath, his shoulders dropping. "You're right, I'm sorry."

He took a step toward me, his face softening. But I held up a hand. Something had snapped between us. I suddenly saw that I could stick with it, let us go a few more rounds of this same argument, which might carry us through a few weeks or even months. Or I could turn and face the writing on the wall. This wasn't a good fit, and it wasn't likely to lever itself into a better one.

"This isn't working," I said, my tone even. "And it's only going to get worse if we drag it out. Sorry, Johnny, but I don't think we should do that."

I knew I should have delivered it with more sensitivity and grace, but even under good circumstances, those weren't exactly in my skillset.

His eyes widened in disbelief and then narrowed in anger. A flush crept over his cheeks as a storm seemed to gather inside him. It all happened in the span of a second or so. His hands tightened into fists as the rest of him seemed to tense up. He stood stock still and unblinking for a moment, and then shook his head and strode to the door and out into the night.

I went to turn the deadbolt and then flipped off the light and sank onto the sofa, weariness returning as my adrenaline drained away. I untied my boots and kicked them off. With my clothes still on, I pulled a blanket over me and sighed deeply. Loki jumped up and settled on the far end of the sofa with his head resting on my ankles.

When I'd first started seeing Johnny, there'd been a spark, but looking back I realized how short-lived it had been. I'd been too busy and distracted to see that we didn't really connect past that initial attraction. He'd helped me through some difficult moments, and he deserved credit for that, but ultimately there just wasn't anything to sustain us. Plus, he'd turned out to be kind of a controlling ass. If he wanted a woman he could keep under his thumb, he'd definitely picked the wrong one in me.

My mind skirted around his accusation about Rogan, and I remembered that second in the cabin after he'd helped me stand up. Perhaps I *had* felt something then but brushed it off in that moment. I didn't have the energy to examine it, and exhaustion did me a favor and pulled me into sleep before my thoughts could begin to swirl.

I awoke to the sounds of Deb rummaging in the kitchen and the smell of coffee brewing.

I stiffly pushed myself up and swung my feet to the floor.

"You're up!" she sang out from the kitchen doorway.

I stood and shoved my tangled hair off my face, and her cheerful expression fell into one of concern.

"Oh no, what happened?" she asked.

"Fought a troll. Lost a ring. Met a hermit mage. Dumped Johnny," I said hoarsely.

Every muscle ached, but my fatigue had vanished for the most part.

"That's . . . concise," she said diplomatically. She tilted her head to one side, and her eyes flitted around me. She was probably reading my aura. "Are you okay?"

"Yeah, I'm fine," I said. "Why didn't you tell me Johnny was such a bad fit?"

"He really seemed to like you," she said gently.

"Eh, I don't know," I said. "Maybe he only liked the challenge of trying to get me under his control. Either way, it was a crappy match."

"Well, you did butt heads quite a bit," she said. Then she shrugged. "Some people like that, though. They mistake the fighting for passion, and they get off on the drama of it. The thing is, if you don't have a foundation of genuine love and respect, the fighting isn't passion. It's nothing but dysfunction in disguise. And that's a doomed relationship, every time."

"How do you *know* all this? Why are you so smart?" I asked. Was everyone in the world better at seeing this stuff than I was?

She gave me a wry look. "Really? Smart? I'm pregnant and in the middle of a divorce from a man who spent all our savings on pyramid schemes."

My phone rang, saving me from having to come up with a response.

"Hey, Damien," I answered.

"We got another message from Zarella, and I think you were right. It seems like the real deal." He sounded excited. "Are you free?"

"Yep, I'll be at your place in forty-five."

On the way to Damien's loft, possibilities whirled through my mind. What nefarious task would a man like Zarella have for us? And what would he offer as payment? He had to know it would be a hard sell.

Not that I was truly considering taking on Phillip Zarella as a client. Hell no . . . Of course not.

When Damien let me in, I saw he was already in work mode. A couple of notebooks lay open on the long kitchen island, and the screen of his laptop was glowing. He picked up a second laptop, closed and sleek-looking.

"Here, this one is yours," he said. He held out the device.

I looked at him in question.

"I'm not sharing, and you need more than just your phone. Business expense," he said brusquely and pushed the laptop at me again.

I took it. "Okay, but how are we paying for it?"

"Leave the finances to me," he said, already turning his attention to his computer screen. He looked at me, his eyes glinting. "Take a look at this."

I expected an email, but Damien had pulled up a web page that was blank except for a short block of text.

Dear Sir and Madam,
As to your inquiry about my needs, I can tell you only that I seek your services for the retrieval of an object. In my current situation, I'm unable to go to get the object myself. And as to why I've contacted you specifically, I will say this: I

can give you both the invaluable things you desire in return
for doing this small task for me. I believe it will be well worth
your time.
P. Z.

I squinted at the note, reading it a second and third time.

"He's a powerful necromancer, though, and he's operating as one even from his confines," I said. "I just learned he drives zombies to proxy for him in underworld council meetings. So why can't he just send a zombie or a demon to get this object?"

"Let's ask," Damien said. He switched to a window showing an email inbox. "His messages are delivered via email. He sends links that go to encrypted web pages, but he said in his first email that we could reply directly as long as we don't use his name."

He started typing.

"Also ask him what exactly he's offering," I said. "He seems to have something specific for each of us that he thinks we can't turn down. I want details."

My stomach was slowly winding itself into a knot. Zarella's offering to me would somehow relate to my brother, I was almost sure of it. I had a vague idea about what he might be offering Damien, too. As I watched Damien type and send our reply, I felt a distinct falling sensation. Not a rollercoaster plunge, but the start of a gentle descent, as if gravity had taken a tighter hold and was beginning to pull me downward.

I knew we shouldn't pursue this particular white rabbit, but I needed to know what Zarella thought he could give me. I *had* to know, and I kind of hated it.

"It might take a while for him to respond," Damien said. "Last time it was almost twelve hours, so we might want to—"

His laptop pinged, and we both whipped around to stare at it. There was a new message from Zarella. It contained only a link. Damien tapped it.

Neither a zombie nor a demon would be able to gain access to my desired object without attracting considerable notice. And neither one would be able to protect it the way a living human can. But I need both of you to have full possession of your magical abilities in order to complete my request. And to that need, I must supply the lady with the solution to her reaper problem. Up front, she will receive a fix that will keep the reaper from consuming any more of her soul. It also will allow her to retain the abilities the reaper has bestowed.

After the retrieval of my desired object, I will complete my payment. That will be thus: to the lady's partner, the means to the magical power he so deeply desires, though I feel obligated to warn you that it can't be achieved without a steep price that even I would not wish to pay.

For reasons that will become clear later, I also must require the lady to join the Society of the Underworld and pay her requisite visit to the dragon oracle.

Another demand? Zarella sure was bold. And how the hell did he know about the dragon? My scalp crawled, and I felt slightly sick as I absorbed what Zarella was offering. I shifted my attention to Damien and furtively watched him out of the corners of my eyes. He was leaning in, reading the message over and over. His full lips were parted slightly, and I could see his faint, quick pulse on the side of his neck.

"Oracle?" Damien asked, turning to me.

I explained about the dragon and told him about the visit with Switchboard. Damien's straight blond brows lifted as I spoke. I could tell he was intrigued.

"We don't even know where we'd have to go or what we'd have to do in order to get this thing for Zarella," I said. "It might be a trap."

"I don't think it's a trap," Damien said, finally straightening and tearing his eyes away from the screen. "The payments really don't cost him anything. If he were offering a giant sum of money or something that was of great value to him, *then* I'd think it was a trap."

"I don't know if I totally follow your logic, but my gut tells me you're right in that he would deliver on his promises . . . *if* we were to take the job."

We looked at each other as the silence grew heavy in the room.

"He'll tell you how to control the reaper," Damien said softly, his voice almost soothingly hypnotic. "That, along with Jennifer's spell for stemming the tide of the ley line magic . . . you'd get your magic back, you'd never have to worry about the reaper killing you, and you could go after your brother. Zarella himself said he has to give you that up front. We wouldn't even have to follow through with the job." He added the last almost as an afterthought.

My throat was too dry to respond. He was trying to convince me, and in spite of the way he put the focus on what I would gain, I was fairly sure that once we agreed he would want what was promised to him, too.

"We have to take that, at least," he said. "This is your life we're talking about."

He was right. I knew nothing about the dragon and what he might or might not give me. An oracle was just some sort of fortune teller, and the fact was I didn't care about hearing my fortune. I needed a real solution to my reaper problem, and that was exactly what Zarella offered. I needed to take it. If I didn't, my brother would slip away from me again, and I felt certain that I wouldn't receive another chance to save him.

A few seconds ticked by, and a sense of dread began to fill me.

"Okay," I said, my voice barely above a whisper. "Tell him we accept."

Damien sent a message to Phillip Zarella telling him we would take the job.

We watched his laptop expectantly but after a few minutes figured we needed to at least pretend to do something else or we'd go nuts waiting.

I sent a quick text to Rogan.

I've found a different fix to the reaper threat. No need to see the dragon now.

My phone rang almost immediately.

"Sorry, but it's too late," Rogan said. "You don't cancel on the oracle."

I growled a frustrated noise. "Oh, come on, there's got to be a way out of it."

"Nope," he said with finality. "Remember the part about cooking like a rabbit on a spit? The dragon already knows who you are. Trust me, if you tried to get out of this, it would likely be the last thing you did. I don't think even your reaper soul could save you from getting cooked in dragon fire."

I huffed a loud sigh. "Wait. Did *you* try that route? To, you know, get back to the *in-between*?"

"Actually . . . yeah, I tried to provoke him," he said reluctantly. "But he knew what I was doing and wouldn't take the bait. He doesn't like being manipulated."

"Ugh, fine, I'll go," I said. "By the way, in return for the reaper fix, I'm gonna have to join the underworlders."

"Hey, cool," Rogan said. "You're a necromancer, after all. Practically one of us already. You'll fit right in."

I snorted. "Oh, that makes me feel *so* much better about all of this," I said sarcastically.

He chuckled, taking no offense at my tone, and we ended the call.

Lately my life had become one stupid, unwanted obligation after another. Lynnette's coven. Zarella's demand that I join the Society of the Underworld. And now this audience with the oracle.

"Um, I have a favor to ask you," I said to Damien. I explained how I needed three others to accompany me to see the damned dragon.

Damien leaned a hip against the kitchen counter, and his mouth twitched as he did a poor job of holding back a grin. "You're picking me as the good guy? The shining light of goodness in your unholy trinity of friends?"

I rolled my eyes, relieved to see his posture loosening and some of the intensity fading from his expression. "You're going to make us call you by some stupid title, aren't you? What, Bearer of Light and Goodness? Damien the Innocent and Fair?"

He snorted. "Nothing lame like that. You can call me The Ethereal Prince. You know, something with real dignity behind it."

I snickered, and he laughed with me, and for a moment, everything felt good. But as our laughter trailed off, a sense of weighty anticipation crept back in like a dark sea reaching high tide.

I held a breath for a second and then let it out. "He's saying he can make you a mage, Damien."

It wasn't phrased as a query, but the inherent question seemed to hang in the space between us. Was Damien planning to go for it?

He pulled his bottom lip in between his teeth and shifted his sky blue eyes to gaze out the tall windows overlooking downtown.

"I won't do anything stupid," he said finally, with forced lightness in his voice that I didn't buy for a second. He smiled at me, but his eyes looked haunted. "Don't worry."

A swirl of disquiet seemed to gather strength around my heart. "Don't agree to anything without me, okay? I'm serious. Promise?"

"Yeah, I promise," he said.

Usually he was the one trying to get me to swear I wouldn't go off and do something impulsive on my own. I wasn't a fan of this reversal, and I didn't like the gleam in Damien's eyes. But I'd be able to keep tabs on him. We were partners, and this was a job we had to work together. That was what I told myself, anyway.

"I can't take all this standing around," I said. I tilted my head toward the staffs mounted like pool cues on one wall. "Spar?"

He grinned, and to my relief, the old Damien seemed to return. "Oh, yeah. I owe you an ass-kicking."

We moved barefoot to the mats and sparred until my arms shook with fatigue.

When we stopped for water, his laptop pinged.

Excellent news, I am so pleased. As soon as the lady pays her visit to the oracle and enters the Society of the Underworld in earnest, I will deliver the reaper fix. She shall not ever again have to worry about her reaper causing her untimely death.

I don't know what I was expecting from Zarella, but the short note felt like a bit of a letdown.

"What's with the lady this and the lady that?" I asked irritably. "Is he mocking me?"

Damien crooked a half-smile at me. "I think he's just trying to avoid using our names."

I gathered my hair off my neck and held it up, my mind already spinning ahead. "I need to talk to Jennifer. If she's willing, then I have my team, and we can check off this oracle visit. The sooner the better."

I texted Jennifer while Damien worked on mundane business setup stuff. My conversation with Jen turned into a call when her reluctance became obvious.

"That oracle has close ties to the Society of the Underworld," Jen said. "The Society has tried to recruit me. Several times, in fact."

I didn't know about that connection, but also didn't see why it was relevant.

"But my visit to the oracle has nothing to do with the underworld," I said. "It's just a, uh, thing I have to do. But out of curiosity, what turned you off of the underworld?"

"I'd feel like a tuna in a tank of sharks."

I frowned. "Huh? Sorry, but I don't get it. I know you're sensitive about your vampire-witch status, but . . ."

She made an exasperated sighing sound. "The underworld is full of necromancers. *Necromancers*, Ella. They can control the minds of the undead."

I slapped a hand over my eyes. "Oh crap. I'm so sorry. I'm a total ass. I'll find someone else to go."

She started to protest, but I cut her off.

"Seriously, Jen, I didn't mean to be insensitive. Does it help at all to say that I don't think of you as undead? To me, you're just as alive and vital as I am." I went for a comically contrite tone, and thank the universe it elicited a throaty laugh from her.

"And you're pretty cool for a necromancer," she shot back with another laugh.

I felt like a total idiot. But I had a new respect for Jen's willingness to be my friend.

"You've got another option," she said. "Lynnette is death-touched."

I grimaced at the mention of the coven leader's name. "Oh. Yeah. I guess that fact slipped my mind."

"Don't sound so excited."

"No, it's just . . ."

"I'm kidding. I get it. You're not besties." Jen paused. "But you know she'll say yes."

"True." I stifled a sigh. "I'll see you soon at some coven thing, I'm sure."

"Bye, Ella."

Damien glanced up, his eyes snagging on me when he took in my expression. "What's with the puke face?"

"Jen doesn't want to do it," I said. I pulled one hand down the side of my face. "But she reminded me that Lynnette qualifies."

His brows drew together. "Huh. I guess as an exorcist she would have be death-touched. I wonder how death marked her."

The pit of my stomach constricted. "I don't know, but it wouldn't surprise me if it wasn't an accident."

He gave me a doubtful look.

"Really. She's that power hungry," I said slowly, my eyes glazing over as I tried to imagine how Lynnette had gained her death-touched status. "She lives for it. She'd do just about anything for more power, even risk death."

My gaze sharpened and darted to Damien as I realized what I'd just said and how blatantly the accusation could apply to his longing for mage magic.

He shifted his weight as an uncomfortable silence seemed to suck the air out of the room.

I lifted my phone. "I guess I'd better get it over with."

I called Lynnette, and of course she agreed immediately. I tried to focus on the task in front of me rather than the fact that I'd just handed Lynnette yet another opportunity to gather more personal information about me that she'd no doubt use against me later.

I sent Rogan a message to tell him my group was complete. He replied with a smiley face, and then a message about how we'd have to wait for the hermit mage to tell us where to go for the rip that would take us to the dragon.

"We're still pursuing paying contracts, right?" I asked Damien. "Even if we accepted Zarella's so-called payments, those aren't going to keep the power on in my apartment."

"I've got some feelers out to Supernatural Crimes," he said. "Maybe Johnny knows some other avenues?"

"Uhh . . . we broke up."

Damien groaned.

"What?" I said, trying not to sound defensive. "We don't need him to get work."

"I've been using him as, well, not a reference exactly, but I've *referenced* that we worked together on the Gregori gargoyle case and it would be easy to hire us together, seeing as how our services are complimentary."

I put on a nonchalant expression. "Well, I can be a professional about it. If he can't, that's on him."

"Sorry about your breakup, though. I assume you did the breaking?"

"Why do you say that?" My voice took on a snarly edge.

He raised his palms defensively, and his eyes widened. "Because you're an independent, strong woman who's too good for any man alive, and how dare he even exist? Also, you're super pretty, and you smell nice."

I gave him a withering look. "Yeah, well, you guessed right."

"Sorry," he said.

"I'm not. It's good. I'm fine."

I made a frustrated noise deep in my throat and started pacing around the loft. Talking about Johnny had soured my mood.

"I miss being on the move all day, Damien," I groused. "I liked patrolling the beat. All this waiting and talking and standing around and staring at a laptop bullshit makes me antsy. Maybe I'll go get Loki and take him on a trail run. Might be my last chance before spring."

I started to go for my keys, which I'd tossed on the counter, but Damien stood with a sudden look of urgency on his face.

"No, you can't go home," he said.

"Huh?"

"I mean, how about we go get something to eat instead?"

I narrowed my eyes at him and folded my arms.

He scratched at the back of his head. "I'm sorry, I can't let you go home."

"Why?" I demanded.

"I . . . promised someone."

I let my head drop back and moaned at the ceiling. "Oh shit. My surprise birthday party is going to be tonight, isn't it?"

His shoulders lowered with relief. "Oh good, you know. She can't blame me for spoiling it. Hey, how did you figure it out?"

I arched an eyebrow at him. "Deb is like an open book. Also, I saw the party decorations."

I let my tongue loll as I made stabbing motions at my chest and shot a finger gun at the side of my head.

"You've got a best friend who wants to throw you a birthday party, you poor, poor thing," he said with mock sympathy.

"Whatever." I waved a hand at him. "If we're stuck here for a while, let's get something done."

I went over to peer at his laptop. We spent the next couple of hours scrolling through a database of government contracts available for freelancers to bid on. Most of them weren't a good fit for us, either too far away or requiring magical talents we couldn't provide. Damien tagged a few with potential so he could come back later and begin the lengthy application process.

After a while he pushed back from the counter and stretched.

He slid a glance at me. "Ready to put on your surprised face?"

I gave him a glowering glare.

"C'mon, you can do a lot better than that." He giggled gleefully at my misery. "Practice on the way home. I'll see you at your place."

Once in my truck, I seriously contemplated jerking the wheel in the opposite direction of my apartment and hightailing it out of town. But knowing Deb, she'd probably spent too much money and way too much time on planning this little shindig, and I just needed to suck it up and try to enjoy her efforts.

When I got to my block, there was no row of cars out front to give away the surprise. But I thought I passed Rogan's Jeep a couple of streets away from home, and I caught a glimpse of Jen's SUV around the corner. And was that—?

I groaned and swore under my breath as I recognized Johnny's Mustang two blocks down. Deb knew we'd broken up. Johnny *sure* as hell knew we'd broken up. I couldn't imagine why he'd show up at my birthday party.

I parked in my usual spot and killed the engine, watching the front bay window out of the corners of my eyes. It looked dark inside, but I thought I saw the blinds twitch. Damien parked behind my pickup and then came up to grin at me through the passenger window. He made a slow beckoning motion. With a heavy sigh, I got out and dragged myself up the front walk, pausing with my hand on the doorknob.

"C'mon. Just rip it off like a Band Aid," he stage-whispered over my shoulder.

I lifted my hand to flip him off and then shoved the door open.

The lights flicked on, and I staggered back a step as what seemed like a hundred people hollered, "Happy birthday, Ella!" in unison.

Damien jabbed me in the spine with what felt like his key fob, and I winced.

"Smile," he muttered in my ear.

I did my best as Deb rushed forward to grab my arm and drag me into the living room. I looked around wide-eyed as I realized just about everyone I knew was gathered in my tiny apartment. Okay, so it wasn't a *hundred* people. But it was quite a few. The whole coven, some old coworkers, even Rafael St. James and a couple of his crew had shown up.

Somebody turned on music, and Sasha Bowen from Demon Patrol came up to shove a bottle of local lager in my hand. I spotted Johnny talking to Lynnette over by the TV. I scanned the crowd for Rogan but didn't see him. Maybe I'd been wrong about the Jeep parked down the street.

"Deb," I said urgently. "What the hell is Johnny doing here?"

She gave me a baffled look. "He told me you guys were cool and wanted to stay friends."

I didn't have time to respond before a blond teenager dressed in a baggy hoodie rushed me. Roxanne burst through the crowd. I threw my arms around her as if she were my life raft in this sea of people.

"Come and see the cupcake tower we made," she said, her eyes sparkling as she pushed her corn silk blond hair behind her ears with impatient swipes.

She pulled me into the kitchen, where the meager counter space was covered with all kinds of food. The mismatched unfamiliar dishes told me it was a potluck affair, which gave me a small measure of relief. I'd have killed Deb if she spent a ton of money on this.

"Look!" Roxanne held up her hands ta-da style at the tiered stand that stood on my tiny dining table. "Deb and I and some of the coven witches did it. We had to mix the frosting ourselves, 'cause you can't buy it that color."

The stand was stacked with purple-frosted cupcakes topped with sprinkles. I managed to summon up a shred of genuine appreciation as I admired Roxanne's work. While I was oohing and ahhing, I happened to glance out the window into the back yard. Rogan was tending the barbeque, stacking hot dogs into a glass baking dish.

"How've things been at home with your brother?" I asked Roxanne.

She grinned. "It's so good to have him back!"

I returned her smile. "Good to hear. No ill effects from being stuck in the gargoyle?"

"I don't think so. He sure seems like his old self."

I couldn't help thinking of Evan and hoping his would be a similarly happy homecoming. It wouldn't be as simple as Nathan returning to Roxanne, of course—my brother was going to need a lot of help to get his life on track—but I felt a rare swell of optimism.

After I'd paid the cupcake tower appropriate homage, I excused myself and slipped out through the back door, closing it quietly behind me.

The soft glow of twilight washed the back yard in muted tones that belied the chill in the air. I pulled my jacket tighter around me against the December cold. Rogan hadn't heard me come out, and he was turned away from the door while he concentrated on flipping hamburger patties.

I stood where I was, drinking my beer, watching him work, and enjoying the peace.

Perhaps sensing my presence, he twisted around and brightened when he spotted me. The fading light cut angular shadows under his cheekbones and jaw, and his deep-set eyes were nearly hidden. His face relaxed into an easy smile.

I walked forward, and the hint of a grin—a real one—tugged at the corners of my lips. For some reason it amused me to see him doing something so mundane.

"Deb put you on BBQ duty, huh?" I asked, my words puffing out in ghostly white clouds that quickly dissipated into the evening.

He lifted a shoulder. "I volunteered."

As usual, he was wearing only a t-shirt under his duster, seemingly impervious to the freezing temperature. I moved to the side of the barbeque so I could watch him. The duster had grown on me. It gave him an outlaw vibe, and somehow made glimpses of the thin cotton stretched over his obviously toned chest that much more interesting.

"Happy birthday, by the way," he said. "How old are you?"

"I'll be twenty-five in six days," I said.

"Just a kid," he teased. He glanced up when I didn't respond, and his tawny eyes reflected a tiny flare from the grill.

"I don't feel like a kid," I said seriously, shifting my gaze to stare away into the dark yard.

Something I'd been avoiding chose that moment to hit me. My brother would be turning twenty in January. For some reason it had always felt very important to find him before that happened. He'd disappeared when he was fourteen. Still just a kid but old enough to start getting in some real trouble, which he'd managed plenty of even at that tender age. I wanted to save him while he was still a teenager. I knew it was irrational, but there was some part of me that felt sure I could preserve some of his innocence if only I could find him before he turned twenty.

When I looked up, I saw Rogan had paused his burger flipping and stood very still, watching me. The tongs looked almost miniature in his wide hand.

"What's on your mind?" he asked quietly.

I shook my head. "Just a sudden need to get on with things. Any word from Switch about where we'll go to meet the dragon?"

"He's going to let me know tonight."

I sucked in a slow breath of icy air. "Good."

"Ella?"

I jumped at the sound of an unexpected male voice speaking my name. My shoulders tensed, already anticipating who I was going to see standing behind me. Johnny. I hadn't heard the door open, and I had no idea how long he'd been standing there.

With his back to the porch light, his face was cast in shadow.

"Yeah?" I held up a hand to shield my eyes from the glaring bulb.

"Could we talk alone?" He sounded contrite on the surface, but something about his tone sparked my irritation.

I flashed back to the times I'd been with coworkers at our favorite watering hole and watched him zero in on an attractive woman. I'd been within earshot enough times to know the sound of Johnny Beemer trying to work his magic. That was what I heard in his voice.

What had Deb said? Something about how he had a Don Juan complex. He'd been flirting with me for years. But when I'd given in and we started seeing each other, the spark between us had fizzled. It should have been obvious. I should have seen it earlier. Don Juan didn't get dumped. He was always the one to do the leaving. The only lingering question was why he hadn't beaten me to the punch. Not that it really mattered now.

"We don't have anything to talk about, Johnny. And I'm busy helping Rogan."

"Please," he crooned, his voice as smooth and sweet as melted chocolate. He took a few steps toward me.

I tried to give him the benefit of the doubt. Maybe he really was confused about why I'd broken things off, or he genuinely wanted to try to patch things up.

I faced him, my free hand planted on my hip. "Maybe later, okay?"

"Ella, come on. Let's just talk. Give me one minute, that's all I ask. Please?"

"Are you deaf?" Rogan had moved next to me. "She said no."

Johnny's arms stiffened at his sides, and for a split second, I thought he might stomp forward and try to sock Rogan in the jaw.

But instead, Johnny rocked back on his heels. He looked back and forth between the two of us and then barked a short, humorless laugh. "At least now I know what's really going on here."

He turned on his heel and stalked inside.

I pushed my fingers against my temple and groaned. "God, I can't believe he just did that," I muttered.

"Was he implying what I think he was implying?" Rogan asked.

I glanced up at him. "Yeah. Apparently he's been suspicious of the two of us."

He turned back to the barbecue, but not before I caught the amused twitch of his lips.

I reached for the platter of cooked hot dogs. "I'm really sorry about that. I kind of want to die right now, so I'm taking these inside, and I'm going to drown my sorrows in beer and purple frosting."

In my haste to escape, I rushed into the kitchen and nearly plowed into Lynnette. Awesome. One pain in the ass after another.

"Ella, happy birthday," she said. Her eyes took on a predatory gleam. "So sorry to hear about your Patrol job. At least you have the coven to support you, though, right?"

I ground my teeth as I set the hot dogs next to a couple of bags of buns.

"I don't need the coven's support, and I don't need you," I said. "I'll manage just fine."

"Oh, really?" She tilted her head, her kohl-lined eyes widening. "But you just asked me to join of your little oracle party."

I slammed a lid on my temper, forcing it back to a simmer.

I smiled sweetly at her. "I thought you'd appreciate going along for the ride. The oracle has connections to the underworld, and seeing as how you're death-touched but don't have the right qualifications to join the Society, well . . . I figured you'd be glad for any little glimpse of something that's off limits to you."

It was a bit of a stab in the dark, but not really. If she were eligible to join the Society of the Underworld, she would have done it long ago. Lynnette coveted power, and connections were a great source of what she craved. I knew she wouldn't back out of my invitation, even if I pissed her off.

My suspicion was confirmed when her face flushed and she huffed indignantly, but couldn't come up with a retort.

Rogan came through the back door with a platter of burgers, distracting me for a moment. Lynnette took the opportunity to slip away.

Pent-up frustration prickled along my veins. Let's see. In the past few days I'd been fired, lost one of my charms to a troll, gotten forced into a surprise birthday party I didn't want, fended off an asshole ex trying to manipulate me, and been jabbed at by a power-hungry witch I couldn't seem to get away from. I wanted to punch someone. Instead, I waited for Rogan to set down the dish, and then I grabbed his sleeve and dragged him back outside. On the way, I killed the outdoor light. This probably wasn't the smartest thing I'd ever done, but at that moment I didn't really care.

I pushed him up against the side of the house and crushed his mouth with mine. He got over his surprise much faster than I'd expected. Lacing his fingers into my hair, he pulled me to him even harder. Desire shot through me in a white hot flash, and his body seemed to respond immediately. He bit down on my lip with almost enough force to draw blood, which only fueled the fire between us. One hand stayed tangled in my hair, and his other hand moved down to the small of my back to yank my hips against his.

The back door swung open, and we both let go. I staggered back a step, breathing hard.

"Hey, birthday girl!" Roxanne's voice sang out. "Time for cupcakes! I convinced Deb that cake is a side dish, so no need to wait for dessert."

"Okay," I said raggedly. "I'll be right in."

Rogan and I stared at each other, both of us panting. I pressed my fingertips to my mouth, which was still throbbing from the pressure of his lips. An unexpected laugh bubbled up as I blinked a few times. Everything was cast in odd yellow and blue hues.

He arched a brow at me. "So you thought that was amusing?"

"No, not at all," I said. "I just realized my necro vision kicked in, but there aren't any demons around. Guess it was you."

He stepped into my space and reached one arm around my waist, nearly lifting me clear off the ground as he pulled me against his chest.

"Give me another fifteen minutes, and you won't be able to see straight," he said roughly, his lips inches from mine.

I actually stopped breathing for a second or two.

Every cell was thrumming with desire, but I could hear the voices of people gathering in the kitchen. He set me down, and still reeling, I went back inside. I had to grab the edge of the counter to catch my balance.

Roxanne and Deb were lighting the last of the birthday candles that were stuck into the towered cupcakes. Everyone started singing, and I felt a stupid smile stretch across my face. Deb looked so thrilled, but I'd never be able to tell her that my expression had very little to do with the happy birthday serenade. I blew out the candles, and then Deb and Roxanne started to pass cupcakes around.

Roxanne handed me two cupcakes, and I turned to give one to Rogan. When our eyes locked, I saw desire—and the promise of more to come—still smoldering in his. He'd been holding back, I now realized. I'd assumed that his reaper nature meant he was, well, mostly passionless. He'd embraced the physical nature of his human existence far more than I ever would have guessed. If I could have snapped my fingers and magically cleared the house in an instant, I would have thrown him down right there on the kitchen floor. But until then, I'd just have to endure the torment of anticipation.

I peeled the paper away from my cupcake and bit into it, reveling the jaw-locking sweetness of the frosting.

I skirted another look at Rogan, who had moved to the edge of the kitchen, somehow making himself an island in the midst of the crowd. His attention was aimed at the back door.

He was looking through the window out into the dark back yard, and even though my charmed ring prevented me from sensing hellspawn I guessed what had drawn his notice: a demon messenger. I watched as his eyes unfocused and took on the intensity of concentration, as if he were listening carefully. He stayed that way for almost a full minute before his awareness snapped back. When it did, his gaze sought mine across the kitchen.

I made my way over to him, and he leaned down to whisper in my ear.

"It's time to go to the dragon," he said.

Rogan told me the location, and that we had only a brief window of time to get there.

"Get the others and I'll drive us," he said.

I found Damien first.

"It's go time," I said, my voice low in his ear. "We have less than an hour to get out into the area between here and Mountain Home."

He nodded. "Ready when you are."

Feeling someone's eyes on me, I looked around to find Deb watching us with her head tilted in question. Damn. I hadn't told her about the oracle yet, knowing she'd be put out that I wasn't asking her along. And to make things worse, I was going to have to bug out of the birthday party she was throwing me. I forced myself to trudge over to her.

"I need to tell you something." I pointed in the direction of the bedroom, likely the only place we'd have any privacy.

Once we were in there with the door closed, she folded her arms and raised her brows, waiting.

"I want you to know how much I appreciate this." I gestured at the door. "I seriously don't deserve a friend like you."

One corner of her mouth quirked. "But . . . ?" she drew the word out.

I blew out a breath. "I have to go somewhere, and it can't wait."

I gave her the short version of the stuff about the dragon.

"Wait, you're going *through* a rip?" Her eyes widened in alarm.

I scratched at the back of my neck. "Apparently, yeah. This is how it's done. But it's not like I'm the first to do it. Rogan's already been through this rite of passage, and he obviously survived it. Don't worry, it's all going to be fine."

She shook her head slowly. "This is crazy."

"I know. But does that really surprise you?"

That got a small smile out of her.

She rubbed her upper arms as if chilled by a draft. "At least you won't be alone. That's something."

"I'm sorry I have to sneak away," I said.

She shrugged and then snorted a laugh. "Hey, I'm just glad you didn't sprint away screaming when you got here. This was the coven's doing, by the way. I told them a surprise party wasn't really your cup of tea, but they were hell bent on it, so I had to go along."

My phone was vibrating in my pocket. I pulled it out but gave her one last look to make sure she was okay.

"Go," she said, shooing me toward the door and glowering with fake menace.

I had a text from Damien: *Found Lynnette, she's ready to roll.*

And from Rogan: *We're waiting on the side street. We need to go.*

I threaded through the still-crowded apartment toward the back door. It would be too obvious if I tried to leave through the front, and I didn't have time to answer questions. I called Loki, and he eagerly followed me out the back.

Adrenaline pushed through my veins as I let us out the gate and dashed toward the idling Jeep. I tried to get Loki to jump in the back, but he whined and protested. Not wanting to waste time, I hopped into the front seat next to Rogan, and my giant hellhound-doodle got in on top of me. Lynnette and Damien were jammed into the small back seat, both forced to sit with their legs folded up. The dog probably wouldn't have fit back there, anyway.

Lynnette popped her gum. "Did you bring something shiny? Dragons like shiny shit."

I glanced at Rogan. "Was I supposed to?"

He winced. "Probably a good idea. I forgot to mention it. She's right. Dragons do like sparkly things."

"Here." Lynnette's hand appeared between the seats. She held out a ring she often wore, a silver skull with pink crystals for eyes.

I twisted to look at her. "You don't have to do that."

She shook it at me. "Take it. I've got more goth jewelry than an angsty thirteen-year-old girl. It's not expensive."

I snorted a laugh as she dropped the ring into my palm. "Thanks."

"No problem." She snapped her gum again.

I appreciated the gesture, but I knew better than to get all gushy over Lynnette's offering. She wanted to make sure this little adventure happened. I could practically feel the eager curiosity oozing from her pores.

"The dragon and I first met while we were in the coven-sealing circle," I said to her. "I thought you'd called it."

"Ha, I *wish* I could call an oracle," she said with undisguised zeal, her voice edged in something akin to hunger.

Out of the corner of my eye, I caught her drumming her fingers in a fast tempo against her shin. She was keyed up, and I didn't like it.

I pulled out my phone and kept it down by my right hip so the others couldn't see what I was doing. I typed out a text to Damien.

Got a feeling L is up to something. Not sure what.

A few seconds later my screen lit up with a reply: *She keeps reaching for her magic and then releasing it, like a nervous tic. I'll keep an eye on her.*

If I didn't know better, I'd guess she was on something. But most serious crafters avoided drugs because they could dampen or otherwise interfere with their magic. I doubted Lynnette would do anything to negatively impact her power.

My attention slid over to Rogan, which summoned up thoughts of our crazed make-out session in the back yard. My body was still humming with the memory. When he crooked a slow smile at me, I knew he was thinking of it, too. I did my best to turn that energy into focus on what was ahead, but it was hard with him sitting there right next to me. The drive into the desert east of the city was laced with more than one kind of tension.

"You need to ask the oracle the right kind of question," Rogan said, turning business-like. "You can't ask about when you'll die or anything like that. You're not asking the dragon to look into a crystal ball, but to give you insight into something important to you personally. Think of it more like asking for advice. You can also ask for information about something in the past."

"Ask for advice? Not sure I follow. What did you ask?"

He hesitated, and then his tongue flicked over his lips. "What do I need to do or understand in order to be released from the realm of the living back to the realm of reapers?"

It surprised me that he'd said something so personal in front of Damien and Lynnette. I wasn't sure Lynnette even knew that Rogan was a reaper trapped in a mage's body.

"And what did the oracle say?" I asked.

It was so silent in the car, and for a moment, all I heard was the sound of my own heartbeat.

"He said I must find someone like me in this realm and through that person fully embrace my humanness. That person would be the key to getting my wish," Rogan said in a low voice.

A tiny pang gripped my heart. I didn't know how to grant his wish, and I was relieved to not be the one in the dragon's prophecy. I really didn't want Rogan to go.

He turned off the freeway at an exit that didn't seem to lead to much except farm roads. It literally felt like the middle of nowhere, with no buildings or city lights within miles. The sagebrush that dotted the landscape was skeletal this time of year. It looked ghostly silver in the dark.

"Who opens the rip?" I asked him as he pulled off a two-lane dirt road.

"I'm pretty sure it's opened from the inside."

He put the Jeep into park and killed the engine, and we all piled out into the cold winter night. He began to stride in a seemingly random direction.

"This way." He beckoned us to follow him over the uneven, rocky terrain.

Shivering as much with adrenaline as chill, I trotted to keep up with him. Loki kept pace right beside me.

When Rogan tipped his head back to look at the dark sky, I squinted to follow his gaze. I thought I saw the movement of flying creatures above. His demon minions must have been helping him navigate.

He stopped and looked around, and Damien, Lynnette, Loki, and I huddled at Rogan's sides. Rogan lifted his arm and pointed off to the left.

"There. The rip is beginning to form."

At first I didn't see anything, but then my eyes snagged on a faint vertical line that was little more than a thick black slash in the already dark night. We all took off at a jog in that direction, and Loki gave a little yip of excitement. I watched, transfixed, as the black line split and then bowed outward at each side, stretching into an oblong shape with the lowest point hovering just a few inches off the ground. Neon blue magic licked through the rip like a bunch of forked tongues.

Damien gasped. "Whoa."

We pulled to a stop. Loki was wagging his tail, and his pupils had begun to burn orange. Part of me noted with amusement the contrast between the eager doggy wag and the flames of hell licking in his eyes.

"How do we know when to go through?" I asked

"Not yet." Rogan's eyes were intent on the rip. "You'll go in first with Loki."

I'd forgotten a leash, which inspired a brief pang of pet-owner anxiety. What if he ran up and snarled at the oracle? Or tried to lift his leg on the piles of gold or whatever it was dragons surrounded themselves with? I pushed the worry away. Switchboard had seemed confident it was a good idea to bring my hellhound-doodle, so I had to trust it would go well.

"Okay." Rogan nodded at me. "We'll be right behind you."

I touched Loki's head, and he stayed at my side as we moved forward toward the dark oval. I could see nothing within it. As I stepped through, I was disappointed to feel no change—no shiver of magic in the air, no heat, nothing to indicate I was passing from one dimension to another.

Perfect darkness swallowed me, and for a dizzying moment, I thought the ground had fallen away. But I kept walking, taking some solace in the firm surface beneath my feet. I reached for Loki and felt his furry neck under my fingertips. Two red-orange eyes looked up at me.

By the soft scuffing echoes of four pairs of shoes, it sounded as if we were in a large, hard-walled space. It was noticeably warmer than where we'd come from, and a faint aroma of sulfur, smoke, and spice hung in the air. It wasn't an unpleasant smell, but it was wild and exotic in a way that made my pulse tap a little faster.

"Okay, Rogan, now what?" I asked, focused on keeping my balance in the disorienting dark.

"Stay here and wait," he said. He sounded calm, and his voice seemed to help orient me, even if it was just to know he was nearby.

"Is it as pitch black in here to you guys as it is to me?" I asked.

"Black as night," came Lynnette's voice from behind me and a little off to the right.

"Yep," agreed Damien. "Can't even see the rip magic from in here."

One of the guys—Rogan, I thought—quietly whistled a few notes of Darth Vader's theme.

I snorted. "You're hilarious."

As my eyes adjusted, I became aware of very faint points of light domed around us, and it gave me a sense of the space in which we stood. It seemed to be a cavern, and the tiny lights glowed like the most miniaturized Christmas lights imaginable. The lights began to brighten and break into facets, revealing that it was no ordinary cave we stood in. Each light was centered in a pointed crystal attached to the cavern walls and ceiling. The space was enormous, half a football field long and maybe half that high.

I gasped as I took it in, astonished at the sheer magnificence. It was as if we'd been transported into the middle of a geode shot through with rainbows.

But there was a negative space ahead, a huge widening column of darkness.

I gripped Lynnette's ring tightly in my fist.

The dark column bowed out at both sides into an oblong. It was an enormous rip. The widening void was suddenly punctuated by two hellfire eyes the shape of sideways teardrops.

Loki gave a sharp bark and then whined. It wasn't a warning so much as the sounds of an excited canine. There was a cracking sound and then something fell to the floor. I saw Loki moving in my periphery and almost reached out a hand to grab his collar and try to still him when I realized he had no collar. The pop I'd heard was the plastic buckle breaking, and his collar lay on the ground. I peered at my dog.

My Loki was no longer there. Instead, a taller, shaggier beast stood next to me. I sucked in a breath, wondering if bringing him along had been a mistake after all, but he looked up at me and panted a doggy smile. Stunned, I bent to pick up his collar.

"What the hell . . . ?" Damien whispered. He wasn't staring at my dog. He hadn't even noticed the change. His head was tipped back as he gaped up.

I looked up to find something had materialized within the huge rip. It was the scaled creature I'd seen in the coven circle and later in a dream.

An acrid smell reminiscent of a struck match filled the cavern. The temperature was rising rapidly. The creature ducked its serpentine head and stepped through the rip with an almost delicate movement. When the great dragon moved, there were faint metallic clicks and scrapes. Its hide looked to be made of soft gold scales, and rip magic licked the air around it as if the dragon were on fire.

"Ella Grey."

The beast's voice was something between a rumbling growl and a loud exhale, and it was like nothing I'd ever heard. Hot breath washed over me, like a fiery draft following the dragon's words.

The rip behind the beast narrowed and disappeared behind its body. The dragon's legs seemed too slender for such a massive body. The lizard-like tail curled around toward us, revealing its bulbous end, which bristled with nasty-looking spines each at least a foot long. The creature wasn't brandishing his tail though. He was making himself comfortable. With the tail curled around the body and the great leathery wings folded along the sloping back, he lowered himself into a reclining posture, like a cat curled on a pillow. His head towered twenty feet overhead, the claws tipping one front appendage only half a dozen feet away from my boots.

I swallowed, uncertain if I was supposed to respond, and if so, what would be the proper thing to say. Again, I squeezed my fist around the skull ring. Without moving my head, I flicked a glance at Loki. He lay flat on the floor with his head ducked, almost as if prostrating himself.

"Pose your question," the creature intoned, lingering on the hissing s sounds. Steam rose from the nostrils on the end of an alligator-like snout.

Pose . . . ? Okay, then. The dragon wasn't into small talk. Fine by me.

I tried to work some moisture back into my mouth. I didn't want advice. I wanted real answers. How to get out of the coven. How to save my brother and get him healthy. How to get the business with Damien off the ground so I could help Deb and the baby.

Everything seemed to come back in some way to my magic and surviving my own power. I had a plan for that, between Jennifer's spell and Phillip Zarella's offer, but additional backup from a different angle couldn't hurt.

"What do I need to do or understand in order to get my magic back and survive its power?" I asked, remembering how Rogan had phrased his own question.

The creature's head darted forward so quickly my reflexes weren't fast enough, and I stayed rooted to the spot. He angled his head slightly so one giant teardrop eye filled my vision. I watched the hypnotic dance of flames in the vertical reptilian iris.

"Wrong question, Ella Grey," the dragon roared. The force of the creature's breath blew my hair back, and the searing heat made my eyes stream and my skin burn.

My heart bumped, and I sucked in a breath, trying to imagine what the punishment would be for asking the wrong thing.

"Why?" The word slipped out before I could catch it.

The dragon's eye squinted at me.

"Why is that the wrong question?" I tried again.

"There is a deeper, wider, more urgent understanding you must gain," the dragon whispered. "You must look back in time to understand what happened then."

A bigger mission? Back in time?

I shook my head, trying to guess what the creature meant. "Do you mean my . . . uncle?" I asked, my voice dropping. "The original Rip?"

The creature huffed steam but didn't answer.

"A gift," the dragon said finally, and I swear he actually sounded a little petulant. He turned his head away. "I require a gift."

I blinked, not following.

"The ring," Rogan whispered behind me. "Offer him the ring."

Oh, right. I opened my fist and held up the silver skull ring.

"Please take this gift," I said. I stretched my arm out with the ring pinched in my fingertips.

The dragon peeked around to see what I held. I tilted the ring, and the pink crystals caught the light of the creature's great eye. The fire in the iris flared.

I froze as the dragon shifted its great body, my eyes growing wide as it lifted one alligator-like arm. A claw as long and sharp as a steak knife extended toward me. My hand only trembled a little as I gingerly placed the ring onto the tip of the claw.

"You may ask another," he said, tucking his claws around his body and hiding Lynnette's ring.

I drew a breath. "Who stole my brother five years ago?"

The dragon's eye loomed closer as he pushed his face so near I could have reached out and touched the gold-encrusted scales on his snout.

"Wrong. But closer, so I shall answer," he said.

Then he reared back, stretching tall on his hind legs. He spread his wings as far as they could extend within the confines of the crystal cave, and he loomed high like a phoenix ready to rise.

"One . . . of . . . your . . . own . . . blood." Each word boomed like a boulder falling from a great height and then echoed in the cavern so violently that sediment shook loose from the ceiling and filtered down through the softly lit air.

Something harsh and buzzing, like a swarm of angry bees, seemed to descend on my head and downward to surround me. Some sort of magic? It beat against my skin, and I imagined this was what it might feel like to go through a car wash naked.

I ground my teeth and swung out with my arms, trying to fight it off, but they hit nothing. The sensation intensified to the point of becoming maddening, like being pricked by a million tiny needles.

Cracking my eyelids open, I saw the black vertical line form in between me and the dragon, so close I could have reached out and brushed it with my fingertips. It yawned into a huge black disc, cutting me off from the creature. With the violent formation of the rip, there came a rush of air.

I staggered, squeezing my eyelids closed against the gale of air that sucked my hair forward and sent it whipping across my face. The dragon's departure was creating an awful vacuum within the cavern. My eardrums felt like they were on the verge of bursting in the negative pressure.

I whirled around, trying to look for the others just as a hand closed around my wrist.

"C'mon, Ella!" Rogan's words seemed to get whipped away almost immediately.

He dragged me back toward the rip that had reopened behind us. Through it I saw Boise's city lights in the distance and stars above the horizon.

Damien went through and then Lynnette with Loki right on her heels. Rogan dragged me out of the crystal cavern, and I sucked in a deep lungful of winter air. I didn't even care it was freezing out. I was so relieved to have escaped with my eardrums still intact. We all stood there catching our breath.

There was a soft rustle in the sagebrush off to the right. I spun around. I'd flipped the strap off my whip, and it was in my hand as fast as a reflex. Loki growled.

"Who's there?" I called out, peering into the darkness.

There was more rustling, and a beam of light cut through the night and flared in my face, blinding me. I threw up my left arm to shield my eyes.

"It's them," came a rough, unfamiliar voice from behind the glaring light. "Go."

The light switched off, leaving me with blinding blotches dancing across my vision.

"What the—" Damien started, but his question ended in a grunt.

Motion and footfalls suddenly surrounded us. I lunged, cracking my whip at the forms emerging from the cover of the bushes. A golf-ball sized blob of light whizzed past my left ear.

I brought the whip around again, striking out at where the light had come from. I felt the whip find its target just as a male voice let out a cursing bellow.

I heard Lynnette let out a frustrated screech, but then she was silent.

White lights were popping like camera flashes around me. I dropped to the ground as I recognized the *click-whoosh* sounds of magic-fueled stun guns being fired. They were weapons used to disarm violent crowds and temporarily cut crafters off from their magic.

Furiously blinking the spots from my eyes, I army-crawled toward the nearest bush, hoping to take cover. Loki was snarling and barking like mad.

"Oh no you don't." An iron grip grabbed my boot and yanked me back, dragging me along the rough, cold desert floor.

I flipped to my back and flexed my wrist, praying my whip hadn't gotten caught on anything. It sang through the air and snapped with a satisfying sound. I thought I'd caught the guy across the face, but he still held on to my ankle. A dark, furry blur flew in from the side and knocked my would-be captor clean off his feet. My boot was free, and I pushed up to my feet and began to run.

"Go, Loki!" I shouted, hoping he'd get away.

"That way!" a female voice shouted behind me.

I could hear at least two people in pursuit. I chanced a look over my shoulder. Big mistake. I turned my ankle and tripped. Seeing I had no chance of staying upright, I tucked my head just in time as I flew into an unplanned roll. The ground sloped away sharply, and I tumbled ass over teakettle into a shallow gulley.

My pursuers veered away from where I lay spread-eagled, my ankle throbbing. Still except for my heaving chest, I listened.

After a moment, I heard nothing, so I raised my head.

A figure appeared to loom above me.

"Gotcha," the guy said with glee.

A bright flash hit me square in the middle of my stomach. Pain lanced through me, and then the world numbed and faded away.

I came to with a pounding headache and my arms pulled around behind me. By the ache in my shoulders, I'd been in that position for a while.

With my head drooping forward and my chin on my chest, I carefully opened my eyes just enough to assess my situation. I could see concrete floor under my boots. I was seated on a metal chair, and a subtle tug of my arms told me my hands were bound to each other but not tied to the chair.

A brain-cramping screech of metal on concrete announced that I had company.

"Sleeping beauty awakes." I recognized the voice of the guy who'd taken me out.

I raised my head to find him straddling a dented folding chair turned backward, his beefy arms folded across the back. A quick glance showed no sign of Rogan, Damien, Lynnette, or Loki. Maybe they'd gotten away.

"Oh my, you turned your chair around. You must be a *badass*," I said with mock wide-eyed awe.

He narrowed his eyes at me and then slapped his knee and let out a mocking laugh.

"I heard you might be difficult, but that was funny." He waggled his index finger at me with a knowing, I've-got-your-number look on his face.

I forced my pulse to stay steady. I didn't know who this guy was or what he wanted, but he'd reveal it soon enough, I assumed. In the meantime, I needed to get my bearings. I spotted my whip coiled on a scuffed conference table that had been shoved to the far end of the room. Next to the table was a door—heavy-looking, with a metal push bar instead of a handle or knob. Faint black tire tracks marked the floor with greasy-looking stains here and there, and the stale smell of motor oil lingered in the air. I guessed I was in approximately the middle of the room, and the two of us seemed to be alone.

The overhead fluorescent lights glared unflatteringly, highlighting barely-visible acne scars on the guy's cheeks. He looked about my age, muscular to the point of being bulky, maybe ex-military and almost certainly a mercenary.

"Who do you work for?" I demanded.

His mild amusement dissolved between one blink and the next. "I'll be asking the questions."

He stood, drew his leg back, and then booted his chair off to the side. It flew out of view and hit the wall with a clanging clatter. Over his shoulder, I noticed a camera mounted high in the corner of the room. He turned to me, and I saw he held a small device that looked like a shortened cattle prod, which had been hidden from view behind the back of the chair while he'd been sitting. But even worse than the torture device was the eager gleam in his eye.

This was not good. Not at all. He was one of those crazies who got off on this shit.

"Just tell me what your boss wants," I said, my voice low and even.

He wanted me to resist. He'd relish it.

He held up the prod, and an arc of light sprang between the prongs, accompanied by electric zaps. I managed not to wince. He strolled forward and stopped in front of me. I had to tip my head back to look up into his face.

"Where's the box?" he asked, his voice mild.

I blinked. "Box?"

He jabbed the prod against the soft spot at the front of my shoulder. Pain exploded through me, and every muscle jumped convulsively.

Breath came raggedly through my nose, and I worked my jaw muscles loose. My brain whirled, trying to come up with something to stall the next jolt. Anything that might convince him to let me go.

"Okay, okay," I said, trying to sound as if I were relenting on the information he wanted. "I don't have it yet, and that's the truth. I don't give a damn about the box. As soon as I get it, it's all yours, I swear."

I wasn't lying. I didn't give a shit about whatever box he was talking about.

He peered at me suspiciously, and then his face hardened and he shook his head. "No, you wouldn't cross him that easily."

He raised the prod again.

"Why not? Why shouldn't I?" I asked, playing along and making it up as I went. I had a pretty good guess about who had sent this guy and the other goons. I carefully flicked my gaze across his clothing, looking for confirmation of who he was working for. "He, uh, hasn't done jack shit for me lately. I have no loyalty to him."

He brandished the prod, but there was hesitation in his eyes.

"You're either really brave or really stupid," he said. "He'll kill you and then turn your corpse into one of his flesh and bone puppets. Or maybe he'll keep you alive. I don't know which would be worse. Evil sonofabitch."

He shuddered, the cattle prod all but forgotten at his side.

A couple of puzzle pieces snapped into place in my mind, more or less confirming what I'd suspected.

"Zarella doesn't scare me," I said. "And you can pass that along to Gregori."

Jacob had sent them. He wanted whatever it was that Zarella had hired us to retrieve, but Jacob had miscalculated, probably mistakenly thinking we'd picked up the item when we'd gone through the rip to the dragon.

"We don't have it yet," I said. "That wasn't what we were doing in the desert. Zarella hasn't even told us where it is."

The door at the end of the room opened, and my captor swung around. It didn't open far enough for me to see who was on the other side.

"C'mere," the unseen person said.

The beefcake with the cattle prod jogged to the door, bent his head and listened for a moment, and then nodded and whispered a few words.

He tossed the prod on the table and stalked toward me as he reached for a knife sheathed on his hip. I drew back, as much as I could in my current position. Knife in his fist, he went around me, and a moment later my hands were free.

"Get your shit and get out," he said.

I jumped up and backed away. "Huh?"

"You're free."

His jaw muscles bulged, and he folded his arms. He looked pretty pissed about losing his opportunity to torture me further.

Keeping my eyes on him, I backed up to the table and reached for my whip. My phone and the knife and sheath that were usually attached to my waistband were nestled in the coils like eggs in a nest. I snatched up my things just as the garage door at the opposite end of the room, which I was now seeing for the first time, began to rise.

With one last look at the guy, I sprinted past him toward the dark night outside. As I passed him, I caught sight of the handgun holstered on his thigh. The leather holster was stamped with a G enclosed in a circle.

The Gregori Industries insignia.

Yep, good old Uncle Jacob.

I spun around in the darkness, looking for any clue as to where the hell I was. Not the Gregori campus, I was fairly sure. I was surrounded by two long rows of garage doors. A storage facility? I took off. I'd worry about everything else once I'd put some distance between me and the guy with the cattle prod.

"Ella?"

I shakily skidded to a halt at the sound of a familiar voice calling out my name. Lynnette came running up behind me.

I looked beyond her. "Were the others with you?"

She bent over and placed her hands on her knees, shaking her head. She was trying not to puke, I realized. I edged back a step.

"What happened? Are you okay?" I asked. As much as I wanted to hightail it as far away as possible, I was actually glad for an excuse to just stand there for a second. My legs didn't feel entirely stable.

She held up a finger, silently asking for a moment.

A scrabbling noise against the pavement sent my pulse flying. I squeezed the handle of my whip, my arm tensed and ready to lash out. I wasn't sure how long I'd last in a physical confrontation. My muscles were still shaking from the zap from the cattle prod.

A couple of little yips announced that the dark blur bearing down on us was no threat. Loki flew at me, hitting my chest with his front paws and nearly taking me down. He was back to the hellhound-doodle form I recognized.

I knelt and wrapped my arms around his shaggy neck. "I'm happy to see you, too, boy." He lapped at my arm with his tongue.

"Where are the guys?" I asked. Turning my attention back to Lynnette, I realized she was still dry-heaving. "Geez, what did they do to you?"

"The guys got away." She shook her head. "This will pass in a minute. I'm just having some major after effects from getting my magic back so abruptly when they released me." She straightened and pushed her dark hair away from her face. "I've never been cut off for so long. I don't know how you've survived it for days on end."

"It's better than the alternative," I said grimly.

I pulled out my phone and saw a series of messages from Rogan and Damien. They'd escaped, and they were looking for us.

I beckoned to Lynnette. "Let's get out of here."

I called Damien and told him we were at some sort of storage facility. I checked my GPS and found we were about a mile from where we'd entered the rip, and I relayed that to him.

"They're coming to get us," I told Lynnette.

Lynnette and I ran toward the end of the row of storage units with Loki loping along with us.

I glanced at her. "Did they ask you about a box?"

"Yeah. What was that about?"

"No idea," I said.

"So you think, what, they had the wrong people." It was so clear she didn't believe me that she didn't even bother phrasing it as a question.

"I don't know what they were talking about. You don't know what they were talking about. So yeah, I'd say they had the wrong people."

We'd reached the end of a row. I slowed to figure out which way to go.

"There." Lynnette pointed at what looked like the entrance.

I nearly sagged with relief when I saw we wouldn't have to scale a fence to get out. My legs still didn't feel quite right. It was more than just the shock from the prod. I suspected I was also still suffering the residual effects of the blast that had knocked me out in the desert.

We ducked under the bar that blocked the driveway into the storage facility. I scanned down the road and realized headlights were bearing down on us. I wasn't sure if it was our ride or not. I was just about to pull Lynnette behind the facility's sign when Loki gave an excited bark and wagged his tail.

The vehicle screeched to a halt, and I let out a breath. It was Rogan's Jeep.

The driver side door swung open.

"Hop in!" Rogan shouted.

I saw Damien in the passenger seat.

I jerked open the back door, shoved Loki in ahead of me, and dove in. Lynnette crammed in behind me, and Rogan took off before she had the door closed.

"Did you guys get away before they knocked you out?" I asked. My heart was still slamming in my chest.

"They got Damien, but I managed to steal him back before they took off with him," Rogan said.

He was driving like a bat out of hell. I squinted into the dark, trying to figure out where we were. Still a couple miles outside of the city, it looked like.

Damien twisted in his seat. "Are either of you hurt?"

"Not permanently," I said. "You can slow down."

"What?" Rogan glanced at me in the rearview mirror.

"It's okay, they let me and Lynnette go. They're not going to come after us."

He eased off the gas pedal a little.

"What in the hell *was* that?" Damien asked. He pulled his hands down his face. "I seriously thought we were going to be corpses buried out there in the desert."

"I think it was mistaken identity," I said. I'd fill in Damien later on my real suspicions about what had just happened. "We both got questioned, but when they realized we didn't have what they wanted, they let—"

"I disagree," Lynnette cut in. "I don't think it was a mistake, but I do know it wasn't *me* they wanted." She peered at me sharply.

I exhaled loudly. I was not in the mood for this. "I don't have a box, and I don't know about any box. Seriously, lay off, will you? I think we've all had enough for one night."

We crossed over into the city limits. Returning to humanity made it a little easier to shake off the crawling in my brain ever since I'd spotted the Gregori logo on the beefcake's holster. But I really needed to talk to Damien alone. I was pretty sure that Jacob had accidentally tipped his hand.

"Drop off Lynnette first," I said to Rogan.

"Nope, my car is at your place," she said, folding her arms with a self-satisfied little smile. "Remember? I was at your birthday party, and then I left with you to do you a favor in the middle of the night. Oh, and then I got knocked out and tied up for my trouble."

"Look, I'm sorry about what happened," I said. "But it wasn't my fault. It was just an ugly misunderstanding."

We mused over what had happened as we made our way back to the city. The front window of my apartment was dark, and it appeared the party was over.

"See you tomorrow at the coven meeting," Lynnette trilled in an overly cheerful voice as she got out of the Jeep.

I swore under my breath as I watched her stride down the street toward her car. I wasn't going to the damn coven meeting no matter what she threatened. I had more important things to do.

Loki hopped out and bounded around in the grassy area in front of the porch, and I leaned forward between the guys.

"Let me know tomorrow about what's next?" I asked Rogan.

He nodded and gave me a look from under hooded lids. In spite of my current condition, heat stirred through me. This night might have ended differently if I wasn't still suffering the aftershocks of the various weapons I'd been subjected to. Personal indulgences would have to wait.

I wearily dragged myself out of the car and to the sidewalk, and Loki came over to bounce circles around me.

I waited until Rogan had pulled away and then grabbed Damien's sleeve and pulled him close.

"It was Gregori," I whispered. "He thought we had something from Zarella. A box."

He grasped my elbow before I even realized I was swaying on my feet.

"You okay?"

I briefly closed my eyes and nodded. "I'll be fine. Just a little shaky. Count yourself lucky you didn't get taken in."

"So you think Gregori knows Zarella hired us, and Gregori wants whatever we're going to be hunting down." His brows pulled low over his eyes. "Gregori must not have great info if he didn't know we don't have it yet."

"And it must be pretty damn important for him to jump us that way, and torture—" I cut myself off with a growl. I'd almost said, "Torture his own niece." Damien didn't know that Jacob Gregori was my uncle, and I preferred to keep it that way.

"Wait, *torture*?"

I shrugged. "One of his lackeys hit me with a cattle prod."

It was Damien's turn to curse. "Are you sure you're not hurt? I can take you to the emergency room."

I waved a hand in the air, brushing off his concern. "Nah. But we're going to have to tell Zarella he's been made. Gregori's going to be breathing down our necks if he thinks we'll lead him to the box. Hell, he might even kill us for it if he wants it badly enough. He could easily make us disappear. He could have done it tonight if we'd already had what he wanted. We can't go forward with Zarella's job."

"But Gregori doesn't know that we know he's behind it," Damien protested. "We can use that to our advantage. I bet Zarella can help. I say we go ahead with it."

I had no idea how Damien thought we could use the knowledge to gain the upper hand, but I knew he couldn't stand the thought of giving up what Zarella had offered.

We stared at each other by the weak light of the front porch fixture. Zarella had dangled the ultimate power in front of Damien, and he wanted it—badly.

Maybe we were both stupid for wanting impossible things.

"I'll tell Zarella what happened and see what he says," Damien finally said.

"Okay. It's fricking freezing out here," I said. "Let's get some shut-eye, yeah?"

He nodded, turned, and flipped a wave at me over his shoulder as he trudged toward his Lexus. "Talk to you tomorrow."

Loki and I went into the dark apartment, and I beelined to the kitchen, suddenly in dire need of a sugar fix.

"Oh, thank god," I whispered as I spotted a plate with half a dozen cupcakes on it. I peeled part of the paper away and ate half of it in one bite. I finished it off, licked purple frosting from my thumb, and took another.

Loki sat, transfixed and unblinking, watching me chow down.

"Hey, I earned this," I said around a mouthful of cake. "Don't judge."

The next morning I was rudely awakened by my phone buzzing against my cheekbone and jangling in my ear. I didn't even remember falling asleep with the thing on my pillow.

It was Rogan.

I sat up, raking my tangled hair off my face with one hand and holding the phone up to my ear with the other.

"Hello?" I croaked.

"Morning, sunshine," Rogan said. "The underworld council is convening a special session to usher you into their ranks. Today."

"Today?" I repeated stupidly, still trying to clear the fog of sleep from my brain.

I'd agreed to join the underworld to appease Zarella, but I hadn't really given it much thought beyond that. Suddenly it all started to feel a whole lot more real.

"Tonight, actually. The council meets at eight," Rogan said.

Rogan and I arranged to meet up and then go to the location of the council meeting, which would be held at some sort of facility in the hills.

I had no doubt Zarella had his own reasons for wanting to pull me into the underworld. I wondered how long before he'd reveal them. In any case, once I was officially inducted, he owed me the big fix to my reaper problem. And with Jen's help, I was on the verge of getting my magic back. I'd deal with the consequences of it all later.

I went to Damien's to work, and he showed me Zarella's reply, which essentially said that we didn't have to worry about any more interference from Gregori. I didn't know if I wished he'd said otherwise or not.

Damien and I passed the day applying for contract jobs. It was mundane work, but there was a moment, just a few seconds really, when I looked up from my laptop. I watched him as he typed, his brow furrowed in concentration. A strange sense of pause came over me, as if a ball had been tossed in the air, and that very second was the one where the ball stopped its ascent and hung there, suspended, before gravity pulled it back down.

Things were going to change. If Zarella offered Damien a way to become a mage, he would take it. Even though Zarella had warned there would be a cost.

Our deal with Zarella was going to restore me to who I was supposed to be. It was going to give me a chance to survive and live the new life I'd been given since my accident. But it was going to turn Damien into someone else, and it wasn't going to come cheap.

An uncomfortable sensation of weight settled in the center of my chest.

Back at home that evening, Deb and I made an early dinner. Lately she had an insatiable appetite for mac and cheese and fresh arugula salad drenched in some gross-looking greenish dressing. I couldn't complain though because at least it was an inexpensive meal. I wasn't sure what we would have done if her pregnancy cravings were filet mignon and caviar.

When we started cleaning up, I knew I couldn't procrastinate any longer.

I turned to her. "I'm not going to the coven meeting."

She paused with the faucet running into the bowl we'd used to mix up the macaroni, and her eyes found mine.

"Tonight I meet with the underworld council for some kind of induction ceremony," I said.

She shut off the water and slowly scrubbed at the bowl.

"I don't like this," she said. "Any of it. Zarella, that dragon creature, the underworld necro creepers who'll do who-knows-what to you. After last night . . . "

Earlier that morning I'd told her all about the crystal cave and our misadventures in the desert. I'd tried to downplay the hands-bound cattle prod incident, but Deb had gone pale and had to sit down when I got to that part.

"I won't be all on my own," I said. "Rogan is taking me. He's already part of the underworld, and he'll have my back. I know the idea of the underworld is a little unsavory, but they're not out to harm me."

I was talking out of my ass. I had no idea what the Society of the Underworld was really like or how the membership regarded or treated one another. For all I knew, they gathered every full moon to sacrifice small animals and dance with demons around a burning effigy. The only shred of reassurance I felt about any of it was because of Rogan.

"I hate that you're missing coven activities, too." She pouted. "I like that we do those things together."

I gave her a wry look. "Deb, we live together. We see plenty of each other."

"I know, it's just, well, things are going to change, you know?" She absently rubbed one hand over her pregnant belly. "Things are *already* changing. You're not on Demon Patrol anymore. You're going to bring Evan home. I'm going to be a mom soon. It's all going to be different."

I forced a smile. "You and I will still be the same, though."

I couldn't help noticing how closely her sentiment echoed what I'd felt earlier at Damien's. An uncomfortable tightness spread through my chest. I knew change was inevitable. Some of it, like Evan's return, I welcomed. But uncertainty seemed the prevailing theme in my life these days, and as much as I wanted to feel sure of *something*, I knew I had to ride it out the best I could.

We both fell into quiet pensiveness until she had to leave for Lynnette's. By the time Rogan came to get me, I was more than ready to get out of the silent apartment. Ironic, considering how I used to covet my space. I ran out before he had a chance to come up to the door.

My pulse jumped when I got into his Jeep, and it wasn't just because of nerves about the underworld council. My brain insisted on calling up in great detail the feel of his lips crushing mine and the pressure of his chest against me.

"Are you sure you're up for this?" he asked, casting me a couple of quick glances.

I cleared my throat. "Yeah. The quicker the better."

"So, um, you're going to get marked. It's part of the ceremony."

"What?"

He gave me an apologetic look. "It's small."

"Where's your mark?" I asked.

He reached around to the back of his neck and pulled down the collar of his duster. I leaned over, squinting. It looked like there was some sort of red-inked design.

"I can't really see it," I said.

"Hang on." He pulled up to a stoplight, switched on his phone's flash, and handed me the device. He twisted around so I could get a better view.

I used his phone like a flashlight and saw an impossibly intricate, slightly raised geometric design about the size of a nickel just above the neck of his t-shirt.

The light turned green, and he let go of his collar so he could drive.

"Each one is slightly different, like a fingerprint," he said.

"Did it hurt?" I asked.

"It didn't tickle. It's fast, though."

Awesome, I was going to get *branded*.

"So what's the draw of the underworld?" I asked. "Why did you join up?"

"I was looking for a way out," he said. "I thought I might find someone who had the answer."

It took me a second to realize what he meant. "Obviously you didn't find what you were looking for."

"No."

"What about for others? Why do they want into this club?"

He shrugged. "Exclusivity makes it desirable, of course, like with any other human club. And there's a lot of opportunity for networking with people who are knowledgeable, rich, powerful, you name it. Another thing humans seem drawn to."

We were heading up in elevation on Bogus Basin Road, which led to a recreation and ski area. But about halfway up, Rogan took a turn onto an unmarked dirt road.

"This place is pretty wild," he said. "You ever play Dungeons and Dragons?"

I gave him a baffled look. "Um, no. When I was a kid I was too busy working and trying to keep my brother from doing anything too stupid." A slight grin formed on my lips. "You play Dungeons and Dragons?"

"I dabbled, decades ago."

"What does D and D have to do with anything?"

"Let's just say the owner of the place we're going is very wealthy and has a penchant for the fantastical. You've been warned." He gave a low chuckle.

We were winding along a well-groomed dirt road through the trees, our route giving no clue as to what waited ahead.

When the trees parted and revealed a clearing, I expected to see either a medieval castle, based on Rogan's warning, or a log mansion tastefully designed to blend in with the natural surroundings.

What I saw was neither. It looked more like a huge, modernized Egyptian tomb. A roughly pyramidal shape, except with the peaked top lopped off, it was all smooth stucco surfaces and sloping lines, with no discernable roofline and few windows. There were two large lit torches marking the entrance. It looked like something from a Disneyland set.

Half a dozen cars were already parked off to the side. As Rogan pulled up next to a late model Hummer, I thought I saw something moving through the trees just beyond the light cast by the torches.

I shaded my eyes, peering into the forest. I could have sworn it was a person.

"Ready?" Rogan asked.

I turned and followed him toward the entrance, where the front door was set so far in it was almost like a cave. There was no bell, but a camera was mounted over the ten-foot tall, bolt-studded, wood plank door.

He flipped a little wave at the camera, and a moment later there was a mechanical *thunk*. He reached for the metal handle that bore rune carvings and pushed the door open.

Inside was a corridor lined with smaller glass-enclosed versions of the torches we'd seen out front. I couldn't imagine the ventilation system that kept each individual sconce free of smoke.

The walls were painted with scenes that did indeed look like they were lifted from fantasy video games and fairy tales. A bearded sorcerer standing on a mountain. An armored knight on a black stallion. A maiden with long golden hair sitting beside a pond and trailing her fingers in the water. It would have been beautiful if not for her ridiculously huge breasts spilling from her corset. A mural of a battle scene featuring dragons, elves, trolls, fae, vampires, and just about every other supernatural creature I could imagine stretched for a dozen feet.

We passed a handful of heavy-looking wood doors that were scaled smaller than the front door but still oversized enough to make me feel like I was walking through a giant's house. They were all closed and bore keyed locks.

The floor began to slope downward, and I couldn't help imagining an honest-to-god dungeon waiting somewhere below.

What I actually found brought the start of a grin to my face. The corridor ended at a room that could have held about ten of my apartments. It was part pub, part man cave, and all fantastic whimsy. A bar lined a good portion of one wall, but it wasn't like any bar I'd ever seen. The entire thing was upholstered in gaudy gold vinyl. An iron sculpture of a dragon's skeleton hung suspended from the vaulted ceiling like a dinosaur display at a natural history museum. Medieval weapons mounted in glass cases decorated the walls. A giant TV screen hung like a dark window, with three rows of recliners set up like movie seats below it.

There were three pool tables, one of which was in use by a woman with gray-streaked dreadlocks and a guy who I could only describe as swashbuckling. He wore a loose-fitting white shirt, dark leather pants, tall boots, and a red bandana around his head like a sweatband.

Half a dozen men and women were gathered at the far end of the bar. One of the women was dressed in flowing fabric and a headscarf that made her look like a palm-reading Gypsy wannabe.

A clean-cut man in his late fifties with neat salt-and-pepper hair and a paunch that hung over the front of his pants strode forward. He was wearing an actual velvet smoking jacket and held a lit cigar in his left hand. He looked vaguely familiar.

He extended his free hand. "Ed Jensen. Welcome to my playground."

Ah yes, the third generation owner of Jensen Motors, a huge local car dealership.

I grasped his hand. "Ella Grey."

"We'll get started in just a few minutes," Ed said. He made a sweeping motion with his cigar. "Please, make yourself at home."

"Thanks," I said.

Ed drifted back toward the bar, and I turned to Rogan.

"Is he on the council?" I whispered.

Rogan shook his head. "Nah, he's just a member like me. He likes to play host."

I looked around at the others.

"Only one council member is local," Rogan said. "Well, aside from Zarella. The rest will send their proxies. The other ones gathered are part of the society membership."

"Okay, let's get this over with," I said and headed toward the group at the bar. Rogan trailed after me.

The Gypsy lady was the first to notice us.

"It's the guest of honor," she said in a thick Eastern European accent that sounded genuine. Maybe the Romani costume wasn't a costume after all. She took one of my hands in both of hers. "I am Florica."

I shook her hand, and to my relief, Rogan stepped up and introduced me to the rest of the group, an eclectic mix of people who at a glance I would have assumed had nothing in common.

Mark, a slight pale guy with thinning hair and glasses, who reminded me of a junior high math teacher, went around to the other side of the bar.

"What's your poison?" he asked.

I didn't really feel like a drink and nearly waved him off, but everyone else was holding a glass or a bottle. It dawned on me that this crowd was probably much more my style than the tea-and-mulled-wine drinking coven.

"A lager?" I said.

"Oh no, you must have something stronger than beer," Florica insisted. "Give her a swig of Ed's Five Points."

Mark gave a little *heh-heh* laugh and reached under the counter. He produced a clear bottle, with nothing but a pentagram on the label, and a shot glass.

"Ed's potato vodka. He distills it right here." Mark poured a generous shot.

I tilted my head and eyed it. "This isn't going to make me go blind, is it?"

Everyone chuckled.

"Ed would be walking around with a seeing-eye dog by now if that were a danger," someone said behind me.

"I heard that," Ed called from a few feet away, where he was talking on his cell.

I picked up the shot glass and raised it. "*Salud.*"

I knocked it back, and my eyes bulged as fire hit my throat. The vodka was flavored with something spicy enough to make me want to dunk my head in a bucket of ice water. I coughed, and someone clapped me on the back.

"Cinnamon with a dash of jalapeno," Florica said.

"Why would anyone do that to perfectly good vodka?" I choked out.

She laughed good-naturedly as Mark popped the top off a bottle of beer and slid it across the counter to me. I caught Rogan's broad smile—a rare sight, but one I wouldn't mind seeing more of.

I downed half the beer in a couple of gulps just to put out the flames.

By the time Ed began rounding us up, my head felt pleasantly warm and thick.

He led us to a door at the back near the pool tables, which opened into a small, round room with a domed ceiling and high stained-glass windows. The room was empty, the only real decorative flourish besides the windows was a many-pointed star integrated into the design of the marble floor. There was nothing overtly religious in sight, but the space had the feel of a chapel. The low conversation of the group hushed.

The room was dim when we walked in, with only a strip of tiny lights around the edge where the floor met the wall, so it took my eyes a second or two to adjust. I'd entered at the back of the crowd, and it also took me a moment to realize that our numbers had grown.

Too-still figures stood at intervals around the star on the floor. When I got a little closer, I sucked in a breath, automatically reaching for my whip. They were zombies. My vodka and beer-induced buzz vanished in a bolt of adrenaline.

Rogan placed his hand on my arm. "They're the proxies," he said quietly.

I'd seen zombies plenty of times on the news or in pictures on the internet but never in person.

The scent of burnt sage had already crept through the room. It was the aroma of the strong magic that up to that point I'd only heard of. It kept zombies from smelling like grave rot. There was an underlying note to the smell, something wild and fleshy that I preferred not to dwell on.

A door opposite the one we'd used to enter cracked open, and I nearly jumped as another zombie slipped in.

They were sometimes called braindead-undead, which was bluntly accurate. NECR2 kept its victims' bodies stubbornly alive, but the person inside was gone—lights were on, but nobody was home. It was like viral life support. And the virus was tenacious as hell in its purpose. Zombies could be killed only by incinerating their bodies to ash. As a general rule, all were put down because they were cannibals and obviously dangerous if left to roam free, not to mention the risk of infecting more people with the virus.

But some were kept for study, and there were rumors that others were occasionally acquired illegally by private citizens. I was presumably looking at twelve such specimens, controlled remotely by necromancers. The memory of the figure stealing through the forest outside flashed through my mind—I'd bet money it was one of these creatures.

"You're in the middle." Rogan gestured to the center of the star. He stepped close and whispered in my ear, "Just embrace it. You're going to be a great underworlder."

I flicked him a grateful glance and then turned sideways to move between two of the zombies, cringing internally. Contrary to how zombies were often portrayed, real ones didn't have special strength and weren't particularly fast. I could kill one before it had a chance to bite me. Still, the things were damn creepy, standing there dressed in regular clothes with vacant looks in their glazed eyes, staring at the floor.

One of them looked up, right at me. It opened its mouth and spoke with perfect enunciation. "Nice to see you, Ms. Grey."

I shuddered. Zarella. It wasn't his voice, but they were his words. I gave him a tiny nod of acknowledgment.

Twelve zombies were arranged around the star's points. To my surprise, Mark took the final position. For some reason he was one of the last I would have expected to be the one human representative of the underworld council in attendance. Rogan and the other non-council members lined the walls.

I couldn't help comparing this gathering to a coven circle. Zombies preceded by vodka shots at the bar versus witches and mulled wine around the kitchen island. It wasn't that I didn't appreciate the power of a coven. But it was painfully obvious that I seemed to fit in better in one scenario than the other. I wasn't exactly comfortable with that light-bulb moment, seeing as how the underworld gathering included animated corpses and Phillip Zarella as part of the leadership.

Ed joined me in the middle of the room.

"Death-touched necromancer Ella Grey joins our ranks today," he said, his voice carrying with a master-of-ceremonies tone to it. He winked at me. "It's going to pinch a little. Just stay right here."

He pointed to the starburst that formed the center of the larger design in the floor. I moved over so the soles of my boots nearly covered it as Ed stepped out of the zombie circle and went to the wall.

I inhaled slowly. Time to get the mark of the underworld.

Florica took a step away from the wall and raised her arms like a conductor ready to signal the first note of a symphony. The fabric of her flowy dress trailed from her arms, her garb adding to the drama of the moment.

I saw her magic glowing in strands that stretched between her hands. Half expecting her to zap me with it, I braced myself. But instead, she sent it upward to the domed ceiling, where the colored streams seemed to play and dart for a moment like fish in a bowl. Then the magic gathered at the apex and arrowed down on me like a bolt of lightning.

My entire body stiffened as hot pain lanced through me. The sensation swam through my veins and then retreated to a point at the back of my neck. It was like a hundred electric shocks concentrated in a single point. I squeezed my eyes closed and dug my nails into my palms, refusing to wince or reach up to touch where the pain was centered.

Then in the next breath it was gone.

I inhaled slowly through my nose and opened my eyes. The room was filled with the sounds of chanting, and it took my still-crackling brain a second to realize that I didn't recognize the language. I watched the jaws of the zombies move mechanically as their drivers spoke through them.

I stayed where I was until the chant ended. Rogan stood at the wall directly ahead, and the slow smile that spread over his face sent a thrill of heat through me.

Actually, my entire body felt hyper-awake and sensitized, as if a Roman candle had been lit inside me and its sparks surged through my blood.

I looked around, and everyone seemed to relax. Amid smiles and a few cheers, the underworlders clapped. I couldn't help a grin as my body buzzed. I hadn't felt this alive since I lost my magic.

A few people came up to shake my hand or clap me on the shoulder, and everyone began filtering back into the game room. I lingered, still getting my balance after the brief but powerful slap of magic. I reached up to touch the back of my neck. The skin was smooth but so sensitive my eyes widened.

"The sensation will fade some after a while," Rogan said. He lifted his chin, indicating something behind me. "Looks like someone wants to talk to you."

One of the zombies—Zarella's—was crooking its pointer finger at me, beckoning me closer.

Rogan stayed close as I moved toward the creature.

"I need to speak to Ms. Grey alone," Zarella's zombie said.

I nodded at Rogan. "I'll see you in there."

The zombie waited until the room had cleared. My eyes slid over the leathery skin, and I fought the urge to take a step back.

"Welcome to the underworld," the zombie said.

"Jacob wants it," I whispered urgently. "The thing you hired us to get for you."

"He does, he does." The zombie nodded, seemingly unconcerned.

I raised my hands "So? Doesn't that present a problem? Damien and I can't take the job if Gregori is going to be on us like white on rice."

The zombie folded its arms and then lifted a hand to tap at its chin, as if thinking.

"As I told your partner, you don't need to worry about that," Zarella said finally.

I shook my head.

"I don't think this is going to work," I said. "Sorry, but the job's off."

"Well, it would be your choice to not fulfill with my request. Of course, that would mean your partner would not receive the thing he desires."

"He'll get over it," I said.

The zombie chuckled. "I doubt that. In any case, you have fulfilled the first part of your obligation by joining us here, and I owe you something for it."

The zombie reached into the small satchel that was slung over one shoulder and across its body. It produced a tiny canvas drawstring bag the size of a coin purse.

"It contains what you seek, something that will keep your reaper from consuming you completely," Zarella said.

I grasped the bag. It felt like it had a few marbles inside.

"And what's the catch?" I asked.

"No catch, Ms. Grey. I'm confident I will get what I need without any trickery."

I eyed the zombie but of course couldn't read anything in its expression that might enlighten me to its driver's sincerity. I didn't believe he would purposely do me mortal harm. There was no benefit to him if I died.

There could be some other catch in the future. But the fact was, I had to try Zarella's fix even if it ended up having unwanted consequences. I had no other choice.

"I want to know about Damien's part of the deal," I said.

The zombie tilted his head in a gesture so normal and human it gave me the willies. "Meaning?"

"Meaning the price he'd pay. If he went through with it and got the power he wants, what would happen to him as a consequence?" I was trying to be as clear as possible. Zarella struck me as one of those people who could get slippery with language, finding loopholes in the semantics and the spaces between words.

"He would not be the same man afterward," he said. "A good friend would strongly encourage him not to take the opportunity. If he does it, he will no longer be the type of person you will want to associate with. I can almost guarantee that if he survives it, he will be lost to you."

Anger flashed though me. "Then why in the *hell* did you offer him a deal with the devil in the first place?" I said hotly.

"Because I need something. Surely you can relate to that, Ms. Grey."

I seethed silently for a moment, but what could I say? I'd made my own deal with Zarella with almost no hesitation. I was holding evidence of it in my hand that very second.

I lifted the drawstring bag he'd given me.

"No instructions?" I tried not to grip the pouch too tightly.

"Instructions are inside."

I'd always known I'd do anything to bring my brother back, but I hated the gratitude I felt. The irony wasn't lost on me that it looked as if Phillip Zarella had turned out to be my savior. I hastily pushed those thoughts aside.

Between the magic of the branding ceremony still zipping through me and the promise of what the pouch contained, I could barely hold still. With our business concluded, I left the zombie, and I went into the game room, where music was playing, the huge TV showed a football game on mute, and everyone had refreshed their drinks.

Florica strode to me with folded papers in one hand. She held out the packet.

"Rules and charter of the Society of the Underworld for your perusal. Nothing too serious, I assure you. We're a pretty casual group," she said. "And I need you to sign the official copy of your membership certificate. I'm the record keeper for this chapter of the Society, by the way."

Words began to appear in the air between us, as if drawn with a flame-inked pen. It was the certificate, and it bore a seal with the same design that was on the floor in the room where I'd been branded. Using my index finger, I traced my signature on the line at the bottom. The words vanished, leaving a wisp of vapor and a whiff of decaying leaves hanging in the air.

The energy from the ceremony seemed to be growing within me, rather than receding as I'd expected. My eyes sought Rogan. I spotted him leaning against the bar, not quite part of the group gathered there, but not quite separate from it either. As if sensing my gaze, his attention turned to me. He strode toward me, and I swear there was a sultry sparkle in his eyes. It set off my internal fireworks anew.

"Mind if we take off?" I asked when he got close enough.

He cocked a smile at me, and his lids lowered partway. "Quick goodbye to our host. He'd be offended if we disappeared suddenly."

I nodded and practically dragged him over to Ed. We made our pleasantries, and I begged off from the group when Mark offered another drink, and then Rogan and I hightailed it out of the game room.

We were barely out of sight of the others when Rogan turned to me, grasped my shoulders, and pushed me back against the wall. The back of my head smacked the stucco, but I didn't care. I twisted the lapels of his duster in my fists and pulled him roughly against me. Our lips met, and his fingers laced into my hair.

My pulse raced on the wave of the heat surging between us, and the world seemed to shrink down to only him. I was drunk on the smell of his skin, the taste of his lips, the pressure of his chest holding me against the wall. A throaty moan welled up through me.

He pulled me away from the wall, and we stumbled a few steps to one side and into the alcove of a nearby door. His hands roamed my body, leaving fire in their wake. I tugged at the hem of his shirt, half ready to rip it open.

Laughter and voices made us both freeze. Breathless, I listened. Rogan's lips were next to my ear.

"Let's get the hell out of here," he whispered, his words feathering against my cheek and hair.

He grabbed my hand, and we took off toward the front door. I surreptitiously righted my shirt and jacket as we ran. We hopped into the Jeep, and I grabbed the oh-shit handle as Rogan tore out of the parking area, the tires spitting gravel behind us and the back fishtailing for a second.

He flashed me a hooded grin. We made it down the mountain road in record time, and instead of heading to my neighborhood, Rogan turned onto Reserve Street. We passed the corner where I'd dropped him once, and I realized we were going to his place.

By the time he pulled into the driveway of a small house in an older part of Foothills East, the blaze between us had become a smoldering burn.

Silently, he took my hand and led me inside. The place was sparse, as I'd guessed. He drew me through the dark house and into a bedroom with a bed so neatly made it looked like it'd never been slept in. He let his jacket slide off to the floor.

"Sure you don't mind if we mess this up?" I whispered with a smirk, gesturing to the perfectly made bed.

He responded by sweeping me into his arms with a grin and a low growl, and we landed together on the bed.

When I woke up later, it was early morning but still dark and Rogan was asleep next to me. My body still hummed gently with the afterglow of the night, and I lay there for a moment to soak it up. A delicious shiver passed over my skin. Maybe it was because he'd been in his human form for decades, or because he wasn't really human at all, but his complete abandon to the physical experience was unlike anything I'd encountered before. He hadn't a shred of insecurity, and it was incredibly sexy.

With a soft sigh, I pushed the covers away, slipped out of bed, and found my clothes. I didn't have the luxury of lolling around in bed.

Once outside, I nearly wheeled around and went back in. It was probably below thirty degrees, but I had on my thigh-length, lined leather coat. I zipped it up all the way and tucked in my chin, pulled on the gloves that were stuffed in a pocket, and set out toward home at an easy trot.

It was freezing out, but Zarella's drawstring pouch was burning a metaphorical hole in my pocket. Besides, it was less than two miles to home. On Demon Patrol I'd spent entire shifts out in much worse winter conditions.

Memories of Patrol brought me around to my new business venture and Damien. I had what I wanted from Zarella's deal, but Damien's prize would be awarded only at the finish line. Could I convince my partner to let it go, to give up Zarella's promise of mage power? If not, I'd have to refuse to finish the job with him.

I couldn't do it, knowing that Damien would turn into someone I wouldn't want in my life.

I wanted to think that I could persuade him, that Damien would see it wasn't worth it. In my imagination, we had the conversation and agreed on it and moved on to our boring government contracts. But I had feeling it was nothing more than a wish, a fantasy. He'd tried to hide it, but I'd seen the fervent light in his eyes at the prospect of mage power.

When I got home, Deb was up.

She looked at me with groggy eyes and her strawberry blond hair spiked and messy from sleep, but then her attention snapped into focus.

She gasped and then let out a little squeal. "Somebody got some!" she sing-songed.

Loki looked up in alarm.

"What? No," I said with exaggerated denial. "I'm an underworlder now. That's what you're seeing in my aura. The underworld is super sexy."

Her face pulled into a horrified expression. "Did they make you do an orgy?"

I let out a peal of laughter. "They're not like that. At least, not that I saw."

She narrowed her eyes, raised her coffee mug to her lips, and giggled softly behind it. "Rogan, huh?" She took a long sip, still eyeing me.

I pressed my lips together and ducked into the bedroom to change clothes and avoid responding.

"Ella and Rogan, sitting in a tree." Deb's voice floated in. "K-I-S-S-I-N-G!"

"Real mature, Deb."

I couldn't help a grin as I pulled off my clothes and tossed them in the hamper. It had been a very, *very* good night.

"Hell of a lot more than kissing, judging by your aura," she called. "Hope you're on birth control. Or you'll end up like meee!"

She giggled again, a little maniacally this time, as she slammed the bathroom door closed and started the shower.

I chewed my bottom lip. I wanted so badly to open the pouch and do whatever I was supposed to do with the contents. But I had to wait until I could get with Jennifer Kane. I wouldn't know if Zarella's fix worked unless I could remove the charmed ring that kept me cut off from magic and my reaper. But as soon as I took off the ring, the *in-between* magic would flood through me, and I might not survive another influx. I needed Jen's spell to stem the tide.

Ugh. Too many steps. Of course it couldn't be simple, oh no.

I texted Jen and then forced myself to go pour a cup of coffee instead of sitting on my bed clutching my phone like a teenage girl waiting for her crush to respond. After a few minutes with nothing from Jen, I went sat cross-legged on my bed, opened the pouch, and carefully poured out the contents. No harm in looking.

There was a little scroll of paper rolled up tightly, plus three smooth, flat stones about the size of my pinkie nail. The stones were nearly identical, opaque black with a silvery, darkly mirrored surface. Hematite, maybe. And there was a single wooden matchstick.

I unrolled the piece of paper.

Swallow them. Burn this.

I turned it over. That was it? Zarella was succinct, I had to give him that. I stared at the paper. I'd expected a few lines to chant. Maybe a ritual to be performed under moonlight. Something more than some pebbles and a piece of paper with four words on it.

With a shrug, I tucked everything back into the pouch and tightened the drawstring.

"Okay, Xaphan," I whispered to the dormant reaper. "Ready for a truce?"

"What're you mumbling about?" Deb appeared in the doorway in a bathrobe and a towel turbaned on her head. "Reliving your night of passion?"

I threw a pillow at her head, and she caught it easily.

"I got the reaper cure from Zarella." I held up the pouch.

Deb sobered and took a few steps toward me. "What do you have to do?"

"I'm not sure," I lied. "I have to get Jen's spell before I can do anything with this, and I don't want to mess with it until I was ready to actually use it."

I wasn't sure why I didn't tell her I'd looked in the pouch. I think I was afraid she'd see the stones and say it was a trick. Or find some other reason to insist I shouldn't do it. But I didn't want any warnings, and I couldn't deal with anyone else's fears. I just wanted it done.

She nodded soberly.

"Just . . . listen to your gut, Ella. Don't do anything that feels wrong," she said.

"I won't. I promise."

I left her alone in the bedroom so she could get dressed for work.

When I finally heard from Jen, I hollered a quick goodbye to Deb and headed out with Loki, relieved to escape before she decided we should discuss Zarella's cure.

The sun was barely cracking over the horizon, and it was still just as cold as it had been when I started my trek home in the dark.

On the way to Sunshine Valley, I got a text. My pulse gave a little bump when I saw Rogan's name.

You could have stayed. I happen to make quite a decent espresso.

I crooked a small smile and replied when traffic stopped.

I'm not afraid of morning-after coffee. Couldn't sleep. I'm headed to Jen's now. Wish me luck.

He responded: *I would, but you don't need it. You'll be good as new in no time.*

At least someone besides me had confidence that this was all going to work out.

I pulled up to Jen's and snapped a leash onto Loki's collar.

Jen answered her door dressed in athletic shoes, canvas cargo pants, and a ski sweater, and I saw a parka and knit hat with little pompom tassels on the sofa.

"Getting back from somewhere?" I asked. It was an odd hour to be returning home, but Jen was a vampire, so who was I to assume anything about her nights.

"This spell is likely going to produce a big blowback," she said, going to put on her coat. "I thought it'd be best to go up into the hills a ways so we don't piss off the neighbors."

Powerful spells were sometimes accompanied by a noise almost as powerful as a sonic boom, especially if the spell created a very swift change. Not having much power myself, I'd never cast magic strong enough to cause one.

We went out the back door, across her yard, and through the gate. Low-angled morning sun greeted us. There was a tree-lined, paved pedestrian road there that ran along the back yards of the houses on Jen's street, but beyond it the rolling foothills were undeveloped. The brush and boulder-studded land seemed to go on forever. There were paths carved in the dirt by hikers and wildlife, and Jen picked one of them.

I let Loki off the leash, and he gleefully raced ahead, circled back to do a quick fly-by, and then bounded off in another direction.

Jen and I hiked side-by-side.

"We missed you at the meeting last night," she said.

In the midst of everything else going on, I'd nearly forgotten I'd skipped the coven gathering.

"Ha, I bet," I said. "What'd I miss?"

"Lynnette told everyone about your induction into the underworld. And about losing your job."

"Awesome," I said sarcastically.

It wasn't that either of those things were private information. I just didn't like the idea of being discussed.

"I'm sure Lynnette is glad she has you to keep an eye on me," I said, sliding Jen a wry look.

She let out a throaty laugh. "Well, duh. You and I both know that she loves to be as far up in people's business as possible."

She said it with a carefully mild tone, but I thought I detected an edge of something. Maybe resentment.

Jen slowed and turned to look back the way we'd come, walking backward for a few steps, probably judging whether we were far enough from humanity.

"This spell you're going to do, is it something that the coven could help with?" I asked, the idea suddenly dawning on me.

"How so?" She faced forward again, and we began climbing up a ridge.

"I don't know, forming a circle and doing the spell as a group?"

She shook her head. "This isn't something that can be done with collective magic. It's too delicate. Even the most honed coven can't work in perfect synchronicity. It'd be like trying to perform brain surgery with thirteen different doctors' hands on the scalpel at the same time."

I took a deep breath, trying not to get hung up on her all-too-vivid metaphor for what we were about to do.

"Okay," she said. "I think we're good here."

We both stopped. We'd hiked up over a ridge and then followed the path down a gentle slope. The hills completely blocked any view of the Sunshine Valley development. I couldn't help thinking these hills would be a good place to bury a body. Close enough to civilization to make it a quick haul but easy to hide in the expanse of undeveloped land. I wasn't looking for a place to hide a corpse, of course, but it made me a little edgy to be this isolated.

Jen had moved over to a boulder and was pulling some things out of her coat pocket and lining them up. There were two milky white crystal orbs about the size of ping pong balls, a plastic zip bag filled with what looked like salt, a small folding knife with a pearl handle, and a clear stone wand. She glanced up at me, and her face was tensed, her eyes focused.

I swallowed as my pulse kicked up. I was putting it all in her hands, and this was the moment of truth. I trusted that she wouldn't deliberately harm me, but I had no idea of the odds of success.

"Not that I doubt your abilities," I said. "But how sure are you about this spell?"

"I've only had the opportunity to perform it once. But I'm one for one." She gave a little shrug and a faint smile. "You should probably show me what you're going to do for the reaper part. We'll have to do the two spells in very quick succession."

"Mine's not much of a spell." I pulled out Zarella's pouch and emptied the contents in my hand so she could see. I unrolled the scroll and showed it to her.

Her brows lifted, and she leaned in to peer more closely at the three dark stones. "Swallow those?"

"Yeah, I guess."

She frowned and then straightened. "Odd, but not unheard of."

I placed the items back in the pouch and set it on the rock next to her things.

She twisted off one corner of the baggie of salt and let a thin stream of it fall to the ground, using it to draw a line around us that also enclosed the boulder where our magical items sat. Then she used the stone wand and cast a quick circle.

She reached for the two crystal orbs and held them out.

"Palms up, and hold one in each hand," she said. "When your power starts to flow in, I'm going to catch it and then direct it between these two crystals. I won't be able to hold it there forever, but hopefully long enough to keep the magic from frying you while I perform the spell. The idea is that I'm putting in place a sort of permanent sieve which will squeeze down the flow of the magic to a manageable trickle."

I held the cool stone spheres in my hands and wondered how they could possibly hold the torrent of magic from the *in-between*. But Jen was living proof that this type of spell had worked once before, and I'd have to take that as good enough.

"As soon as I've finished, you need to go for the reaper spell right away."

I nodded, too keyed-up to speak.

She picked up the folding knife and held it and then drew a deep breath with her eyes closed and began centering herself for magic. When she opened her eyes, her pupils glowed with power.

"The charmed ring," she said in the monotone of trance.

I adjusted the orb that was in my right hand so she could grasp the ring on my index finger. Her hand paused there, and she began to glow with neon pink magic. It was so concentrated, and even in daylight, I had to squint as my eyes began to tear up in the intense light of her power.

Her fingers tightened on the ring and pulled it off. She let it fall to the dirt, and it hit with a faint metallic ping.

She began to chant, but I lost all sense of her words as magic began to flow into me. At first, the sensation was a sweet, poignant joy. I reveled in the feel of the power like a junkie in the first seconds of a hit. But within seconds the sensation began to shift. It scraped through me like sandpaper. It intensified, clawing at my insides and filling my head with impossible pressure.

I gritted my teeth and squeezed my eyes closed, trying to focus on Jen's voice. Her chanting was my life preserver in a violent sea of magic that threatened to tear me apart from the inside.

The pain eased by half, and I cracked my eyelids open.

She'd managed to trap at least some of the magic in between the crystal spheres. A current of silver swelled between my hands, and the stones became heavier and heavier. The spheres now looked mirrored, and magic swam furiously around in them.

Words spilled from her lips at a hurried pace, barely intelligible. She opened the folding knife and drew the blade across her palm. The cut was shallow, but blood beaded and then dripped to the ground. She let it fall on the charmed ring.

Within half a minute, the intensity began to swell again. My head felt like an overfilled balloon ready to pop.

I groaned through my teeth, not sure how much longer I could hold onto consciousness.

A new sensation caught my attention and sent my heart racing. There was a stirring in the center of my chest. The reaper was awakening.

"Hurry," I whispered.

An explosion rocked the ground and pummeled a blast of freezing air against me. I staggered but kept my feet under me. Dust kicked up all around us, blowing grit into my eyes and making me cough.

Suddenly the pressure was gone, and the world snapped back into focus.

Jen had sagged to the ground, her head hanging.

The most intense sensation was now centered in my chest. It was as if a fist was squeezing my heart. The reaper.

"Go, do it," she ground out, gesturing with one hand without lifting her head.

Zarella's spell.

I dropped the crystal orbs and reached for the three black stones, quickly centering them in my palm so I could toss them back like aspirin.

As I swallowed them, it occurred to me that Zarella had no magical ability. Who had created this spell for him? Whose magic had touched the stones I'd just swallowed?

They seemed to expand as they went down, painfully pushing against my throat. My stomach jolted, trying to rebel.

Resisting the urge to double over and puke up the dark stones, I reached for the piece of paper and the match.

Swallow them. Burn this.

The next few seconds seemed to stretch out in slow motion.

With trembling hands, I struck the match against the rock. It flared to life just as Jennifer raised her head.

I watched the flame consume the paper, hypnotized by the rainbow colors of the fire.

There was a pinprick sensation in the center of my forehead. It swelled until it was a nail driving into my skull. I dropped the smoking match. The last remnant of the paper slipped from my fingers. It extinguished as it fell.

The pain in my head felt like it wanted to devour my sanity. Dropping to my knees, my muscles gave way and I fell forward. I caught myself on my palms and stayed there, panting, until the pain receded. As I stared at the patch of dirt between my hands, something dark dripped onto it. I reached up to touch my nose, and my fingers came away smeared with blood. I pulled the cuff of my sweatshirt down over my hand and used it to pinch my nostrils.

Jen let out a soft moan.

I went over and squeezed her shoulder. To my enormous relief, she raised her eyelids and sat up.

"Are you okay?" I asked.

She sighed heavily. "I think so. Just give me a sec." When she reached up to brush her hair from her face, I saw that the cut on her palm had already healed.

I sat back on my butt, my arms circling my knees. I wasn't so hot on the idea of trying to stand up just yet. I didn't think either of us were ready for the hike back.

Jen and I stared at each other for a moment. She started pushing stiffly to her feet and then stood with her hands on her generous hips.

"Well," she said. "How do you feel?"

I let out a long breath. The stones still felt lodged in my esophagus, like when a large pill goes down wrong. But maybe it was just my imagination. I tentatively reached for magic, and easily caught a thread of earth power. I sensed the reaper's presence, and I wasn't dead, so something must have gone right.

"I can grasp magic, and the reaper hasn't eaten the rest of my soul, so . . . pretty damn good."

She gave me a tired grin.

"You need healing, though," I said, noting how weariness seemed to drag at her.

"I'm not going to argue," she said.

I bent to pick up the two crystal orbs and my ring, and she collected her knife and wand.

When I straightened, she gestured at my face. "You're bleeding. It might be a good idea for you to see a healer, too."

I used my sweatshirt cuff to wipe at my nose. Damn. I hoped the nosebleeds were just a temporary thing. They could be a sign of brain damage from magic overuse . . . no, I wasn't going to think about it. I was alive and had my magic, and I chose to focus on that victory.

A curious mingling of buoyancy and fatigue filled me as we made our way over the ridge and back to Jen's house.

I had the mark of the underworld, my magic was back, and my reaper was going to let me live.

For the second time in a matter of months, I felt resurrected. And I was ready to go kick some vampire ass and free my brother.

After i'd sent off a text to Deb, Rogan, and Damien to let them know that I survived the spells and was back in action magic-wise, I contacted the healer who had treated me after the battle with the Baelmen. I was trying not to dwell on it, but the nosebleed wasn't a good sign, not for a crafter who'd recently been subjected to some crazy-ass magic.

Gina, a magical healer as well as a conventional nurse, ran a small supernatural healing clinic out of her home. She said she could fit me in for a session in twenty minutes.

I didn't say anything about the nosebleed beforehand because I wanted to see what she might pick up in her healing.

When she finished, I sat up on the treatment table and looked at her expectantly.

"I know enough about your recent history to know that you've experienced some . . . *unique* magical stress and strain," she said tactfully. "Contrary to what you might think, being cut off from your magic for extended periods can actually be quite damaging. It's not exactly like magical exhaustion, but it's an unnatural state for a crafter. It's almost like using magic allows certain supernatural toxins to be expelled, and by not crafting at all, those toxins build up in your system. This is a case where your lower natural ability was actually an advantage. If you were a Level II, you could have some permanent damage at this point. If you were a Level III you'd likely be in a coma."

I let that sobering info sink in for a moment. My fingers had curled around the edge of the table, gripping it hard as she spoke.

"So now that I have my magic back, do I need to worry?" I asked.

"I strongly recommend you take it easy for the next few weeks at minimum. Use your magic daily, but very gently. Don't push your natural limit or get yourself into high-stress situations."

I swallowed, my throat suddenly dry. "What if I do?"

She lifted her hands. "I can't predict exactly what might happen, especially in your unusual circumstances. You could accidentally blow out the magical sieve that's been put in place. Or burn out and lose your magic permanently. Maybe trigger a sudden aneurism. The possibilities are all pretty dire."

I stifled a sigh. Just when things started looking up, the universe had to deliver another sucker punch.

I paid for the session and on the way out to my truck got a call.

"Hi, Damien," I answered.

"We got another communication from our client," he said in a tense voice.

"Okay," I said, drawing the word out with apprehension clear in my voice.

"I don't want to say anything more over the phone. Come to my place."

The line went dead. I stared at my phone for long moment.

I hated that I could read the tight eagerness in his voice. With a heavy feeling in my chest that had nothing to do with the three black stones I'd swallowed, I headed to Damien's.

When he answered the door to his loft, his face was still and he appeared composed on the surface, but his sky-blue eyes flicked around restlessly, gleaming with pent-up energy. I got the sense he'd been pacing as he'd waited for me to arrive.

Inside, I faced him.

"Damien, you can't go through with this," I said quietly. "At the underworld meeting, Zarella warned me that whatever he offers you will change you, and not just in the ways you're hoping for. If it doesn't kill you, you won't be the same person anymore. He's dangling this in front of you, hoping you'll take the bait. Don't do it. Nothing bad will happen if we don't finish the job. It's not like Zarella's going to sue us for breach of contract or anything. Officially he's dead. Dead people can't sue."

I finished with a small laugh, but Damien's tense-eyed expression didn't budge.

Misery gripped my heart in a tight fist as I remembered Zarella's warning. I couldn't let Damien do this.

"Please, just say you'll think about it," I pleaded in a low whisper. "Promise me you'll take some time and think it over. I've got to get my brother, and then when I get back we can talk again. Okay?"

"When are you leaving?" he asked.

"Rogan has some of his demons set up around the vampire compound keeping watch. He's trying to determine the best time for us to go in. As soon as he's figured that out, we'll leave."

"You're not strong enough yet." His gaze roamed over me, and he gave a slight shake of his head.

"Come with us," I said brightly. "We could use you."

He gave me a narrow smile. "Wait a month until you're stronger, and I'll go."

I snorted a laugh. "So now you're trying to bargain with me?"

He shrugged sheepishly, and for a moment, his zeal for Zarella's offer was gone, and he was the old Damien. His eyes shone but only with amusement.

"Could you at least spare a couple of hours?" he asked. He went to his laptop, which was open on the kitchen island. "We're actually in the running for a job we bid on with Supernatural Crimes. They want to meet with us as a sort of interview. It would be good to have some work in place when you return with your brother, don't you think?"

I couldn't argue with that. I really hadn't even thought about the fact that I'd be supporting another person. Not that I minded. I'd do whatever it took to get Evan back on his feet. My apartment was going to be busting at the seams with three of us living there, but we'd make do.

It seemed a little odd, though, getting into Damien's Lexus with him and driving to the SC station. It was as if we'd agreed to go through the motions of business as usual, when I wasn't even sure about the future of our venture. If he went through with

Zarella's job, was there any way Damien would still be my partner? Would I still want him to be?

When we got to Supernatural Crimes, I actually welcomed Detective Barnes's sour face as a reminder of a time when Damien and I had been firmly united.

Detective Lagatuda, in one of his ubiquitous suits—navy, this time—shook hands with both of us.

"I see you've made a recovery," Barnes said, looking me up and down. The gesture was no small feat, considering I was nearly a foot taller. "Good thing. We couldn't hire you if you were still powerless."

"Nice to see you too, Detective," I said in my sweetest voice.

The job we'd bid on involved an odd predicament. There'd been an accident at a construction site when some young crafters had snuck in at night, started fooling around with magic they couldn't control, and a spontaneous rip had opened suddenly. Although the rip wasn't large, it was a recurrent one, meaning that it continued to pulse open and closed. Unfortunately, there had been casualties.

The authorities had managed to retrieve the bodies, but there were a couple of lingering problems. One, the rip itself. And two, the souls of the people killed were lingering. SC speculated that the souls hadn't been reaped because of the rip. So they wanted us to deal with the rip as well as reap the souls.

Really, we couldn't have custom ordered a more perfect job for me and Damien. We had experience with demons and could handle the creatures that flew through the rip whenever it pulsed open. With Damien's knowledge and strong magic, we should be able to figure out how to seal a minor rip. And I, of course, could reap the souls.

We finished with the official interview, and Lagatuda walked us to the main entrance. After we bid him goodbye, he called out to me and beckoned me back.

"How's your friend doing? Deb?" he asked.

I folded my arms and narrowed my eyes. "Fine."

He drew a breath. "I know this is a little weird, but I've thought of her a lot since the Baelmen case, and I was just wondering if she was okay."

"She's doing fine," I repeated.

He reached up to rub at the back of his neck. "I noticed she wasn't wearing a ring. Is she . . . ?"

I let a second or two pass as his cheeks pinked.

Finally, I relented. "She's in the process of getting divorced. It should be final soon."

He nodded and cast his gaze off to the side with a sad puppy-dog look.

I rolled my eyes and stuck out my hand. "Do you have a card or something?"

"Huh?"

"Give me your card. And then I will give it to Deb." I spoke slowly and deliberately.

"Oh! Yes." He fumbled around, first checking one of his pants pockets and then reaching into his blazer. He produced a dog-eared business card. "Thanks, Ella. Really, thank you."

I took the card and then held up both hands as if to ward off his gratitude. "All I'm gonna do is give it to her."

I started to shoulder the door open but then paused to glance back. Lagatuda was still standing there.

"If you so much as look at her cross-eyed, I will murder you in your sleep," I said, just loud enough for him to hear.

His eyes popped wide.

I shoved the card into my jacket pocket and went out into the December cold.

"Let's get a drink," Damien said once we were in the car.

"Now?"

"Sure, why not? I'm pretty sure we've got the SC job. We should celebrate." He gestured to the dash. "It's after four. Officially happy hour."

"Let me check with Rogan and make sure he's not going to want to take off in the next couple of hours."

I sent a quick text.

After a minute or so, Damien shot me a questioning look. "Well?"

"Haven't heard back." I shrugged. "One drink isn't going to hurt anything."

He nodded and steered to a parking garage downtown.

We walked down to a pub that was a favorite of Demon Patrol officers, but first shift hadn't let out for the day so the place was pretty quiet. At the bar, we claimed seats and then ordered beers.

"So what's the worst that would happen if you didn't take Zarella's offer?" I asked while we watched the bartender at the taps.

He looked down at his hands and traced a stain on the wooden bar top for a moment.

"Imagine if there was one thing you wanted your whole life. Just one thing that you dreamed about and wished for every night as a kid. One thing you devoted your education and all your free time to, and then one day someone offered it to you." He lifted his gaze to mine. "What would you do?"

"I'd think really, really hard about the consequences," I said.

Two beers appeared in front of us, and I took a sip and then wiped the foam from my upper lip with a finger.

"Aren't there other important things in life?" I asked.

He gave a shrug. "Like what? I'm estranged from my family. I'm not in a serious relationship. It's not like I really even have a social life."

"Yeah, but those things are choices you made," I said. "You can't use them as a reason to throw everything away and lose who you are."

He looked at me with eyes so haunted my breath went still.

"This is all I have left." He said it so quietly I barely caught the words.

"Damien—" I started but didn't know what to say.

Why was I trying so hard to talk him out of it, if this was the one and only thing in life that he wanted? Was I really trying to help him, or was it more about what I wanted?

"Look," he said, straightening. "I've been studying magic, and specifically aptitude transformation, for years. If there's anyone who has a chance to successfully transition from sub-mage to mage, it's me. It's not like I have a death wish. If I do this, I'll put all of my knowledge to work. I'll do everything I can to do it safely."

"That's true." I raised my glass in a little salute. I forced back the lump in my throat. "If there's anyone who could pull through, it's Damien Stein."

He managed a faint grin and clinked the rim of his glass against mine.

"To achieving our highest goals," he said.

With a silent resolution to refrain from nagging him, I took a long pull of lager.

My phone vibrated with an incoming text from Rogan.

The vamps have kept the victims inside for the past twenty-four hours or so. I need to see why before we storm the place. Earliest we would leave would be late tonight.

"We're good for a while," I said to Damien. "So. What's the first thing you'd do as a mage? Join the Order?"

The Order of Mages was a very old, very secretive organization.

"If they invited me . . . maybe," he said. His tone implied he might not accept the invitation, and his smug expression said he'd possibly relish turning it down.

"Is this really just about revenge?" I asked. "Getting back at your family for treating you like an outcast?"

"Maybe in part, but it's also to prove something." His brow furrowed, and his face darkened as he spoke. "I want to show them that they're not as special as they think they are. If it's possible to achieve mage power without being born with it, that kind of takes the shine off the whole thing, doesn't it? It's the superiority complex that I hate the most."

His jaw worked for a moment. I waited, sensing there was more coming.

"They didn't just treat me like I was different," he said. "They treated me like I was inferior. A mistake of their genetic line. Growing up, we had family portraits taken every year. They always did one without me in it. That was the photo displayed in the formal rooms where my parents received their mage friends."

My mouth fell open. "Damien, that's . . . it's just flat-out *cruel.*"

He gave a little shrug. "That's just one example of many. Oddly, they still fund my trust. I haven't touched the money since I left home, though."

"Huh," I mused. "You're not quite the silver-spoon baby I thought you were."

He let out a bark of a laugh that made me jump. "That's really what you thought?"

"Well, yeah. I mean, the nice clothes, the Lexus, the expensive downtown loft . . . I figured that in spite of your strained relationship with your family, you must be living off a trust fund."

He laughed again. "I guess I do let people think that. The truth is, I have family money but I don't have to rely on it. I sold some magical technology patents when I was still in college. I invested the money and hit pretty big with those investments, and, well . . ." He trailed off and gave a modest little shrug.

I shook my head. "I'm sorry I assumed all those things. Here I thought you were a spoiled rich kid, and you're actually a self-made man."

A raucous bunch of people entered the pub, and we both twisted around to see a crowd of first-shift Demon Patrol officers crowding in.

A couple of them spotted us, and a moment later we were surrounded by former coworkers.

Sasha Bowen grabbed my shoulders from behind. "We never got to give you guys a proper send-off!"

I waved a hand, scoffing. "Aw, no need for that."

"Oh no," she laughed. "We're going to make up for it."

I groaned as she ordered a round of shots.

Two shots and another beer later, I clutched Damien's arm.

"We've gotta get out of here while I can still walk," I said, my head fuzzy and warm. He'd managed to beg off after the first shot, but drinks kept appearing in front of me. "There's still a chance Rogan might give the go signal late tonight."

"Okay, you leave first," he said. "I'll meet you outside."

With what I hoped was a nonchalant expression, I vacated my spot, wove through the crowded pub to use the restroom, and then slipped out the delivery entrance. I jogged down the alley and around to the front of the building where Damien was already waiting.

"I don't think they even noticed," he laughed.

The alcohol had lifted his mood and seemed to have loosened the previous tension between us.

"Let's go back to my place," he said. "I have an idea."

"As long as it doesn't involve any more shots, I'm game." My head was spinning a little more than I'd have liked. I really needed to down some water.

Back at Damien's loft, soft atmospheric lights came on automatically when we entered. He went to the fridge and tossed me a bottle of water.

"Ah, mind reader," I said, and twisted the lid off.

I chugged half the bottle, watching him, and then took off my jacket and lay it over the back of a rich person's version of a La-Z-Boy recliner. He had his notebook out on the counter, and he was flipping pages slowly with a studied furrow of his brow. Leaning my forearms on the counter beside him, I peered at the neat rows of handwriting, diagrams, and symbols.

"What's all this?" I asked.

"Notes on exactly what I did to increase my magical aptitude," he said mildly, still concentrating on the notebook. He straightened and turned to me, his eyes glittering. "How would you like to become a high Level I tonight?"

That sobered me up.

I stared at Damien for a couple of heartbeats, playing his words over again in my mind to be sure I'd heard correctly.

"Seriously?" I asked.

The prospect of raising my magical aptitude both freaked me out and piqued my curiosity.

"Sure," he said. "What, you don't want to?"

"I do, but . . . I don't," I said honestly. I pressed my hand against my stomach in an attempt to still the fluttery sensation there. "The healer said I shouldn't do anything strenuous."

He gave me a look out of the corners of his eyes. "Like go challenge a bunch of wild vampires?"

He had me there. I couldn't come up with a snappy response, so I just lifted a shoulder and let it drop.

"This won't hurt you," he said. "It should be pretty simple. Well, relative to what I did to adjust my own aptitude. If it were *simple*, everyone would be doing it. I hesitated before because of the reaper soul. But that's under control now, right?"

I nodded, and I swear I could still feel a vague lump at the base of my esophagus, as if the three stones had settled there. The reaper soul had been very quiet since Jen and I had performed the spells out in the foothills. I could feel it, though. Maybe that was just how it would feel forever.

"I'd like to do this for you," he said quietly.

My gaze had dropped to the floor, but his tone brought my attention back up. Our eyes locked for a long moment, and I felt words trying to bubble up because I knew what he was doing, and I didn't want it to happen.

Damien was offering me a parting gift.

I opened my mouth, intending to refuse, but then I closed it again. A slow, sad smile tugged at my lips.

"Okay, let's do it," I said.

He rubbed his hands together and let out a little cackle. He pointed to the sofa.

"Let's move this so it's lined up with magnetic north," he said.

"Huh?"

"Just help me swing it around so it lines up this way." He drew an invisible line with his arm.

We scooted the low profile dark gray leather sofa around, nudging it this way and that until he was satisfied. Then he started gathering props. He produced a bowl full of lava rocks, which went on the floor at the north end of the sofa.

He stood. "This is for earth."

"Ah, gotcha."

He wanted representations of the four basic elements.

He had me fill a large white ceramic salad bowl with water. I set it on the west side of the sofa. An empty bowl for air in the east position. And he set up a plate with pillar candles at the south point.

"This is just to help me focus," he said, lighting the candles with little sparks of fire magic. "But we won't even need to cast a circle or anything."

"What do you want me to do?" I asked.

"Lie down with your head at north, and relax," he said. "I'm going to read my notes one more time."

Relax, right. I was about to undergo a magical procedure that literally only one other person had experienced. It was like Jen's spell all over again. My heart thudded dully, and I couldn't help wondering if maybe I shouldn't push my luck. I'd already subjected myself to two questionable spells today. Could I really expect another one to go off without a hitch?

"Ah, screw it," I mumbled softly to myself.

I trusted Damien. In spite of our recent difference of opinion on finishing Zarella's job, Damien was still the expert. He'd devoted his entire life to this type of magic. He'd never do this if he didn't have complete confidence in it.

The soft brush of Damien's power moved through the air, raising the tiny hairs on my arms and neck and setting off a cascade of shivers over my skin.

"Reach for your magic, but don't draw any," Damien said. His voice had the flat, faraway quality of trance.

I did as he instructed, closing my eyes to center myself and then sending my awareness down as if to draw earth power.

His magic flowed thickly in the room, seeming to saturate the air with a sense of anticipation like a combustible gas ready to ignite at the slightest scratch of friction.

I was bracing myself for a boom like the one that Jen's spell had set off. But instead, gentle tendrils of magic seemed to drift into my head to curl around like a soothing mist. I sank deeper into my focus, losing track of time and my surroundings as I dipped in and out of the lightest feathery edges of a meditative state.

I began to dream. I felt the top of my head begin to turn, unscrewing like the cap of my water bottle. It lifted away, and the chilly touch of air brushed the top of my brain. The magic drifted in, soaking into the cells of my brain as it had drenched the room. My head felt heavier and heavier, like a sponge taking on water.

Suddenly there was a sharp pop at the base of my cranium. I gasped and bolted upright.

Magic swirled in multicolored streamers, twisting around Damien in a vortex.

"Did it hurt?" he asked, still partially immersed in trance. His magic began to fade.

I blinked rapidly, taking stock of my physical body as if I'd been separated from it for hours. I shook my head.

His power blinked out, leaving us in the glow of the candles still burning at the foot of the sofa.

"Try pulling magic," he said.

I reached for earth, grasped a strand and tugged. The thread turned into a rope that grew into a rush of power. I rose to my feet and kept pulling, drinking in the earth power and letting it fill me.

It was ten times what I'd ever drawn before. My entire body began to glimmer with magic, casting a pallor of green light around me. I felt powerful enough to take down a building.

Damien was watching me intently. He cracked a grin and nodded.

"Careful," he said. "Don't overdo it."

I let the magic sing through me for another second and then released my hold on earth power.

"Whoa," I breathed. I stared at him. "It worked. And you made it seem so easy."

"Easy?" he scoffed. "That took almost three hours!"

Three hours? It hadn't felt like more than twenty minutes, tops. I looked out the window, but that was no help. It'd been dark when we got here, and it was still dark.

"Damn, if that's what it feels like to be a high Level I, I can't even imagine how it must feel to be you," I said, staring at him.

He sat down heavily and ran his hands through his hair, messing up the comb marks.

"Are you going to be okay?" I asked. "Should I take you to a healer?"

"I'm good," he said. "It was more about complexity than brute force amounts of magic. If I'm tired, it's mostly because it's after two in the morning."

My brows lifted, and I went to my jacket to rummage for my phone. I flipped through a couple of missed texts, relieved to find that Rogan hadn't sent any crucial updates while I'd been high on Damien's magic.

I slipped my coat on. "I should let you get some rest."

He nodded wearily. "You need it, too."

We walked slowly together toward the door. When we stopped, I hesitated for a second and then threw my arms around him. He stiffened, clearly surprised but then wrapped me in a firm hug.

"Don't do anything stupid while I'm out in the desert kicking vampire ass," I said.

"Stupid isn't my style," he whispered back.

I let him go and left. All the way to my truck, a strange, uncomfortable carousel of emotions played through my heart.

Back at home, I pulled my phone and wallet from my jacket pocket, and something fluttered to the floor. I bent to pick it up and realized it was Lagatuda's card.

I rummaged in the junk drawer and found a pen and a sticky note.

Tall Detective asked about you.

I stuck the note to the card and propped them against the coffee maker so Deb would see them first thing in the morning.

The next day was Saturday—actually, it was technically already a few hours into Saturday—and Deb would sleep in. I crashed on the sofa so I wouldn't disturb her, and the thought of sleeping for the next twelve hours quickly pulled me from consciousness.

My plans for a half-day spent comatose were not to be, though. I was dreaming of the compound where the vampires were keeping Evan, watching through the eyes of a small demon perched high in a tree on the site.

I don't know if I jerked in my sleep or if it was a sound that pulled me from the dream, but when I awoke to a tapping noise it was no longer dark out. The weak light of the winter morning told me I'd probably only slept about five hours.

The noise came again, from the front door.

Grumbling under my breath, I stumbled from the sofa, ready to send away the person on the other side. I didn't want a subscription to the Idaho Statesman, I wasn't interested in Girl Scout cookies, and I couldn't afford to buy chocolate bars to support the Boise High School marching band's trip to the state competition.

But it was Rogan.

"It looks like the vamps are planning on a venue change," he said. "Time for us to go get your brother."

I stared at him dumbly for a moment and then blinked several times.

"Come in," I said, swinging the door open wider so he could come in. "Deb's still asleep. Let me just grab my things and we can leave."

I turned and took a step away, but he caught my forearm. With a motion that just skirted the delicious edge of roughness, he pulled me hard against him and covered my mouth with his for a deep, lingering kiss.

That got my blood going and pushed the sleep from my system.

"Something about you has changed," he whispered, leaning back just far enough for his eyes to roam my face.

"I got my magic back," I said. "And, I got a little boost. Apparently I'm a high Level I now."

I couldn't help a grin.

"Damien?" he asked.

I nodded.

"Damn, that guy has some serious tricks up his sleeve," he said.

"No shit," I said. "Keep this one to yourself, though, okay?"

I reluctantly pulled from his embrace as the press of the task ahead cut through to the forefront of my mind.

I seemed to blank for a moment as I looked around the weakly lit apartment.

Loki whimpered and trotted a circle around me, snapping me out of my stupor.

This was the moment. It had finally come. We were going to bust Evan out of the vampire den and bring him home. Now, what does one need to take to such a rescue?

I sprang into motion. I found my whip, and it sang like a plucked string in my hands when I touched it, as if recognizing and relishing my newly amped-up magical ability.

I strapped my knife sheath to my ankle and pulled on my boots. My rarely used Sig Sauer was locked in a box stashed in a cubby at the back of the coat closet. As soon as I'd discovered Evan was in a vamp den, I'd gone about procuring black market anti-vamp bullets. They were made with a silver alloy that guaranteed they'd penetrate the skin, but they were designed to lodge within the body and explode with a giant burst of UV light. With the right kind of hit, one of those babies would nuke a vamp's insides. It wouldn't kill it, but a well-placed torso shot would do enough damage that a vamp would stay down for hours, if not a day or more, before he regenerated. Vamps were very, very hard to kill.

The bullets were an incredibly intricate creation of technology and magic—not to mention illegal—and their price tag had reflected all of these things. As such, I could only afford three of them.

They were packed like the precious jewels they were—in a little box with molded foam depressions.

I cinched the Sig holster around my waist and snapped the coiled whip on my other hip. With no access to a service belt, I didn't have a good place to stash the Brimstone burner, so I'd just have to tuck it in my waistband before we stormed the vampire den.

Loki came to stand next to me, and when he looked up, I saw hellfire flicker in his eyes.

Rogan looked me up and down with a gleam of approval in his eyes. "Ready to go, Indiana Jane?"

I nodded. "Let's go kick some vampire ass."

Loki seemed to sense the gravity of the situation as he jumped in the back of Rogan's Jeep and sat there like a sentry, with none of the eager tongue-lolling and panting he usually displayed when I took him somewhere. I'd hesitated at first about bringing him, but he'd gone to the door with an expectant look back at me as if there was no question he was coming along, and I decided to trust his impulse.

We had a five-hour drive ahead of us, and Rogan began making use of the time by briefing me on what he'd discovered and what he thought the best approach would be.

"There's been a lot of activity, and it looks like they could be in the process of changing locations," he said. "I wish I knew what spooked them. It must be a serious threat because the compound is the perfect setup for a vampire den. I can't imagine they're going to find something better."

He talked about the layout of the place, which I already knew in part from my visions of Evan.

"Any idea who the compound actually belongs to?" I asked, imagining the owner must have been very wealthy and had some major pull to keep the house obscured from public aerial photos.

Maybe the owner was now a vamp. Or maybe the vamps had killed him or her and taken possession of the compound.

He shook his head. "I'm not sure, but the place looks kind of ragged, like upkeep stopped a while ago."

We were alone on the road in a particularly dull stretch of desert highway when something ran out in front of us.

Rogan jammed on the brakes, swearing. The Jeep fishtailed on the sandy pavement, and skidded to a stop about twenty feet away from a man standing in the middle of our lane.

"What the . . ." I leaned forward, squinting.

He was just standing there, unnaturally still. Then he raised an arm and crooked a finger in a beckoning motion.

"Shit," I muttered, unbuckling my seatbelt. I reached for the door handle.

Rogan grabbed my arm. "Wait, what are you doing?"

"It's a zombie," I said. "I'm betting it's one of Zarella's. Pull off to the shoulder, and I'll go see what it wants."

I got out of the Jeep, slammed the door, and unfurled my whip. I reached for earth magic, added a filament of fire, and pushed some of the power down my arm and into the whip.

Properly armed, I stalked toward the zombie. I stopped about eight feet away from it, and over to the side. The zombie sidestepped out of the way of potential traffic, too.

"What's up, buttercup?" I called.

"Ms. Grey, good morning to you," the zombie said with Zarella's voice, its jaw moving in a way that was only a little puppet-like but still enough to give me the willies. "There is something you should know about your family."

With an eye roll, I spread my arms. "Right now? I'm a little busy here." Not to mention it was damn cold out.

The Jeep idled behind me, the headlights lighting up the zombie's vacant eyes.

"I'll make it as quick as I can. I believe you will find this interruption worth it."

I made a rolling motion with my free hand, indicating he should get on with it.

"I will cut right to the heart of the matter," the zombie said. "You and your brother were conceived for a specific purpose."

I blinked. "Huh?"

"You and your brother were experiments. Your mother and father conspired to create a person uniquely powerful, a hero of the ages who could sew the big rips closed for good. You were the failure. Your brother was the success. However, your mother had regrets and decided to hide that fact from everyone."

My mouth dropped open, but no words came for a few seconds. "What in the *hell* are you talking about?" Anger roughed my voice.

Heat rose to my face in a flush of irritation. Why was Zarella screwing with me now of all times?

"If Jacob Gregori were to find Evan, your uncle would have his greatest prize. The one thing he's been seeking to atone for his sins," he said slowly and clearly, as if loading each word with importance.

"Stop talking in riddles," I spat.

Zarella knew Jacob was my uncle. I clenched the handle of the whip as my pulse pounded.

"Your brother holds the power—the right kind, and in sufficient quantities—to close the rips permanently," he said with surprising patience. "But it would require him to sacrifice his life. Your uncle would be more than willing to kill your brother if it sealed the rips. He's willing to pay any price. Jacob will do everything he can to get your brother."

I took a shaking breath as my brain chugged to try to make sense of it. Jacob wanted Evan and would kill him in the name of closing the rips. That was the critical thing here.

"Does Jacob know where my brother is?" I asked as calmly as I could.

"If he did, he'd have Evan already."

"With all of Jacob's resources, how can he have not found Evan?"

"Some of us have been ensuring that he didn't."

My breath stilled. So if all of this was true, Zarella had his own reasons for keeping Evan away from Jacob. Foreboding tightened its chilly fingers around my heart, slowly squeezing into a fist.

"Why would you do that?" I asked. "What could possibly be your motive?"

The zombie tsked. "So suspicious."

With a motion so quick it was only a blur, I raised my right hand and gave a little flick, cracking the whip about a foot in front of the zombie's nose. It didn't even flinch.

"Tell me now, or I take your pet's head off," I warned.

"Some of us believe in the joining of dimensions. We believe that chaos and darkness are a natural part of the order of things. We do not want it suppressed. Ergo, we desire the rips remain open," he said, and even through the zombie, I could sense the pleasure in the words Zarella spoke.

A writhing shiver worked itself over my scalp and spiraled down my spine.

If Phillip Zarella wanted to keep the rips open, that was reason enough to side with my uncle . . . except for the part about sacrificing my brother.

Other implications of Zarella's information tried to crowd into my thoughts, but I had to keep focused. I had to get Evan. I had to protect him.

"Perhaps I owe you my thanks for keeping my brother hidden from Jacob, if what you say is true," I said. "But you clearly have your own reasons for what you do, and I'd be an idiot to put my complete trust in you."

"You may not have a choice, if you want to keep your brother alive," he said.

"That remains to be seen."

I flicked my whip again, this time sending fire magic crackling down its length. Sparks flew off the end as if it were a downed live wire.

The zombie nodded once, pivoted, and sprinted off into the desert.

I coiled my whip as I returned to the Jeep.

"Are you okay?" Rogan asked, his hands gripping the wheel, and his tawny eyes focused and steady as he watched my face.

"I'm not sure," I said truthfully.

I repeated my conversation with the zombie word-for-word, as best as I could recall it. I needed someone else to know what I was facing, even if it meant exposing things I'd rather keep hidden.

"You're Jacob Gregori's niece?" he asked.

I nodded. "Surprise," I said dully.

I closed my eyes and ran my hands down my face.

Rogan blew out a low whistle. "That's a lot to take in."

"If any of it is true."

He went silent, chewing his lip.

"What?" I asked.

"I think the part about protecting Evan may be accurate. There have been rumors for the past few years among underworlders, talk about Zarella and others like him guarding someone important. Sinister and very hush-hush."

"What do you mean by 'others like him'?"

"You remember I told you the underworld is a mix of people. Some good, some not so much. Some straight out of a nightmare." He hesitated, his eyes darting to the windshield to stare down the highway.

"Yeah?" I prompted.

"It's one of the rifts within the underworld. There are the ones like Zarella who'd be thrilled to see more chaos unleashed on our world, and, well, the rest of us who aren't insane."

I snorted an unexpected laugh but quickly sobered.

"So maybe Zarella bringing me into the underworld has something to do with his wish to keep Evan out of Jacob's hands," I said.

"Could be." Rogan checked for traffic and then pulled off the shoulder and back onto the highway.

I cast one last look off to the right in the direction the zombie had gone. I saw a tiny figure moving in the far distance, toward what I wasn't sure. Sagebrush and thin patches of snow stretched out for miles, with a backdrop of snow-tipped mountains.

As the tires on the highway lulled us into our own separate thoughts, I played my conversation with Zarella back in my mind.

You and your brother were conceived as experiments. Your mother and your father conspired to create a person powerful enough to sew the rips closed. You were the failure. Your brother was the success.

Evan and I were experiments? Could there be any shred of truth to that?

I searched my memory for everything I could recall about my father, which was, of course, filtered through my mother because he died when I was very young. I replayed random scenes from my childhood. It had always seemed as if my mom loved me and Evan. I couldn't remember anything that might have hinted she'd had us only as science projects.

Zarella had said she later regretted something, though, and out of that regret had protected Evan.

I tried to imagine the conversations between my parents before they had me. I tried to picture them talking about creating a child with specific magical gifts, ones that would be powerful enough to close the rips. And after I was born, how did they even know that I was the "failure?" Magical abilities didn't kick in until puberty, and by that time my father was long dead.

My thoughts jumped to what the dragon had said when I'd asked it who had taken Evan five years ago. Someone of my own blood. Jacob?

I was trying to fill in blanks with too little information, which was a pointless exercise in insanity. Yet I couldn't help my spinning thoughts.

I needed to know the truth, but who could I ask? My parents were both deceased, my grandmother gone, too. Jacob and my brother were the only living relatives I knew about. Evan wouldn't know any more than I did. Jacob was the only option, but I wished there was someone else, anyone in the world who knew the whole story.

My thoughts spiraled over to Evan. If Jacob wanted my brother, how in the name of the universe would I keep him safe? Was I delusional, thinking I could bring him back to Boise and my home, which was mere miles from Gregori Industries?

I took a long breath in as the weight of the world seemed to begin to settle on me. I looked at Rogan. "Should I leave Evan there?"

He flicked me a glance, frowning. "What?"

"Maybe I should leave him where he is. If Zarella is telling the truth, he and his cronies have managed to keep Evan out of

Jacob's clutches. If I get my brother out of the vampire den, how long before Jacob realizes he's with me?"

"Could you really do that? Just walk away, knowing where Evan is?" Rogan asked quietly.

"Maybe, if I'd discovered he was in a good place," I said. My visions of Evan's slack body rushed into my mind's eye. "If I knew he was happy. But if I leave him where he is, he'll probably die anyway. He's not living any sort of life in a vampire feeder den."

"I think you have your answer," he said.

A new, even more disturbing thought pinged like a tiny bell in my head. Why *had* Zarella kept Evan alive all this time if he was a threat to what Zarella and his buddies wanted? He must have some plan of his own for Evan.

All I wanted was to give Evan a chance at a normal life. But one thing was becoming frighteningly clear: my brother was a prize in a dangerous power play I didn't fully understand.

Rogan and I passed the next several miles in silence. He turned off at a rest area.

"Could you take over? I need to focus on my spies for the rest of the way."

"Sure." Maybe taking the wheel would be a good distraction.

We got out, let Loki run around for a minute in the dog area, and then Rogan and I switched seats.

Rogan sank into trance with his eyes closed and his body so still he appeared to be sleeping. After about forty-five minutes, he took a deep breath and shifted in his seat.

"They're definitely restless, but obviously with the sun up they haven't made a move to leave yet," he said. "It's a little hard to tell what's going on inside, but I think we need to go in while it's still full light outside."

I squirmed a little. "Makes sense, but I hate the idea of storming the castle in broad daylight."

"I know, it goes against our instinct to use darkness as cover, but the sunlight gives us an advantage over the vamps. If they try to attack or pursue us outside, they won't be able to put up much of a fight."

"You think we'll be able to surprise them at all?" I asked.

He shrugged. "Hard to say. We'll have to park at a distance, though, if we want any hope of gaining that edge."

Shit. In my visions it looked like Evan was barely capable of standing under his own power. A full-speed sprint away from the vampire den? I puffed my cheeks and blew out a long breath.

"The turn-off is coming up." Rogan pointed at an exit marking a town that was little more than a truck stop.

We stopped for a fuel refill, and then he gave me directions that eventually took us to a one-lane dirt road that looked as if it hadn't been graded in a decade.

I shifted the Jeep into all-wheel drive, but Rogan had me stop only about twenty feet down the dirt road.

As I killed the engine, I looked at him in question. "How far are we from the compound?"

"About five miles," he said.

My heart sank. "There's no way my brother will make it from there to here. I'm not even sure he'll be able to walk without help."

"I've got a plan," Rogan said. "It involves some, uh, demon flight."

My brows shot up. "What?"

"I'm going to command a few arch demons. I've been holding the minds of three of them, one for each of us. They'll pick us up, fly us here to the car, and drop us off."

He pointed to the hills in the distance, and I stretched my awareness in that direction. It took a moment, and I was rusty with my necro senses, but I felt them if only faintly. The presence of three distinct arch-demons.

A grin spread over my face. "Nice. Creepy, but good thinking."

I let my senses range around our area and picked up the presence of many smaller minor demons. Most of them were concentrated at a point northwest of us. Rogan's pet spies around the compound, I assumed.

Part of me expected a twinge that would tell me the reaper was watching, too, but it didn't come. I could feel it there in the center of my chest along with the black stones, which still felt lodged behind my breastbone.

Loki stuck his face in between me and Rogan and whined, as if prompting us to get on with things.

I scratched behind Loki's ear and peered around him at Rogan.

A dark smile spread across his face, and his tawny eyes glittered in the light of the mid-day sun.

"Let's roll out," he said and reached for the door handle.

Rogan and I took off at a jog in the direction of where I'd sensed the cluster of minor demons. Loki loped along easily beside us.

Running through the open desert in broad daylight set my nerves on edge. But as Rogan had said, this was the time of day the vampires would be sluggish, and the sunlight gave us a weapon against the vamps. We moved in silence for a while, both of us breathing in rhythm to our footfalls.

"What do you make of the lead vamp?" I asked Rogan.

"He's powerful. Older than most."

"But not VAMP1 old?"

Modern vampires had been infected with VAMP2, a virus unleashed when the first Rip split Manhattan. VAMP1 was the strain that had infected the original vampires of Europe and all of their descendants. Most of the new generation of vampires was like Jennifer Kane—rendered docile with an implant and able to live more or less normal lives. But some had evaded capture and remained rogue, reliant on the blood of their victims for survival.

"Nah," Rogan said. "But even so, I think we're in for an exciting fight."

That was an understatement. In the world of vampires—in most of the supernatural world, actually—age meant strength. Enhanced powers. Cunning, and skills of survival.

"Good thing we get this little warm-up run before we have to face him, then," I said mildly. I punched the air with jabs and a hook like a boxer psyching herself up for the big fight.

Rogan grinned.

"You're kind of looking forward to this, aren't you?" I asked.

"Like a teenage girl going to her prom."

I laughed outright but flicked another glance at his profile.

"Why?" I pressed. "This isn't your fight."

He went a good dozen paces before responding.

"I've spent decades looking for ways to die, and I failed," he said frankly. "I figure I might as well make use of my immortality. You know, use my powers for good."

Immortality. My stomach dipped as the word seemed to hang in my mind. I pushed it away. This definitely wasn't the time for meanderings of philosophical thought.

I reached out with my necro senses, searching for a minor demon away from Rogan's flock. I knew he was keeping an eye on things, but I wanted to look for myself. Finding what I sought a couple of miles to the south, I probed into the energetic center of the creature's mind until I felt it give into my control.

I took a few stutter steps as my sight blurred and darkened. My right eye shifted to necro vision as seen through the creature's viewpoint while my left stayed as it was and kept me from stumbling over the uneven ground. I blinked several times as my brain adjusted to the double vision.

I sent the creature into flight toward the compound, which gave me a bit of time to work through the dizziness and make sure I kept my feet under me. Running and controlling a minor demon at the same time pushed the limits of my coordination and necro abilities. I couldn't even imagine how much focus it took for Rogan to hold the minds of three arch-demons, umpteen minor demons, and run along beside me like it was all a stroll in the park.

Just to see what would happen, I reached downward for earth magic. I caught a small strand of it for a split second before I tripped over a stick.

Rogan was there, with one hand clamped around my upper arm and the other on my waist. One of my knees hit the ground, but he pulled me upright before I could go sprawling.

He gave a low chuckle as he let go of my arm and reached down to brush off the knee of my pants. "Trying to get fancy, are you?"

I gave a breathy laugh that got lost in my panting. "Kinda stupid, I guess."

He straightened, his hand still on my hip and his face close enough for me to see tiny reflections of myself in his irises.

"You're sexy when you sweat," he said. The corners of his eyes crinkled with a genuine smile.

I wrinkled my nose, feeling my cheeks begin to flush at the odd compliment. "Gross."

He stepped in and pressed his lips to mine, gently at first and then more urgently. Forgetting my focus, I nearly lost my hold on the demon. When Rogan pulled away, his eyes glinted with desire.

With a quick squeeze of my hand, he was off again. He looked at me over his shoulder.

"Keep up, Grey!"

With Loki keeping pace with me, I sprang into a run and pulled even with Rogan, my heart still pounding from his kiss.

My demon was nearing the vampire den. I watched through its eyes as it circled high over the compound, making a lazy spiral downward. With careful steering, I landed the creature on the high wall surrounding the property on one side of the courtyard where I'd seen Evan months ago. The courtyard was empty. Rogan had told me the routine of letting the human victims use the outdoor area only at night, when their vampire captors could safely walk outside.

Unsurprisingly, blackout shades were drawn tightly over every visible window.

I sent the demon across the winter-brown grass of the courtyard, landing it on the cement slab of the covered patio. At my will, it hopped like a bird toward the door, turned its head, and pressed it against the surface. I strained to hear through its senses, to pick up anything, any clue to what was going on within.

There was a shuffling sound, and was that a muffled moan?

I squinted, struggling to pick out the sounds. I thought I heard a low voice and was just about to send the demon up to one of the window sills to listen when the door flew open.

I felt the creature's alarm. It strained against my control, and I tried to pull out of its mind, but I wasn't fast enough.

Legs. Hands reaching down. A hand covering the demon's head, tightening into a fist.

Squeezing. Horrible pressure.

An explosion of pain.

I screamed as my vision went blank. Sightless, I stumbled and fell, skidding my palms against the rough desert floor.

I slammed my hands against my ears and folded into a ball. I recognized my own voice, still screaming in terror, but I couldn't seem to stop it.

Someone was shouting my name.

I'd run out of air. Had to inhale.

A sharp smack across my cheek, and the world reappeared.

I looked up, my face stinging. Rogan held my shoulders.

"Ella, say something!" he yelled even though our faces were only inches apart.

"I'm here, I'm okay," I said as much to reassure myself as to get Rogan to stop hollering at me.

I pushed shaking fingers into my hair.

It was him. Just before I lost contact with the minor demon, I caught a glimpse of the lead vampire's face.

"The big vamp twisted the head off the rip spawn while I was still linked with it," I said, my mouth dry as the grit now embedded in the heels of my hands. "I shouldn't have pushed it so close to the house and definitely not in the shade."

I realized how stupid I'd been. If I were going to spy, I should have picked a spot in full sunlight, where a vamp would be less likely to reach outside.

Rogan gripped my face in both hands and tilted it up, squinting into my eyes. Loki whimpered and nudged my elbow.

"You made it out in time," Rogan said, relief replacing some of the tension in his face. "Lesson learned, huh?"

I drew a trembling breath and nodded. "Yeah. That was scary as shit." I touched Loki's head, which seemed to reassure him.

Rogan stood and helped me up. "You okay to go on?"

I looked off to the distance toward the vampire den and then dropped my head. "I'm fine, but I've tipped them off."

"We don't know that," Rogan said. "He was probably just playing it safe."

He was trying to reassure me, but I recognized the worry in his eyes.

I planted my hands on my hips and let out a sharp stream of four-letter words.

"Well, if I did tip them off, it's too late now," I said. "Nothing to do but keep on."

We resumed our cross-desert dash. Getting back into the rhythm of my boots pounding the ground, I tried not to waste energy beating myself up. But I couldn't help wondering if I'd just put the entire rescue mission in jeopardy.

When Rogan slowed his pace, I knew before he said it that we were close to the vampire feeder den. Down in a shallow gulley, I didn't have a direct line of sight to the compound, but my necro senses were alive with the presence of his demon spies, and I felt the larger arch-demons waiting on the other side of a ridge about a mile away.

"You're sure they don't have guards posted?" I asked, still breathing hard from the long run. I hadn't seen any guards through the eyes of my ill-fated demon, but I was getting jumpy about the whole endeavor.

"Nah," Rogan said. "The place is pretty well fortified, and anyone dumb enough to bust in would be vampire meat."

"Dumb enough to bust in, huh," I said, pretending to be insulted.

He shot me a withering look. "You know what I mean."

He bent to pick up a twig and then knelt and began drawing a diagram in the hard-packed, sandy dirt. I dropped to one knee beside him.

"This is the main gate," he said, pointing to one end of his sketch of the compound. "And here's the drainage outlet I told you about. That's where we're going in."

As he'd explained before, it was a small tunnel that went through the outer wall. When he'd been out here before, he'd actually shimmied through it so we knew it was passable.

"You think Loki will be okay on his own?" Rogan asked, glancing at my dog. "I didn't arrange transportation for him."

Remembering how Loki had transformed into a big, dark beast during our visit to the oracle, I nodded. There was more to him than met the eye, and I was confident he could take care of himself. I couldn't imagine he would tolerate being carried away in the clutches of an arch-demon anyway.

"I think he can handle himself," I said. "He'll meet us back at the car. Right, boy?"

With an affectionate grin, I scratched behind one of his ears.

"We'll have to approach from this direction so we stay out of view of any of the windows," Rogan said, again indicating an area on his diagram.

When he started to rise, I grabbed the lapel of his duster and pulled him closer, planting my lips on his for a long, delicious moment before breaking away.

"Thank you for doing this," I breathed.

His eyes sparkled, and he crooked a half-grin. "Thank you for giving me something to focus on."

In the past few weeks, he had transformed. The reticent, icy man I'd first met had warmed. In his place was a Rogan who actually seemed to care about engaging with the world—*this* world, even though it wasn't the one he believed he belonged in. I began to have hope that he might find contentment in the realm of the living.

Keeping as low as we could, we crept over the ridge that hid the compound. I followed Rogan as we skirted the high wall around the property until we got to a slight depression with a shallow ditch leading away from it. The drainage tunnel.

He looked back at me and pressed the side of his index finger to his lips in a reminder to stay quiet. Vampires had heightened senses, and we'd have to be extremely careful to keep from alerting them.

Rogan went first into the tunnel, and I waved Loki in next. I could see the outlet, but the space narrowed uncomfortably, forcing me to scoot along in an inchworm crawl. At least there wasn't any water actively draining. I tried not to think about spiders or other creepy-crawlies.

The drain let out into a narrow strip of side yard. I gulped when I saw the windows, but the shades over them didn't move. We flattened ourselves against the side of the house, working our way around to where the multi-car garage was. Rogan wanted to jimmy open the side door that went into the garage with a little bit of magic. He was fairly sure the captives were being kept in a bunch of bedrooms during the day, which were in a wing not far from the garage.

I grabbed his arm and pulled him close so I could speak at barely a whisper in his ear.

"Why do we need to sneak in?" I asked. "Can't we just blow the door in with magic and surprise the shit out of them?"

He tilted his head, considering. "Why the hell not?"

I felt a ping of satisfaction. For once, someone wanted to go along with one of my impulses. I loved that he was game. A slow grin tugged at the corners of my mouth as I anticipated our grand entrance.

He beckoned me to follow, and we went around past the garage. He pointed at the oversized front door. The house was a sprawling stucco number with what looked like a vaulted entry.

"I'm going to blast the whole entry out, and I'll take a bunch of roof with it," he whispered rapidly in my ear. "The sudden sun exposure should disorient the vamps, and might even incapacitate some of them temporarily. I'll try to keep all the debris up and out of the way."

He flapped his hand at me, indicating I should back up several feet. Loki stayed by my side, his ears perked and his eyes intent on Rogan.

The air prickled with the torrent of magic that he was summoning. I unfurled my whip, and it fell softly to the ground. Following Rogan's lead, I centered myself and reached deeply for earth magic and then wove as much fire through it as I could bear.

Rogan's arms were bent at the elbow with his palms up and fingers splayed. His hands disappeared in growing orbs of swirling power. The magic swelled until I had to look away or risk temporary blindness from the brightness of it.

The very air itself seemed to tear as he hurled power at the house. The blast deafened me and nearly knocked me off my feet as the ground rocked.

My heart pounding, I formed a shield of earth magic in front of me and over me and charged past Rogan and straight for the dust cloud where the front door used to be. Loki sped along beside me, and my battered eardrums picked up his snarls as if they came from far away.

Rogan fell to his knees as I ran by him. He'd likely spent himself with the blast, but I couldn't afford to stop and check on him. Loki and I were on our own against the den of rogue vamps.

I coughed as dust swirled. Debris rained down on the earth-magic shield. Even through the chaos of the explosion, I could smell the blood. The heavy, nauseating smell of stale blood layered over the more subtle but brighter, metallic scent of fresh blood.

My hearing was starting to recover, and groans and screams filled the air.

Something sped in from my right, and I caught a glimpse of blood-red irises and a pale freckled face framed by red-orange hair. I swiveled my shield. The vamp was small in stature, but she crashed into my wall of earth magic like a Mack truck.

The blow rebounded through my magic and back at me like a punch to the brain, and I reeled as my vision fuzzed around the edges and pain exploded in my head. I lost my hold on the shield, and it winked out.

The girl vamp collapsed to the floor. She'd knocked herself out and landed in a puddle of sunlight. Her skin began to smoke and sizzle like bacon in a fire.

I whirled around just as a growl announced another vamp.

He leapt from eight feet away like a lion attacking its kill. Swift as a reflex, my whip snapped into the air to meet him. It curled around his waist, and I yanked with all my strength. His own momentum and the added power of the magic in my weapon sent him flying by me and slamming into a tall female vamp with a halo of frizzy dark hair. They both crashed into a marble column, temporarily stunned and exposed to the sun.

A compact male vamp with the body of a wrestler ran through the gloom where the roof was still intact.

Loki, in the form of the great beast I barely recognized, charged to meet the vamp. With a swipe of a huge paw, he tore the vampire's head clean off.

Feeling confident my dog had my back, I headed left, where I believed the wing of bedrooms was likely located. So far I'd seen only vampires.

There was a long, dark hallway where Rogan hadn't managed to rip the roof away.

The smell of blood was stronger from that direction.

I looked in open doorways, passing a bathroom, bedrooms in disarray, and what looked like a sauna room.

I kept running. At the end of the hallway there was a short right turn. Through an open doorway, I burst into a room where the smell of blood was thick in the air. It was dark, but I could make out the human forms lying on sofas, chairs, and beds that were arranged at odd angles and had obviously been dragged in from other parts of the house.

I slammed the door closed and formed a seal of earth magic around it.

The blood victims were stirring, some mumbling, a few of them even sitting up to look around. I squinted in the low light.

"Evan? Where are you?" I called, my pulse pounding through my veins. "Evan!"

I went to the nearest male form. No, too old to be my brother.

The door rattled behind me, and something on the other side let out a menacing growl.

I raced to the next person and the next, searching for the face from my visions.

There was a violent blow against the door that reverberated through my magic and into my head like a huge gong. I winced, but tried to ignore the pain. The door still held.

"Evan!" I yelled again.

Where the hell was my brother?

"Ella?"

I straightened and turned. In the corner, a young man stood hunched with his shoulder braced against the wall as if it were the only thing holding him up.

My hand reached for him as a sob tore from my throat. I didn't remember moving across the room to him, but suddenly my arms were wrapped around his too-thin body. He was as tall as me. How could he have grown so much?

He shifted his shoulders, wriggling free of my embrace. I looked into his face but couldn't read his expression.

The door exploded inward, breaking my earth-magic seal and sending my magic rebounding back at me like nails driving into my temples. I winced but reached for my power as a vamp stalked in.

It was the big one. The old vampire.

I shoved Evan behind me and clenched my whip. Something trickled from my nose. I swiped at it, and my hand came away bloody.

The huge vamp took two running steps, blurring with speed, and launched himself at me.

Ignoring the drilling pain behind my eyes, I reached past the realm of the living and into the *in-between*. In a blink I'd grasped the ley line magic and dragged it back to where it shouldn't be. It filled me and flowed down my arm and into my whip.

I lashed out at the vamp. He tried to block the whip with a raised hand, but it snuck past to wrap around his torso, pinning his arms to his side.

I couldn't get leverage fast enough to take up the slack in the whip and redirect his momentum. I reached for my Sig, which was loaded with the anti-vamp bullets, but the vamp crashed into me, still wearing my whip like a straightjacket. The gun flew from my hand and went skittering across the floor.

The sheer mass of his weight pinned me, but I wasn't making it pleasant for him. I punched him in the temple and blasted fire magic at his eyes, singing his eyelids but not managing to blind him. I pulsed more magic into the whip, and it responded by tightening around his torso like a boa constrictor. The vamp's face was inches from mine, and I watched with satisfaction as his eyes bulged.

I'd nearly managed to work myself out from under him when he flexed his biceps and broke free of the whip.

The rebounding magic slammed into my head, and I nearly lost my hold on the world. With blind urgency, I flipped over to all fours and started to scramble away.

I could feel the blood pouring from my nose, and pain lanced from my brain down my spine with every breath.

Shit. This was bad. My vision was still clouded. Also very bad.

I pushed to my feet and reached for more ley line power, trying to gather for one big blow. But I was so disoriented I couldn't tell where my target was.

"You're mine," the vamp snarled from behind me.

A hand yanked my hair, and I fell backward. Then a vice grip closed around my neck.

I clawed at his hands and jabbed my elbows back into his ribs. He lifted me clear off the ground and shook me like a dog with a rat.

My windpipe closed. Oh god, no air.

My head was going to burst from the pressure. If I didn't suffocate first. The room around me began to dim.

Searing agony at the spot where my right shoulder met my neck brought me back, and I let out a strangled scream.

The damn vamp *bit* me.

Pain quickly dissolved into an exquisite high. I knew what was happening, but I couldn't fight it. My muscles went limp with the pleasure of the vamp saliva working its way through my bloodstream.

The world began to clear around me, and I saw Evan. He'd slid down the wall and sat slumped there like rag doll, his face half-turned toward me. The gun was only a couple of feet from his leg. That seemed important, but I lost my grasp on the thought before I could follow it to completion.

I smiled at my brother.

I found you.

I tried to say it, but my lips wouldn't move.

Something large and furry blurred in my periphery, and then I was tumbling to the floor, free of the big vamp's grasp.

I watched through the fog of my high as Loki slammed a giant paw on the middle of the vamp's back. My dog that was not my dog clamped his muzzle around the vamp's neck, bit down, and shook violently.

The pop of the vamp's spine snapped me into reality enough to know that I needed to move. He was down for the moment, but not for good.

Swiping a sleeve across my face and barely noticing the thick smear of dark blood, I forced my legs under me and stood.

I snatched up what was left of my whip and scrambled over to grab my Sig. I reached for my brother and hefted him to his feet.

My heart clenched in my chest as I looked around the room at the blood victims, strewn like discarded toys.

"We'll send help for you," I said, my words muddling with the lingering effects of the vamp saliva.

I wasn't sure any of them actually heard me. Even if they did, they might not remember. I wished I could take all of them with me, but I had to get out with Evan before the vamps regenerated.

I aimed my gun at the big vamp and fired two rounds into his torso. I only had one of the anti-vamp bullets left, but it was worth it. Between the rounds and the broken spine, it'd be a while before he drew any more blood from his victims.

We stumbled down the hallway as fast as I could get Evan to move.

I blinked at the carnage near the entry. Loki had been busy, but some of the vampires were already starting to rouse. The ones I'd left in sunlight had managed to drag themselves to the shadows.

Evan was pulling at me, protesting, and I gripped his arm more firmly.

"We've gotta get out of here," I said, my words slurred. It would be a while before the vamp saliva metabolized completely out of my system.

Outside I found Rogan grappling with a vampire that was sizzling like a pig on a spit in the sun. Loki bounded past me, and Rogan got out of the way just as the big dog slammed into the vampire, sending him flying headfirst into the solid wall surrounding the property.

The vamp went still and continued to cook in the sun.

I stared at Loki, finally getting a good look at him in the light. He looked like a full-blooded hellhound. Black, with wisps of smoke rising from his hide. Eyes of solid hellfire. He turned to me, wagged his tail, and gave me a big doggy grin that showed a row of razor teeth as long as my pinkie.

I swallowed hard. "Good boy," I called to him.

Rogan was doubled over with his hands on his knees, breathing hard. He tipped his head up, and his eyes met mine and then flicked to my shoulder, which was probably a bloody mess. "The arch-demons are on their way."

I nodded and looked over at my brother. His eyes were squeezed shut, and his balance was pitching around as if his knees weren't prepared to keep him upright.

"Evan?" I said softly. "I'm taking you home."

He muttered something unintelligible.

I leaned in. "What?"

"You shouldn't have come," he said through clamped teeth. "Leave me."

I blinked a few times, thinking I must have heard wrong.

The screech of a demon overhead made us all look up.

Evan's whole body went rigid, and he began shaking his head and breathing rapidly.

"It's okay," I said. "Rogan is commanding them. They won't hurt us. They're going to carry us to our car."

My brother broke free of my grasp, wheeled around, and began a shambling run back into the vampire den.

I took two steps after him when a black vertical line split the air in front of me. Rip magic reached out like fiery fingers as the line widened into a gap.

I skidded to a stop, but the rip was advancing on me. I turned to run, reaching out for Rogan.

I saw his eyes go wide, and he shouted my name just before the rip swallowed me whole.

I stood in the crystal cave, and I wasn't alone. A roar shook the floor and sent a furnace blast of air at me that blew my hair back and sent tears streaming from my eyes. The heat was enough to parch my skin, and I could only hope that my eyelashes and eyebrows were still intact.

A very pissed-looking dragon faced me, its eyes flashing and its nostrils flaring with puffs of smoke.

I swallowed hard and blinked tears from my singed eyes. Whirling around, I watched the rip I'd come through sew itself up and then shrink into nothing. What the hell was I doing here with the oracle?

"There must be some mistake," I said, jerking my thumb over my shoulder. "I was in the middle of something pretty important, so if you could just—"

"Silence!" the dragon thundered with another singing puff of breath.

I snapped my jaw closed with a click of my teeth. Words were trying to pile up in my throat, but I held them back. Last time we'd met, the oracle had made it pretty clear he didn't appreciate impatience. So while the giant scaled beast shifted around, taking his time finding a comfortable position, I kept my mouth zipped.

I took it as a good sign that the dragon seemed to derive some pleasure from making me wait. A little passive-aggression was definitely preferable to getting fried in a blast of dragon fire, even if the delay was pure agony knowing that my brother and Rogan were still at the vamp compound. I clung to the hope that Rogan was taking care of my Evan, that they'd managed to escape.

Finally, the dragon turned his great serpentine head toward me.

"What is the meaning of this?" He flicked something toward me, a tiny object that tumbled across the floor of the cavern with faint little clinks.

I stepped forward and bent to retrieve it. With a frown, I straightened, pinching Lynnette's skull ring between my thumb and forefinger. It was the trinket I'd gifted to the oracle.

"You're offended by this gift?" I asked carefully.

"Gift!" The dragon snorted outraged sparks. "It's charmed with trickery!"

Charmed with . . . ?

My hands curled into fists. *Lynnette.* She'd done something to the ring.

"I promise you, I didn't charm this," I said. "And I certainly have no desire to try to trick you. It was given to me by the witch who accompanied me when I came to you before."

The oracle narrowed his eyes at me.

"May I ask, what is the nature of the charm?" I asked. I dared not reach for my own magic to try to probe the thing, for fear he'd take it as an affront, or worse.

The dragon's head darted forward, and I jerked back in alarm. But he wasn't trying to strike. He tilted one eye down at the ring I held.

"It wants to pull my golden magic." His deep voice seemed to reverberate in my bones.

The eye shifted to me. It was bigger than my head, and the vertical slit of a pupil seemed to swirl with the fire of a supernova. For a moment, I could do nothing but stare into it.

"Well, I can't say I'm completely surprised by that," I said frankly. "She seems to be a bit of a collector of rare magic."

"Is that so." The dragon drew the words out.

The great head retreated, and I jumped as the blue-flame magic of a rip appeared next to me. A moment later Lynnette fell through the opening, landing in a heap on the floor. She scrambled to her feet, clutching a toothbrush in her hand. There was a smear of toothpaste foam near the corner of her mouth.

I snorted. Good thing she hadn't been in the middle of a shower.

Her eyes wide with shock, she looked up at me. I fluttered my fingers at her in a little wave.

"Ella. What happened to you?" she asked me. "You look like hell."

Oh my god, you idiot. My appearance was laughably irrelevant.

"Hey, Lynnette." I tipped my head at the oracle and stage whispered, "Someone wants to talk to you about the spell that's in this thing."

I held up the silver skull ring with the pink crystal eyes, and she blanched. Caught red-handed. She straightened and used the back of her wrist to remove the toothpaste smear.

"I meant no harm or disrespect," she said, looking up at the dragon and already composing herself.

"You wanted to steal my magic," the dragon boomed.

Lynnette blinked rapidly. "No, no, of course not. It was an honest mistake."

The dragon grumbled, and I held my breath. But he seemed to be settling into a pout. I frowned. He wasn't going to explode in fiery rage?

"I require a replacement gift," he finally said. "*Now.*"

Lynnette and I glanced at each other. Her hair was piled in a frizzy bun, she had no makeup on, and no jewelry was visible. And I certainly didn't have anything sparkly to offer.

"If you could give us some time, we could return with a proper offering," I said.

"You expect patience from me, yet you want everything immediately?" His voice rose, and the puffs of steam from his nostrils became more violent. "No. I require a gift."

I choked back the string of choice words I wanted to hurl at Lynnette. For shit's sake. I'd finally found Evan, and somehow Lynnette had managed to foil my efforts. Now I was stuck in a glimmering cave with her and a sulky serpent the size of a house who was demanding a pretty present in return for our release.

Exactly how had this become my life?

"Any ideas, since you got us into this mess?" I growled at Lynnette through clenched teeth.

"I didn't exactly have time to prepare for this little meeting." She held up her toothbrush and had the gall to look at me as if I were the idiot in this situation. "This is the best I've got."

"Seriously? Not even a belly button piercing?"

I ran a hand across my eyes. I just needed to get the hell out of here. What did I have on me? A broken whip, a couple of knives, my phone, my ID, some cash, and a bank card. I didn't even have any fricking change in my pocket.

There was only one thing I could think of, but it would require the reaper's cooperation. I faced the dragon.

"Can you come with me to the gray place? The *in-between*?" I asked. "I can give you something that's pretty damned amazing, if I do say so myself. But only in that realm."

My heart was bumping in my chest. I had no idea if I could really pull this off. If I couldn't, there was no telling how the oracle would react.

I swear the dragon perked his head like Loki did when I said the word "treat."

I shot a death glare at Lynnette. She owed me. Like, times a million.

Tuning in to the call of the magic that flowed through the ley lines of the *in-between*, I followed it. My eyelids drifted shut, and I let go of the world of the living.

When I opened my eyes, I stood in the mist of the *in-between*. The cave was nothing but smooth rock, with no crystal formations or pretty lights. The dragon was there with me, but appeared as a smoky hologram of his living-realm self. I felt the reaper stir before I even tried to summon it.

There were no souls nearby to reap, but I didn't think I'd need any.

All I had to do was think of it, and the reaping blade appeared in my right hand. The cloud of souls balanced above the palm of my left. A rush of exhilaration surged through me. This was Xaphan's collection, but I was in charge now, even here in the realm where souls waited for the reaper's knife.

I lifted my left hand, watching the tiny points of light dance in the darker swirling cloud, so the dragon could see. I wished I could set them free, but I somehow felt they'd be safer with the dragon than with Xaphan. The little I'd learned about my reaper didn't exactly give me confidence in its goodwill.

The expanding pressure in my chest was my first indication that Xaphan had taken notice. The jolt of lightning in my brain told me the reaper wasn't as docile as I'd assumed. My body seemed caught between opposing forces—my will and Xaphan's.

"Give it up," I ground out through clenched teeth. "It's time."

The reaper didn't budge.

"I don't need you anymore, Xaphan," I whispered fiercely. "Give up the souls, or I *will* find a way to extinguish you, I swear IT."

The reaper's resistance held for a few more seconds but then began to relent.

I eased back from butting heads with Xaphan, and instead reached for the magic of the *in-between*. The pain in my head sharpened, but I ignored it. Drawing the power hurt, and I knew I'd pay a price for it, but I had to overpower the reaper's will.

I used the magic to counteract the pressure of the reaper, and after a moment felt its presence begin to recede. Still gripping the magic, I walked toward the dragon. The souls brightened and pulsed, swirling like fireflies in an orb of midnight sky.

"This is all I have," I said. "Please accept this gift."

I lofted the cloud of souls gently into the air. As it left my palm, I felt a stab of regret. I wasn't sure if it was mine or the reaper's.

The souls drifted toward the dragon, and he reached one great, clawed hand up to catch it. The points of light reflected in his serpentine eyes.

The gray dissolved, giving way to the crystal cave and the realm of the living.

"I accept your gift, Ella Grey," the dragon intoned. He turned to Lynnette, who still stood where we'd left her. "You will have to answer for your trespass."

Lynnette flicked a glance at me, and true fear shone in her eyes. But I didn't have a chance to react as the blue flames of rip magic consumed me, and I found myself dumped unceremoniously onto the ground.

I pulled my feet under me, still clutching the damn skull ring and blinking as I tried to orient myself. I was back at the compound, standing outside the ruined entry. Time must have compressed while I was with the dragon, because the sun was nearly down.

There was no sign of Evan, Rogan, or Loki. A shuffle of movement and low growl came from behind me. I whirled. A lumbering form emerged from the dingy darkness within. It was one of the vamps Loki had busted up. One leg still dragged, not quite healed, preventing the vampire from its characteristic speed.

I reached for my whip but then remembered that the hulking vamp had snapped it in two.

The sun had set, and it would be full dark soon. If Evan and Rogan hadn't made their getaway already, I wasn't going to be able to help them, not at that time of day and on my own. I had to trust that Rogan had gotten them out.

Springing into a sprint, I ran like hell around the side of the house and straight for the drainage tunnel. I dropped and shimmied through it as fast as humanly possible as I gripped earth magic, ready to sling it behind me at the first sound of a pursuer.

My head throbbed as I struggled to hold onto a thread of magic, and I felt a drop of blood leak from my nose.

When I got through, I pulled myself up to my feet. I looked around, trying to discern exactly which way we'd come. In the failing light, I couldn't make out distinct landmarks in the seemingly endless expanse of sagebrush and the occasional gnarled, wind-beaten trees.

It turned out I didn't have to rely on my internal compass after all.

With a whoosh of great wings, an arch-demon flew low over the wall of the compound. It tipped, turned sharply, and flapped as if coming down for a landing. The turbulence of its movement sent my hair flying around my face. The creature hooked its feet around my shoulders and upper arms. Before it lifted me, I chucked the skull ring into the desert.

As my boots left the ground, I had the strange sensation of feeling like a baby or small child being lifted and carried away. I had to hang there limply, trusting that the arch-demon wouldn't let me slip. We rose, but only a few dozen feet.

The cold air rushed over my face, stinging my skin and drying the blood that had leaked from my nose. It had never gotten particularly warm that day, but with the sun down the temperature was already dropping. A bite of winter moisture in the air foretold snow.

By the time the demon descended and set me on the ground near Rogan's Jeep, my face and hands stung with chill and my teeth chattered.

Rogan emerged and ran to me. Loki in his regular hellhound-labradoodle form went over the driver's seat, jumped out, and followed. Rogan grabbed both my hands and then roughly pulled me into a hug. "It's a good thing you decided to reappear. I wasn't going to be able to stay past nightfall."

I peered over his shoulder, searching for Evan. He was in the back seat and appeared to be asleep.

Rogan let me go, and I began moving toward the Jeep. "Is he okay?" I asked.

"I had to use a mild knockout spell to get him to calm down for the airlift," Rogan said.

I glanced at him, and then it dawned on me. The stories about Evan's disappearance. Witnesses had said he'd been carried off by a giant demon. He'd probably been scared shitless when he saw the creatures Rogan commanded.

I pulled the Jeep door open and slid into the back seat next to Evan. His eyes were closed, his face slack. Rogan had covered him with a couple of wool blankets. I tucked the nearest edges tighter around him.

Rogan put Loki in the front passenger seat and then got in and started the car. I reached forward and gripped his upper arm.

"I don't know how I can ever repay you for this," I said quietly.

He just nodded and squeezed my hand in a touchingly warm gesture.

"What happened back there anyway?" he asked as he steered onto the dirt road that led to the highway.

"The dragon happened," I said. "Actually, no. Lynnette Leblanc happened."

Rogan glanced at me in the rearview mirror.

"That ring I gave to the oracle was charmed. Apparently Lynnette thought she could use it to siphon some dragon magic, though she tried to deny it."

"Holy shit, that was beyond stupid."

"Yeah, tell me about it."

"He didn't . . ." Rogan trailed off forebodingly.

"What, kill her? No. Well, actually, I don't know. The dragon spit me back out, and Lynnette was still there when I left. He was pissed but didn't seem to be in a murdery mood. More pouty than homicidal."

"How did you manage to get away?"

"I had to provide an alternative gift." I told him about the cloud of souls. As I spoke, my eyes stayed glued to my brother. There was a part of me that still couldn't believe he was right there, within arm's reach.

I pressed a hand to my diaphragm and searched my inner sensations as if trying to discern Xaphan's mood. I sensed the reaper's presence, but nothing much beyond that.

"You got the reaper to give up the souls?"

"Yeah," I said. "Xaphan didn't want to, but I didn't exactly offer it as a choice."

Rogan had stopped at the turnoff that divided the dirt road from pavement. He twisted to look at me.

"That's . . . wow," he said.

I tore my eyes from Evan's face so I could peer at Rogan. "What?"

"You got the reaper to give up its most prized possession. I'd say you truly are out of danger. Your soul, I mean."

I gave a wry laugh. "Maybe as far as the reaper is concerned. But I've got this new problem. I think my brain is liquefying and leaking out my nose every time I use magic."

He went still, and for a moment, the only sound was the hum of the engine. I shouldn't have said anything. I hadn't meant to, but our ordeal—and having my brother there, right next to me—had lowered my defenses.

"Ella. You've got to get help."

I waved a hand. "You know what? It's worth it. Whatever the consequences are, I don't even care. I've been through too much to worry about it. I don't want anything to ruin this."

I reached up to touch my brother's shaggy hair, brushing it off his forehead. His brow creased as if something troubled him in his dreams.

Rogan didn't argue, but I saw his jaw muscles flexing over and over as he accelerated onto the highway, taking us back toward home.

Evan was going to need medical care. I was going to have to get him into a treatment program to detox his system and get him to a point where he didn't crave the high that came with vampire bites. He was going to need a lot of support to get clean and back on his feet. It would be a process. It would take time. It—

My brother's eyelids lifted suddenly, and I inhaled sharply.

"Evan?" I reached out to put a hand on his shoulder. "It's me Ella. We're taking you home."

My brother growled and shifted forward. The blankets fell away from his chest. He swung out with a clumsy roundhouse punch that I saw coming but was too shocked to stop.

His knuckles connected with the edge of my jaw, and he drew back for another swing as stars danced around in my vision.

I caught my brother's wrist before he could sock me again.

"Evan, calm down," I said, trying to sound reassuring.

He continued to struggle, and I grasped both of his thin forearms as tightly as I dared. I didn't want to bruise him.

Finally he stopped moving, except for his heaving chest. His eyes flashed with rage, inches from mine.

"You've fucked up everything," he spat with surprisingly clear enunciation considering his condition. "*Everything*. You should have left me there. I didn't ask for this! Why didn't you leave me? You have no idea what you've done! You have *no idea* what you're *doing*."

His voice rose in pitch, and he continued cursing me out and started trying to jerk his arms from my grip.

Magic zipped through the air like static electricity, and Evan's eyes rolled back in his head as he slumped against the seat.

"Just refreshed the sleeper spell," Rogan said.

"Thanks." I took a shaking breath, my heart still knocking at an uncomfortable pace.

"That had to sting a little," he said quietly, and I knew he didn't just mean Evan's punch. Rogan looked at me in the rearview mirror. "The addiction talking, I'm sure."

"Yeah," I said. But uncertainty curled darkly through me as the zombie's warning crept up from memory.

Could Evan possibly know that he was sought after, that Jacob considered him the ultimate prize? Supposedly Evan possessed some special combination of power, some kind of unique rip-ending magic. Did my brother know what he was?

Again, I wondered what the hell I was doing, bringing Evan back to Boise. I pulled out my phone and dialed Damien.

"We've got Evan," I said when he picked up. "But now I'm not sure if I'm doing the right thing by taking him home."

I recounted everything Zarella's zombie had told me.

Damien was silent for so long, at first I thought we'd gotten disconnected.

"I'll set some identity-masking wards around your apartment and your truck," he finally said. His voice was oddly hollow, but his offer of help reassured me.

"Any suggestions for keeping his identity concealed when I have to put him into rehab?" I asked.

"I might be able to pull some strings," he said.

I slumped with relief. "Thank you so much," I said.

After a second or two with no response, I glanced at my phone and found he'd disconnected, probably even before I'd thanked him.

My stomach tightened. I tried calling him again twice, but he didn't pick up.

Remembering my promise to the blood victims, I put in a call to Detective Lagatuda at Supernatural Crimes. Of course he wanted to know how I knew about the vampire feeder den, but I refused explanations.

I dropped my phone in my lap and then pulled my hands down my face, my thoughts going back to Damien. Had he found someone else to help him with Zarella's job and already found the box? Had Damien taken the payment? I couldn't tell by his voice if his magic had changed, but he hadn't exactly been his usual self lately anyway.

I still wanted to believe he wouldn't do it—that he hadn't already gone through with it—but knew it was a childish hope.

There was nothing I could do about Damien, I reminded myself. Especially not now that I had Evan to worry about.

By the time we got back to Boise city limits, it was nearly midnight. Evan was still out cold.

My phone pinged with a text from Deb.

I'm going to Jen's for the rest of the night. There's a huge demon infestation on the block and your apartment—actually all the apartments in the house—got evacuated. Haven't heard from you in a while, I hope you're okay.

"Shit," I muttered and tapped the call button.

"Hey, we're almost home," I said.

"With Evan?" Deb asked.

I glanced at my sleeping brother. "Yeah, we got him. He's in rough shape, but—" My words became unsteady and choked off with the threat of tears. I cleared my throat.

"Oh, Ella, that's amazing," she said, her own voice thick with emotion. "I'm so happy for you. How's he doing?"

"It's going to be a tough road, but . . ." I paused to clear my throat again, trying to compose myself. "We'll figure it out. What's going on there?"

"Huge influx of minor demons," she said, her irritation obvious. "None of the big ones, but there are so many, they're having to evacuate us to clear them all."

"Damn. Well, say hi to Jen."

"You'll be okay tonight?" she asked.

"Yeah, we'll, uh, crash at Rogan's," I said, glancing at him questioningly. He gave me a little nod. "See you tomorrow?"

"For sure. And you know, Evan is really lucky to have you. At some point, he'll understand just how lucky he is."

Tears sprang to my eyes. Leave it to Deb to say the exact words I needed to hear.

"Thanks," I whispered, and we ended the call.

I had to take a couple of breaths to steady myself.

"We can't go to my place tonight," I said. "There's a demon infestation. Are you sure you don't mind if we impose?"

"No problem," he said.

I tipped my head back against the headrest. I didn't like the idea of changing plans. Damien had probably already set the additional wards around my apartment. On the other hand, maybe it was better to hide out in a location that I didn't frequent. I was probably being overly paranoid, anyway. According to Zarella, Jacob hadn't known where Evan was for the past five years, so how would Jacob know that I had my brother suddenly? No one had followed us. Rogan and I had been watching carefully, and he had his demons on the lookout, too.

The attached garage at Rogan's place allowed us to get Evan inside without the risk of neighbors watching. Good thing, because it would have looked odd, the two of us carrying an unconscious person inside. We settled my brother on the sofa, and I covered him with the blankets from the car.

Rogan and I watched Evan for a moment.

"We're going to have to let him wake up sometime," Rogan said.

"Yeah. He needs medical care. Food. Maybe fluids, I don't know." I reached down to touch the side of Evan's neck, feeling for a pulse.

My fingers brushed the raised scar tissue from old vampire bites. Vamp saliva had quick healing properties, often effective enough to leave the skin completely unmarred. To have scars this visible, his neck must have been punctured dozens and dozens of times without fully healing in between. My brother's heartbeat was distinct and steady, his breaths slow and even. He seemed okay for the moment.

"Let's give him one night of peace," I said. "In the morning I'll get him some care."

I planned to call Gina, the healer nurse who'd treated me a couple of times. She seemed like someone who knew how to be discreet. If she could give Evan some preliminary treatment, it would at least be a start. Enough to hold him over until I could get him into a detox facility, I hoped.

"Your call," Rogan said, his voice carefully neutral.

If he disagreed with my decision, he didn't show it. The sudden weight of obligation, the knowledge that I was completely in charge of my brother's care, descended onto me like a lead blanket. It wasn't that I didn't want the responsibility, it was more the sense that where only a few hours before there was nothing, suddenly there was this. Him.

I thought of Deb and her unborn baby, and how there would come a day when something similar would happen for her. There would be the moments before, and then the moments after, when everything would permanently change.

I passed a hand over my tired eyes. Loki had been sniffing around the house, but he seemed to reflect my fatigue as he picked a spot near the sofa, turned three times, and lay down.

"I want to keep an eye on him," I said, tearing my eyes from Evan's face to cast a glance at Rogan. I gestured to the recliner. "I'll stay there for the rest of the night."

Rogan came over to me and reached for my coat zipper. He pulled it down and then took the coat off my arms and tossed it over the arm of the sofa. There wasn't anything suggestive about way he did it, but when he looked into my eyes, there was a hint of contained heat.

He held my face in his hands. "You did it. You saved him. Now let yourself rest, okay?"

He pressed his lips to mine for a long moment. I couldn't even begin to imagine what I looked like—bloodstained, dirt-smeared, and battle worn.

After I pulled away, the tiniest of smiles playing across my face.

"I couldn't have done it without you," I whispered.

I went into the bathroom and pretty much ruined one of Rogan's washcloths in my effort to scrub my face, hands, and the remnants of blood from the vamp bite. Then I actually did sleep for a while, and I dreamed of wandering the *in-between*. The endless gray was somehow soothing, almost meditative, and in my dream I understood why Rogan wanted to return there.

When I woke up, the sharp light of the winter morning slanted through the window behind me.

Evan had pushed himself up onto his elbows, looking disoriented. Loki stood a few feet away, his tail waving tentatively as he watched my brother. When Evan swiveled his head and spotted me, I expected his anger to return. Instead, he just looked tired and almost blank.

He sagged back down, wincing and squeezing his eyes closed. "Where am I?"

I scrambled to my feet and went over to kneel next to him. I wanted to grab him, to wrap my arms around his broad, thin shoulders, but I was careful not to touch him.

"We're at my friend Rogan's house," I said.

Evan's lips were cracked and dry. He looked at me, his eyes glassy and ringed with circles that were bruise-dark. I could see recognition flicker in his eyes. But there was no real warmth.

"Let me get you some water," I said, rising and walking swiftly to the kitchen to fill a glass. I brought it to him and then tried not to hover. "Think you could hold down some food?"

He drank and then sighed deeply. "Is Blossom's Deli still around?"

His voice sounded so strange to me—it had deepened and taken on a rich timbre that hadn't been there before. The fact that I didn't even recognize my own brother's voice pulled at my heart. But I nodded like a bobble head, thrilled that he remembered the deli.

"Yeah," I said. "I stop there all the time. Want the usual? Does that sound good?"

I knew I seemed way over-eager, but I couldn't help myself.

One corner of his mouth stretched a little, almost forming a half-smile, and my heart nearly cracked in two.

"Yeah. I don't know if I'll be able to keep it down, honestly, but it sounds damned good."

I let out a little laugh before I could help myself, as if he'd just told a great joke.

Rogan came out of the hallway leading to his bedroom just then, and catching my expression, his face relaxed into a broad grin.

I made the introductions and went to grab my coat to head out for Evan's sandwich but then stopped short and turned to Rogan as my fears crashed over me again. I couldn't just leave.

Seeming to read my mind, Rogan beckoned me into the kitchen.

"I don't want to leave him," I whispered.

"I'd go," Rogan said. "But I think you've already pushed your limits magic-wise."

My shoulders sagged. He was right. Even the thought of using magic was enough to make my temples throb. I'd be useless against a threat, even a small one, at least until I got treated for magical exhaustion. Even then, I wasn't sure healing would fix me, but that was a worry for later.

Rogan was powerful, far more so than I was. Evan was better off with Rogan watching over him.

He passed me his keys. "You'll be back in no time."

I just stood there for a second.

He made shooing motions. "The sooner you go, the sooner you'll be back. It's just a sandwich run. *Go*, Ella."

"You want anything?" I asked, zipping up my coat.

"I'm fine," he said. "I'll see if Evan's up for bathing while you're out."

"Good idea," I said with a short laugh. "He reeks."

As I pulled the Jeep out of the garage, I felt a sense of buoyancy. Not carefree by any means, but just a little lighter. Maybe it was due to the mundane errand on behalf of my brother. The complete and utter normalcy of it. Perhaps it was because it reminded me of years ago when we were kids. Or maybe because it gave me a tiny glimmer of hope that eventually he would be okay.

Before he'd disappeared, and in the times when he was actually home and lucid, he'd been obsessed with the *number three-and-a-half*, a sandwich on the secret menu at Blossom's Deli. A weird combo of salami, roast beef, and a thin layer of sauerkraut that I personally found a little disgusting. We didn't have much money back then, so even a deli sandwich was a luxury, but given the choice, that was what he always wanted. Not pizza or a milkshake or a fast-food burrito like a normal teenager.

The deli opened early, having a small menu of breakfast sandwiches for the morning crowd. I got my own usual—boring turkey—and Evan's abomination.

On the way back to Rogan's, the wail of sirens forced me to pull over and let the emergency vehicles pass. When I saw the familiar Strike Team trucks, my stomach plummeted. I tried to tell myself it had nothing to do with Evan, that I was just paranoid. But they were heading toward Rogan's area. I watched as they passed, and then everything seemed to speed up. As soon as I could pull out, I jerked the wheel over to get back into traffic and jammed on the gas.

With my heart in my throat, I raced toward Rogan's, swerving through traffic and running stop signs.

"No, please, no," I whispered over and over, as if my pleading could have any effect on what was happening.

I could already see the flashing lights up ahead. Supernatural Crimes cruisers sped around me.

I screeched to a halt half a block from Rogan's, unable to pull up any closer. With my heart slamming in panic against my chest, I threw the door open, jumped out, and ran toward the house.

$\mathcal{S}$trike team and Supernatural Crimes were trying to form a police line around the house. Some of the armored Strike personnel were already storming inside.

I tried to bust through the line, but a couple of the Strike guys stopped me, nearly clotheslining me in the process.

More vehicles were pouring in behind us. Everyone was shouting. It was a madhouse.

"My brother's in there!" I shouted above the commotion, tearing at the hands holding me back. "Let me go!"

Someone was yelling my name, trying to get my attention. I turned, and some part of my brain was surprised to see SC Detective Lagatuda. He turned me around and held me hard by the upper arms.

"Who's in there?" he demanded.

"My brother. Evan. And Rogan. This is Rogan's house." I couldn't seem to spit out more than broken sentences. "Please, you have to let me go in there. My brother's not well."

"No! You can't go in." His eyes were tense and unblinking.

Lagatuda looked scared. At first I thought he was empathizing with my own distress, but understanding began to seep through my panic. There was something really, really bad inside Rogan's house.

The realization launched me into a new bout of struggling to break through the line. Lagatuda grabbed my arm and shoved it behind my back, nearly forcing me down to one knee as his hold strained my shoulder joint.

"Ella, listen to me, damn it," he thundered in my ear. "You *cannot* go in there."

My heart still racing, I relented. "Okay, okay. Just tell me what's going on. Please."

He let go of my arm. "It's bad. Some kind of rip spawn we haven't seen before. Worse than an arch-demon, much worse."

I looked up at the house just as one of the windows blew out, sending shattered glass raining down into the front yard. An armored Strike Team guy had flown through, landing in shards in a heap. He didn't move. A few others in Strike uniforms ran up to drag their comrade away from the house. Dark smoke that crept like fog began seeping out from the busted window. Something flashed inside, like licks of lightning.

I sprang away from Lagatuda, using the diversion and ensuing scramble of officials as my chance to dart across the police line. The front door had been busted open, and I ran through before anyone could stop me.

Inside, the dark mist was filling the house. The nauseating smell of brimstone and rotted flesh permeated the air, and bile rose halfway up my throat. My gaze went automatically to the sofa, but my brother wasn't there. The blankets had been shoved to the floor.

"Evan?"

I ran into the kitchen. It was in disarray, with dishes smashed and one cupboard door hanging askew on a single hinge.

Back in the living room, the black fog seemed to be coming from the hallway that led to the master bedroom, which was where the blown window was. I went to peer down the hall and found a dozen armored Strike Team personnel lined up in formation in the doorway.

"Rogan!" I shouted.

One of the Strike guys turned at the sound of my voice, and I recognized Brady Chancellor through the visor of the helmet he wore.

"Get the hell out of here, Ella!" he shouted at me, his voice muffled.

"My brother was here," I said, babbling in my panic. "That's not him in there, is it? He's nineteen, about my height, and—"

A horrible, deafening noise cut me off. It was something between a groan and a roar, and it was powerful enough to make my teeth rattle.

I looked past Brady and the rest of the Strike Team just as one of the armored personnel was jerked forward and into the bedroom. There was a scream, and the lead Strike members started firing their anti-demon weapons. After a moment the dark mist began to thin, and through it I saw a figure. A man wearing a duster.

I almost spoke Rogan's name. But then I saw the glowing crevices in his skin, like cracks in the earth revealing roiling lava beneath the surface.

Possession.

Rogan had been possessed by a demon. Lagatuda had said they didn't even know what it was.

When I saw the mutilated body of a Strike member at Rogan's feet, a part of my heart died.

Strike had just lost one of their own in the line of duty. And that meant Rogan was as good as gone.

Strike Team was retreating. This was beyond their ability to contain. I got swept up in their rush to get out of the house.

I couldn't fight. I could barely stand as my knees tried to buckle. Numbly, I watched Rogan over my shoulder as I got jostled through the living room and out the front door.

Rogan had been possessed, and he'd killed. He was beyond exorcism. He couldn't be saved.

And Evan was nowhere to be found.

Back outside, I couldn't seem to catch my breath. My chest hitched, and the world tilted.

A tactical team, with their grim faces and precise movements, had arrived.

I turned, feeling torn and lost, as if I'd been dropped into some alternate universe. I thought I glimpsed a Mustang that looked like Johnny's at the edge of the emergency vehicles, which just made the entire scene even more bizarre. Maybe this was just a horrible, vivid dream.

"Ella."

The sound of Deb's voice seemed out of place. Just another inexplicable moment in this nightmare. I turned to find her moving toward me. Her coat gaped open in the cold, her belly too big to accommodate the zipper.

"What are you doing here?" I asked her.

She was pregnant. She shouldn't be around all these guns. And who knew what was in that black mist.

"Detective Lagatuda called me," she said. Then she reached up to wrap her arms around me and pull me to her.

"Rogan was possessed, and he killed. Evan's disappeared again," I choked out, my words nearly unintelligible. "I don't know where Loki is, either."

I squeezed my eyes closed, trying to block it all out, but hot tears began leaking down my cheeks.

I felt like I was collapsing in on myself, but that wasn't an option. Evan wasn't inside. I had to believe he was still alive.

With a trembling breath, I pulled upright and dragged my hands over my face.

"You should go," I said to Deb. I wasn't sure what time it was, but it seemed like past the hour when she usually left for school. "I don't want you to get in trouble at work."

"It's the weekend, honey."

I tried to process that.

Something behind me caught her attention. "Is that Johnny?"

I twisted around to see my ex moving through the crowd of officials and vehicles.

"They must have called him in. Lagatuda said the demon is—" I faltered over the words and had to clear my throat. "He said it's something new. Bigger, more powerful."

Obviously a lot worse than anything that had come through the rip before. In Rogan's quest to return to the *in-between*, he had already determined he couldn't be possessed.

Something thorny curled up through my dazed devastation. Hours after I returned home with my brother, and some terrible new creature shows up right here? No—this wasn't an accident or some terrible stroke of bad luck. I didn't believe in coincidences.

A low boom sounded from within the house, and then the tactical team began trickling out. Four of them emerged carrying a metal coffin-like container by the handles molded to its sides. It rocked and bumped. Rogan—no, the *thing* that had taken Rogan—was still kicking inside.

The tactical team set it down in the driveway, and Johnny went through the police line with his black cases. He opened one and pulled out a familiar tablet. Standing over the metal container, he aimed the tablet at it, and then walked around to another angle and did the same.

I watched him take scans, and then Detective Barnes and her boss, portly Rusty Garcia, went up to talk to Johnny. They were hovered over his tablet and didn't even seem to notice when the metal box was lifted and hauled toward an armored truck.

I kept my eyes on Johnny, refusing to watch the box get loaded into a reinforced vehicle that would take it to its final destination, to a facility where the creature inside would be euthanized.

When the three of them started walking our way, still in conversation and with their faces drawn and serious, I moved to intercept them.

"What is it?" I demanded.

Johnny looked up, distracted, and I could tell by his shift of expression that he hadn't realized I was on scene.

Barnes paused, too, while her boss continued on. She came up to me while Johnny hung back.

"Lagatuda told me you and your brother were in the house earlier today, along with the victim," she said. She was several degrees less frosty than usual. There was even a hint of sadness in her eyes. Maybe Deb had told her and Lagatuda that Rogan and I were close. "Can you tell me what happened?"

"Is there any sign of my brother?" I asked, ignoring her question. "Anything at all?"

She lowered her eyelids and shook her head. "I'm sorry. But the good news is, there's no indication that he was hurt."

I raked my hair back with my fingers. "I went out to pick up food. Rogan and Evan were here when I left. I was gone for maybe twenty-five minutes, thirty tops. I heard the sirens when I was on my way back, and when I arrived . . ."

I gestured at the scene. Then I looked back and forth between Barnes and Johnny.

"Do you know what it is?" I pleaded.

I saw Barnes's jaw twitch, and I knew what she was thinking—I wasn't officially part of any department, and I didn't have clearance. But she decided to throw me a bone and gave Johnny a curt nod. Someone called her name, and she turned to go.

"I'm very sorry about the loss of your friend," she said.

I looked at Johnny, making no attempt to hide any of the misery I felt.

"I'm sorry for your loss, Ella." His eyes cut over to the truck Rogan had been hauled into. He cleared his throat, obviously debating internally about what to say next. "What happened between us before—"

"Please, just tell me," I cut in. I didn't give a shit about the past. "Anything. Whatever you know."

He lifted his tablet, seemingly relieved to have something to direct his attention to.

"It's an unknown species of demon," he said. He tipped the tablet so I could see, but I only gave it a cursory glance. I wasn't in a frame of mind to process technical information. "It's got some characteristics of an arch-demon, but it's been—well, I think it's been modified. That's somewhat of a guess, as I don't have a profile of a modified demon to compare it to."

"Modified?" I squinted at him. "Like, genetically?"

"That's my theory. Could be genetic modification using technology and magic."

I didn't know what that meant, but it didn't matter.

I felt the blood drain from my face. "Gregori?" I said, barely above a whisper.

He grimaced. "Very plausible. We know Jacob Gregori is the type of man who does such things. And Gregori Industries has the resources for complex and experimental magical technology."

I looked off into the distance, as if I could see the answers in the morning sky. But I already knew—Jacob had my brother. He'd taken Evan, and he'd killed Rogan.

Anger began to knife through the heaviness of my grief.

"Thanks," I said to Johnny and stalked toward Lagatuda.

He saw me coming, and I beckoned him away from the other officials he was talking to.

"Jacob Gregori is behind this," I said. "He's got my brother, and he's going to—"

I stopped abruptly. Shit. What was I going to say, that Phillip Zarella's zombie told me Jacob Gregori wanted to sacrifice my brother to close the rips?

Lagatuda's brow wrinkled. "What makes you think Gregori is involved?"

I exhaled loudly. "I don't have proof, but I know it. The thing that possessed Rogan is genetically modified. A new species. You've got to believe me. You have to help me get my brother."

He placed a hand on my arm and said something probably meant to be reassuring. I didn't think he disbelieved me. But even if he could convince his bosses, they wouldn't be able to move fast enough. They'd need proof, a case against Gregori before they could make any accusation.

Too much red tape.

Abruptly, I wheeled around and made my way through the crowd toward the Jeep. Deb appeared at my side, doing a little skipping walk to keep up with my long strides.

"Slow down," she said. "You're still in shock, and you've got major magical depletion."

"I'm not in shock," I said dismissively.

"Ella," she barked so sternly I scuffed to a halt. Her voice softened when I finally turned to her. "At least let me heal some of this."

She waved her hand in the air around me.

All of a sudden, a big four-legged blur bounded in from the right. With a few whining yips of recognition, Loki threw himself at me, his big paws hitting my chest. I lost my balance, and I sat down hard on the asphalt, but I didn't really care.

I wrapped my arms around his furry neck as he licked my ear and cheek. My relief at seeing him was so thick my throat closed for a moment as I fought back tears.

Deb helped me up.

I shook my head as I faced the Jeep. I'd left the door open, and I could see the sandwiches from Blossom's Deli on the passenger seat.

"That's Rogan's car," I said. "He handed me the keys, what, an hour ago?"

Deb closed the Jeep's door and gently pulled me over to my own truck. I blinked stupidly at it for a couple of seconds, wondering how it had ended up here, before remembering that her soon-to-be ex-husband had sold her Honda. She'd driven my pickup here.

I dug in my heels, resisting her. "I have to find Evan," I insisted.

"You're not doing shit until you get healing," she said. I could see the worry in her eyes. She'd recognized something in my aura or energy or whatever it was that she sensed about people. She could tell I'd pushed myself into dangerous territory.

Loki leapt into the bed of the truck and watched us through the back windshield as I slumped into the passenger seat and Deb got in behind the wheel. She started the engine but had to wait because the armored truck was pulling away.

Coffin. I might as well accept what that metal box riding inside really was.

Demon control specialists would take it to one of their facilities where the body in the coffin would be incinerated. It would use a combination of flash-incineration and highly controlled obliteration magic to wipe Rogan from existence.

I watched the truck roll by, and the ache in my chest took my breath away. Deb reached for my hand. After the truck was out of sight, she pulled out and made a U-turn.

I stared dazedly out the windshield without really seeing anything. At home, she took me inside and made me lay down on the bed.

"I'll work quickly, I promise," she said and then began performing a healing ritual.

It wouldn't be enough—I needed to see a more powerful healer—but it was better than nothing.

As she chanted quietly, I felt myself wrapped in numbing warmth. She'd probably woven something into her healing for soothing emotions. I didn't want to be numbed. I wanted to feel the hard edge of grief over Rogan, the hot flashes of fear and anger at Evan's abduction. But it would all come crashing back soon enough, so I let myself drift.

Some time later, I sat up. Deb had finished and had left me alone to rest. I was drained, but at the same time newly energized. In a strange reflection of my own sensations, I felt the reaper stirring.

The presence of the reaper grew more agitated until the pressure in my chest became alarming. My heart thudded, adding to the discomfort. Small tendrils of panic began creeping through me. Had Deb's healing given the reaper too much strength? Oh, shit . . . had it knocked loose the spell that kept the reaper in check?

I tried to get off the bed and stand up but nearly fell on my face. I doubled over, groaning and pinching my eyes closed. I wanted to call out for Deb but couldn't even manage the words.

Then all at once the pressure released. I took a breath and opened my eyes, and found I was in the gray of the *in-between*.

And I wasn't alone.

My apartment building existed in the *in-between*, but none of my furniture carried over to this realm.

There was someone in the bedroom window. At least, there had been.

I went through the living room and out the front, where there was no door in the frame. Loki was there in his hellhound form, and he followed me.

And there, standing next to the *in-between* version of my truck, was a skeletal, hooded figure. There was nothing in particular to distinguish this specter, but I knew who it was immediately.

"Rogan," I breathed.

The figure raised a hand in greeting.

I took a shaking breath, trying to smile. After all, this was what he'd wanted. He was free, and there should be a measure of happiness in that. Maybe someday I'd feel it, but my own loss was still too painful.

He half-turned, as if ready to stroll down the sidewalk, and then extended his hand and curled his fingers, beckoning at me. My eyes wide, I approached him. He began walking, his movements silent. The only sign of his passing was the slight swirling of mist around his ethereal cloak.

My reaper stirred, and I sensed it was displeased and longed to put distance between us and the other reaper.

"Get over it, Xaphan," I muttered.

I remembered what Rogan had told me about his former life, that reapers were solitary creatures and instinctively avoided each other. Their lives were so isolated they had no need for speech.

We walked side by side through the mist, with Loki loping along ahead of us. I was tempted to glance back toward home. Had Deb discovered I was gone? I didn't want to worry her. But I sensed this was important.

We walked into a ghostly version of downtown, stopping at intersections to wait for phantom driverless cars to pass. Rogan led me through my former Demon Patrol beat until we reached a corner that was only a few blocks from my old station. It was a spot I'd passed hundreds of times. There was a large square-tiled fountain that had been there for decades, and next to it a non-descript brick office building with an attached parking garage.

I looked at Rogan in question. He moved to the edge of the fountain and waved me over. We peered down into the water pooled there. He reached out a skeletal hand and trailed it through the water. He tipped his skull-like face up and pointed at his temple, tapping it twice. Then dipped his fingers in the water again.

The surface of the water shivered as if disturbed by a breeze. Then it flattened, and in the reflection, I saw the front of Rogan's house.

In the next breath, Rogan, Loki, and I were standing in the driveway.

I turned a full circle. Apparently he'd just used some sort of reaper teleportation to move us two miles from downtown to his old house. But why were we here? Was he trying to give me a clue to my brother's whereabouts?

"Is there something here I need to see?" I asked.

He shook his head, and my brow furrowed in confusion.

Tipping his face back, he almost seemed to sniff the air. I imitated him, inhaling, searching for . . . what? I turned again, slowly this time, kicking up puffs of mist with my movements. For the first time, I noticed that the gray mist seemed to have a scent. Left undisturbed, it settled low to the ground, but motion stirred it up. It was akin to kicking through dry leaves and sending up the moldy, earthy smell of them.

The mist had a chill, slightly mineral note. Like the smell of cool water bubbling up from deep in the bedrock.

Water . . .

I could smell water nearby. Rogan and I looked at each other, and then silently started off in the same direction. We ended up a block away in front of a split-level house. It looked vacant here in the *in-between*. We went around to the back yard where we came upon a pond. Rocks at one end formed a cascade for a waterfall to trickle down, but either it wasn't turned on, or such things didn't work in this realm.

Together we went to the pond and leaned over it. Two spectral faces stared back at us. He tapped the outer corner of one eye and then his temple.

I looked at him and shook my head. How was he making the images of other locations appear in the water?

He made the gesture again and then pointed at the water. Eye and head. Water.

"Mind's eye?" I asked.

He nodded.

The light bulb blinked on in my head. If I pictured the destination, the water would take us there. My breath caught in my throat. Could I use the teleportation to move around and then come out of the *in-between* into the realm of the living? That would be a real trick.

Rogan gestured at me.

Try it.

"Can I teleport anywhere and then pass between realms?" I asked.

He hesitated but then nodded. My mind spun as I thought it through. Sure, I could teleport myself onto the Gregori Industries campus, for instance, but I'd have to make sure I didn't end up trapped.

"Okay," I whispered, focusing on the pond.

I trailed my fingers across the water, pictured the porch in front of my apartment, and then touched the water's surface again. Nothing happened for a moment, but then it shimmered. It clarified into the image I held in my mind.

And then we were there, standing outside my front door.

I turned to Rogan—Atriul, as he was known here. He stepped away, and with a stab of sadness, I realized he didn't intend to stay.

There were so many things I wanted to say to him. But after everything we'd been through, everything he'd done for me, only one thing seemed right.

"Thank you," I whispered. "Thank you for everything."

Before I totally lost it, I closed my eyes and broke my connection to the *in-between*. Back in the realm of the living, Loki and I went inside. He looked up at me and wagged his tail enthusiastically, as if we'd just been on a great adventure. He wasn't wrong—Rogan had shown me a skill that I never would have dreamed possible. It was only because of the reaper soul residing in me that I possessed such an extraordinary ability.

And the fact that I could take Loki along—he apparently had some connection to the *in-between*, too—made it all the better.

Deb looked startled when she saw me coming through the door.

"I was in the kitchen and didn't even hear you leave," she said, almost accusingly. "Where did you go?"

"Sorry," I said. "I had to say goodbye to Rogan."

Her expression softened into sorrow.

"I'll be okay." I forced confidence into my voice.

"Your magic changed," she said quietly. "Damien?"

I nodded and then found my coat and keys. "I need to get out for a while."

"Do you want me to come with?"

I shook my head. "But maybe you could call Lagatuda and see if they've made any progress on Gregori's involvement?"

She brightened. "Of course."

I called Loki, flipped Deb a wave, and I was out the door. I didn't expect her to glean anything helpful from Lagatuda, but I wanted her to feel useful. If the task distracted her from imagining what I might be doing, then all the better. And I had a sneaking feeling that she wouldn't mind an excuse to talk to the tall detective. I knew *he* certainly wouldn't mind it.

As I drove away from home, I realized that I had a ghostly awareness of the *in-between*. It lurked at the back of my mind, hanging there in vague unrest, like the sensation of a task I needed to do but couldn't quite remember the details of it. If I really quieted myself and focused on it, I could almost swear I felt the rivers of otherworldly magic flowing through the ley lines of that other realm.

It didn't tug at me the way it had probably pulled at Rogan. The *in-between* wasn't my home, and its magic seared me whenever I used it. I was a foreigner there. Well, most of me was, anyway.

I drove to Quinn's Pond, a small body of water just off the Boise River beyond a somewhat seedy edge of downtown spotted with motels, dive bars, and abandoned buildings. During the summer, the pond was a spot where kayakers practiced their rolls, triathletes trained for their swimming legs, and people threw sticks for their dogs to fetch. It wasn't cold enough yet for the edges of the water to be frozen. I parked on the street and then walked swiftly with Loki to a spot where I could look down into the water without getting my boots wet.

It struck me that in order to make the teleporting work I had to know my destination well enough to envision it clearly.

The Gregori Industries campus was huge, and I was only barely familiar with limited areas of it.

Damn. What I really needed was Zarella's help. After all, he lived on the Gregori campus, and he'd wanted to keep Evan out of Jacob's hands. Maybe he could even get Evan out. I didn't know how to contact Zarella directly, though. Someone in the underworld could probably help me, but I hadn't bothered to get contact info from anyone I'd met during my induction ceremony. I'd figured that Rogan was my link to the group if I ever needed them. Sometimes my antisocial ways really came back around to bite me in the ass.

Well, I could at least go onto the Gregori campus and have a look around. I might even get lucky and find my brother on the first try.

I let myself dissolve from the world of the living and transition into the *in-between*. A moment later, hellhound-Loki joined me. I drew my fingers across the surface of the water and began to picture the fountain near the center of the Gregori campus.

But then I stopped. I needed leverage, something I could use against Jacob. I suddenly realized what I needed, and with a heavy heart, I knew where I'd find it. I pictured Damien's apartment.

Holding the image firmly in my mind, I touched the water again. The shimmer came, and when it settled, the image in my mind was reflected back at me.

And then we were there. I blinked back into the realm of the living.

"Damien?" I called. The place felt dead, empty, and I wasn't surprised when there was no response.

I looked around and then zeroed in on a small object sitting on the edge of the kitchen counter. A rectangular box about the size of a stick of butter. It looked as if it were carved out of a solid chunk of black diamond, and I could sense the residual magic clinging to it. The lid was tipped back, and it was empty. I closed it and tucked it into the inner pocket of my jacket, trying not to think of the implications. Trying not to imagine what Damien was doing at that moment. How much of the Damien I knew was even left.

I dropped the rubber stopper into the sink drain, and with Loki beside me, I ran a few inches of water. Then I trailed my fingers in the water, pictured the fountain at Gregori Industries, and touched the water again. In the next breath, we were there.

As soon as I looked around, I realized my mistake. I'd brought us to a very visible spot—not a good place to suddenly appear in the realm of the living. I needed to find a safer location before I left the *in-between*.

There were probably ten multi-story buildings on campus, in addition to smaller outbuildings and garages. I'd only been inside a few of them and didn't know them well. I didn't know all the quirks of the *in-between*, but there were some unpredictable features that could get me in trouble. For instance, the fact that windows were often pane-less in the *in-between*, but doors might or might not be present here as they were in the realm of the living.

Basically, I had to make sure I didn't put myself in a place where I could get trapped.

I squared my shoulders and strode off in the direction of one of the buildings I'd been in before, the one where Roxanne's brother had been held when he was caught inside one of Jacob's genetically engineered gargoyles. He'd held one prisoner there already, so it was as good a place as any to start my search for Evan.

Of course, there had to be a door blocking my entry. I tried it and wasn't surprised to find it locked. Keycard activated, if I remembered correctly.

"We need an open window, boy," I said to Loki.

I took a few steps back and tipped my head up, but all the windows on this side had glass panes. Just as I was about to go around the side to check out the rest of the windows, the door swung open.

I sprinted up and flattened myself against the wall right next to it and then slipped inside with Loki on my heels. Like with the driverless cars in this realm, I couldn't see the person who'd opened it.

I went deeper into the building, searching for an inconspicuous place to pop back into the world of the living. A private restroom or an unlocked janitorial closet would be perfect.

Down a side hallway, I spotted a door that led to the stairs. It was propped open with a chair. That might work.

I sidled through and then went around to the little nook below the first flight of steps, where I released my grip on the *in-between*.

Back in the living world, I held my breath, listening. Fairly sure I had the stairwell to myself, I began sprinting up the stairs with Loki silently following at my heels. As I went, I realized that I'd sent myself on a fool's errand. This was basically a needle-in-a-haystack search. I didn't even know if I was in the right building, and it would take me about a year to sneak around undetected and thoroughly search the entire campus.

I paused three floors up, my pulse thumping from exertion and adrenaline.

I needed to speed things up, somehow. I flashed back to the *in-between*, and Loki appeared beside me.

Bending at the waist, I held Loki's huge hellhound face in my hands.

"I need you to stay hidden, boy," I said. He closed his mouth and cocked his head as if concentrating on my words. "I don't want you to get caught up in this. Do you understand? Go hide in the *in-between*."

He panted with his tongue out, licked at my spectral wrist, and then turned and disappeared into thin air.

I returned to the realm of the living and went through the door that let out into a hallway with a row of elevators. As I moved, I reached into my jacket to pull out the box I'd taken from Damien's.

A bearded man wearing a white lab coat glanced at me, and then did a double-take at my leather combat boots. His eyes scanned up until his gaze met mine.

"Where's your badge?" he demanded. He took a step back. "Do you have clearance to be in here?"

"Nope." I planted one hand on my hip and lifted the box in the other. "Take me to Jacob Gregori."

"The guns really aren't necessary," I said for the third time, my hands still raised in surrender.

Scientist Guy had called security, which had resulted in a dozen of Jacob's crew-cut ex-military guys surrounding me with automatic weapons, and an evacuation of employees from this wing. Through the whole thing, I'd just stood there calmly.

"I'm not going to try anything, I swear. But my arms are seriously getting tired. Has anyone called the boss man yet?" I waggled the box. "He's really, *really* gonna want to know that I have this thing."

My bravado was mostly borne of the knowledge that I could disappear into the *in-between* if anybody tried anything threatening. I didn't want to use that card until I had to, though.

The elevator dinged, and Jacob stepped out.

Damn, finally.

He flicked his hand in a dismissive gesture, and all but two of the crew-cuts lowered their weapons and backed up.

"Ella." Jacob smiled magnanimously, as if welcoming his favorite niece to Christmas dinner.

"Where's my brother?" I demanded. I held up the box. "I want to see him. *Now*."

My heart thumped with anger. I was tempted to draw magic but didn't want to risk that the two crew-cuts that stood on either side of Jacob might have jumpy trigger fingers. I relaxed my arms at my sides and forced myself to stay loose.

Jacob's eyes snagged on the box. I saw his throat constrict as he swallowed. His fingers twitched at his sides. He wanted it. Badly. But to his credit, he didn't make a move for it.

Jacob half turned toward the elevator and swept his hand forward in a beckoning motion. "Please, come with me. I have something very important to show you."

"I don't care," I said. "If you want this thing, take me to my brother."

"Evan is safe. He's resting," Jacob said. "I will let you see him. But first, I need you to see something. I promise the detour will be worth it."

We stared at each other for a long moment, but then I relented. "Make it really damn fast."

Jacob took me down to the main floor and outside. We went into a shorter building, and the entire time the two gun-toting guys followed along as silently as panthers behind us.

My uncle led me into what looked like a mini auditorium. The crew-cuts stopped just inside the door while Jacob went down to the podium and picked up the tablet on it.

"What the hell is this?" I asked impatiently.

"You'll see," he said, swiping at the tablet. "Please, take a seat."

I folded my arms, tucking the box behind one elbow. "No thanks, I'll stand."

Part of me wanted to close my hands around his neck and wring the life out of him. Another part of me had this morbid curiosity about what he wanted to say.

The overhead lights dimmed, and the large screen on the wall began to glow. A spinning globe appeared in the middle, and after a few turns, it flattened into a world map. Red dots began to pop up all over, with bunches of them forming masses in certain areas.

"Each one represents a death due to the interdimensional rips," Jacob said. He came to stand near me so he could look up at the display, too. Dots kept appearing. "In total, over half a million lives lost due to demon attacks, irreversible possessions, zombie virus infections, and euthanasia and killings of those infected with VAMP2 before the implant was invented. In the decades since the Manhattan Rip first tore through the sky, I've spent millions trying to understand the nature of the rips and tried dozens of things to try to close them permanently. The mages of the world have been trying to do the same. But neither the most powerful technology in the world nor the most powerful magic in the world has achieved the goal."

He lowered the tablet and turned to peer at me in the semi-dark, the map with all its dots reflecting off the lenses of his wire-rimmed glasses and obscuring his eyes.

"So you want to sacrifice my brother because he has some special set of genes or magic or whatever, and you think tossing him into the rips will zip them up, and we'll all live happily ever after," I said, practically spitting the words.

His lips pursed for the briefest of moments, betraying his annoyance that I'd undermined the big buildup in his speech.

"That's not precisely how it would work," he said. Then his voice softened. "But the exact details aren't important. It's the larger picture, Ella. Think of it. We could close the rips. Go back to how the world was before. No more lives lost, and no more hellspawn plaguing us. No more rogue viruses claiming thousands of innocent people."

"*Or*, we could just live with what we've done," I said. "And why not? The vampirism and zombie viruses are more or less in check, now. We manage the demon problem. We've made a lot of progress." I gestured up at the screen. "Most of those deaths happened in the first few years after the original Rip. These days the casualties are few and far between."

A pang sliced into my heart as I thought of Rogan getting carted away in a metal coffin. My fists clenched as I remembered the sadistic beefcake who'd tied me up and sapped me with the cattle prod. Jacob might not have been there for either event, but he was directly responsible for both.

"Besides, what proof do you have that murdering Evan would close the rips?" I demanded. "Sounds pretty damned far-fetched to me."

"Because Gregori Industries and the Order of Mages have independently arrived at the same conclusion," he said. "We've both discovered the combination of magical factors needed to seal off our dimension. Believe me, I've spent the last few years desperately looking for an alternative, but there simply isn't one."

I wanted to argue, but his tone stopped me short. There was genuine sadness in it. True regret. Regardless of what I thought of Jacob, I couldn't deny that his focus in life was singular, and he'd thrown everything into it—his time, his extensive resources, and his considerable fortune. He wanted a solution more than anything else in life. He wanted to close the rips, to atone for the actions that had caused the disaster in the first place. He'd genetically modified gargoyles in an effort to use them as live demon traps. He'd sent a horde of demonic assassins when he'd discovered that Lynnette was opening rips. And now he was willing to sacrifice his own blood. It struck me that Zarella might be the psychopath, but Jacob was almost as bad. The main difference was that Jacob wanted to atone for his sins, in his own twisted way, whereas Zarella was happy to let chaos reign.

The deaths, all those red dots on Jacob's diagram, weighed him down every moment of his life. But that was his problem, not Evan's.

Before I could respond, Jacob continued.

"We could, perhaps, go on as you suggest. But there is a new twist, an additional piece that only a few know about," he said. "We're nearing a crisis. Our monitoring of the interdimensional activity shows a change in pattern, one that indicates we're in for a completely new tide of devastation. The mages have detected it as well. A new and much more terrible generation of hellspawn is due to come through soon. Very soon. The mages expect new viral strains, as well."

The foreboding in his voice sent a cold shiver curling down my spine.

"I want to know what would happen to Evan," I said, my voice low and on the edge of trembling. "Not because I would ever agree to sacrifice him, but because I think I deserve to know what you would force my brother to suffer. What you would do to your nephew, your own family, to right your wrong."

His lips parted, but he hesitated.

I faced him, my arms dropping to my sides. "C'mon, Jacob. *Tell me.*"

He gave a small sigh. "He would be a catalyst into which the mages would direct their magic. He would have to go through one of the big rips and then remain there while the mages cast their power into him."

I ground my teeth, trying not to picture my brother burning up in a storm of mage magic.

I pushed the fingers of my free hand into my hair and squeezed my eyes closed for a moment.

"I don't understand," I said. "Why Evan? He's not even that powerful. What is it about him?"

"He's much more powerful than you've seen. His extreme power and the unique nature of it, well, all I can say is there has never been anyone like your brother. Your mother managed to mask his true abilities with a spell." He hesitated. "That spell, and the way it dulls his magical abilities, is likely at the root of Evan's . . . troubles."

I didn't want to believe it, but I couldn't help thinking back to when Evan first came into his magic. That was when all the problems started. The rampant drug use. His seemingly single-minded headlong plunge into addiction and trying to obliterate his own mind. He'd never had a chance. I saw it, and the truth of it stabbed me to my very core. My parents had conspired to create a child who might have the right magic to end the world's suffering. And then my mother had regrets, so she tried to smother Evan's power.

"My parents were truly willing to create a child and then sacrifice it?" I asked, feeling my face twist in horror.

"No," Jacob said quickly. "They believed the child would *wield* the power and thereby close the rips. They hadn't considered that sacrifice would be necessary."

"Why didn't you take Evan long ago? You could have. He was right here for years before he disappeared."

"The spell," he said. "It fooled us for a long time into thinking that Evan didn't have what we were seeking. Then, just as we discovered the truth, your brother vanished. So you see, your mother was trying to protect him, and it actually worked for a few years."

My chest hurt as emotions surged through me. Anger at my parents for treating their children as experiments, regret that I'd never be able to confront them about any of this, and devastation over what it had cost Evan. Fury at all of it surged through my veins.

"Evan's never had any chance at a real life, Ella. He's an addict who will never fully recover. He'd never be more than a burden, a drain on you and on society in general. Would it really be so terrible to allow him to give himself up for the greater good? Let him go. He'll save lives far more valuable than his own."

My rage exploded in a white-hot flash, and the sigils on my arms illuminated even through my jacket. Without conscious effort, I'd reached for the magic of the *in-between*. The silvery power lit up my body like a lighthouse on a dark sea. With it came searing pain, but I didn't care. I relished the hurt.

In a split second, I'd gathered so much power I thought I'd explode. With a scream of rage, I hurled it at Jacob. Agony exploded in my head, but I got a moment of satisfaction as I watched him fly back, slam into the wall, and then crumble to the floor like a rag doll.

Out of the corner of my eyes, I saw a series of flashes. My magic drained away, and I went rigid, and then my muscles all gave way at once.

I lost my hold on consciousness before I hit the floor . . .

Blood.

That was the first thing I noticed when my eyelids cracked open and I lifted my head.

I'd been lying on my side with my arm making a pillow under my head. Blood had leaked from my nose, across my cheekbone, and down onto the sleeve of my jacket. I was painfully stiff, as if I'd been lying in the same position for several hours.

I slowly sat up, and my head seemed to have its own pulse. It was ten times worse than my most epic hangover, and I knew I was in trouble. I'd pulled a lot of magic when I'd lashed out at Jacob. Too much. I swiped under my nose and found that fresh blood was still trickling from my head.

I looked around but couldn't see much in the dark room. The floor beneath my palms was hard, so I knew I was no longer in the carpeted auditorium.

The lights came on, and pain drilled into my eyes as I squinted. Wincing, I stood up, not about to get caught sitting on my ass.

I was having trouble focusing, but when my vision finally cooperated, I found I was in a small room with a horizontal strip of window and a heavy door next to it. I was definitely still on the Gregori campus.

The box was gone. Jacob had no doubt discovered it was empty. So much for any leverage I'd had with him.

Half a dozen people stood at the window, peering at me like I was a monkey at the zoo. One of them was Jacob. Most of the rest I didn't recognize, but there was something oddly similar—

My mouth fell open, and I went completely still.

There, at the left edge of the window, stood Damien.

At first, my heart leapt as I assumed he'd come to somehow bust me out.

But then I saw it. Even from several feet away, I could see the change.

His eyes. The sky blue had paled to a silvery cornflower hue. And his irises shimmered, swimming with tiny points of light.

The eyes of a mage.

He'd done it. He's taken Zarella's deal and received the reward.

Damien was now a mage. But what had it cost him?

The rest of the strangers peering at me were mages, too. Their lips moved as they spoke to each other, and Jacob appeared to chime in, too, but of course I couldn't hear a word of it.

My eyes were drawn back to Damien. His face was stony as he looked at me through the glass, almost as if he didn't recognize me. As my gaze flicked over to the others, it suddenly struck me that there was a strong resemblance between Damien and the stately woman who stood next to Jacob. She had Damien's high brow and cheekbones. And the man on her other side bore an uncanny resemblance to Damien. Remove a couple of decades and thirty pounds, and he could be Damien's brother.

Those had to be his parents, the legendary Steins. What were they doing *here*?

I walked a few steps toward the window.

"What the hell is going on?" I demanded. Even if they couldn't hear me, I was sure they'd get the gist of my question.

I just couldn't for the life of me think of why a group of mages, including Damien's parents, no less, would be interested in me.

I'd been so distracted by Damien and the mages that I hadn't noticed how unhappy Jacob looked. His shoulders tensed, his mouth pinched, his jaw clenched. Not just unhappy, but miserably pissed. That was saying something, considering my uncle normally maintained a façade so smooth it would make a slab of marble jealous.

I went up to the window and rapped on it with my knuckles. I crossed my arms and looked back and forth between Jacob and Damien.

"What. The hell. Is going. On?" I mouthed slowly, exaggerating the words.

Jacob gestured to me through the glass. His mouth moved, and I squinted, trying to read his lips. I was pretty sure I caught the words "her brother."

My heart punched at the thought that they were talking about Evan.

"You don't have the authority to keep him, Jacob! I'm his sister. I demand you release him to me!"

I realized the irony of demanding custody of my brother while I was essentially imprisoned myself, but Jacob had no right. The mages had no right.

I'd found Evan. I'd saved him. Jacob only wanted to sacrifice my brother, and I had no reason to believe the mages had his best interests in mind, either.

God *damn* it.

My gaze locked desperately on Damien's face, but his expression remained impassive. When he glanced at me, it was like he didn't even know me.

Rage began to boil hot under my skin.

I'd searched in vain for five years. Evan was my family. My responsibility. I just wanted him to be left alone.

As my anger intensified, I began to reach for *in-between* magic again. In response, my head thumped as if I'd just been boxed in both temples, and I had to back off. I gritted my teeth, holding back a groan, desperate to keep them from seeing that I was in seriously bad shape.

As I tried to get my emotions under control, thoughts whipped through my mind. Damien had turned. Rogan was gone. Who was left? Zarella. I needed the mad scientist and his underworld cronies. They'd kept Evan out of Jacob's hands for years. They'd help me. Where the hell was Zarella?

Jacob and the mages were shifting around, and I realized they were getting ready to depart from the area outside my cell.

"Wait!" I hollered, but none of them turned.

In desperation, I reached out with my necro senses, searching for a mind to command. There were minor demons lurking outside, but I needed something closer and scarier.

I sensed several large rip spawn grouped together, probably in the same building. I'd never commanded an arch-demon before, but I had to do something.

But then I saw that Damien was hanging back.

He pointed up and said something. I squinted, trying to lip-read.

"Evan is up there," I whispered to myself, imitating Damien's words. "Up? Upstairs."

My heart jumped into my throat as I watched a barely visible filament of white-mage magic curl around his index finger and then snake off to the side and out of view.

With my cheek pressed up against the window, I tried to get a visual angle on what he was doing. Something with the door? I went to it and rattled the handle, but it didn't budge. I moved back to the window and shook my head.

Damien held up a finger, nodded once, and mouthed a word. *Wait.*

I sucked in a breath and stepped back. Damien disappeared from view. My heart pounded in my chest as I waited for a count of five and then tried the door. The handle gave under my hand, and the door opened with a soft click.

I leaned an eye around the doorjamb to make sure no one would see me, and something caught my attention on the floor. A slim line of pale magic led away to the right, the opposite way Damien and the others had gone.

Reaching for the *in-between*, I let myself fade from the realm of the living. A grim smile crossed my face as I saw that Damien's line of magic was visible in limbo land, too. Perfect.

I slipped out of my cell and hurried after Damien's trail.

I sailed through the hallway to the stairwell and ran up three flights taking two stairs at a time, unencumbered by the living and stirring misty eddies as I moved through the *in-between.*

My heart lifted with every step. Damien was helping me. Maybe his transition to mage hadn't affected him in the way Zarella had expected. Whatever the Steins wanted with Evan, Damien was only pretending to be with them. He was on my side.

I followed Damien's line of magic to a set of reinforced double doors. Mage power surrounded the handles in a shimmering white cloud. I grinned, sure I knew what it was. A spell to let me into a secure area.

Sure enough, the handle released under my touch.

The trail led me around a few corners and then stopped at a solid door. Again, the handle was dripping with mage magic. I let myself in to a space that reminded me of a hospital room. There was an adjustable bed and a partially open door at the back that revealed a small bathroom.

When I transitioned back into the realm of the living, I saw that my brother lay still on the bed, sleeping.

I went to him, trying to read his physical state in his face. He was pale and rail thin, his lips were cracked, and bruises in a variety of states of healing showed on the little bit of bare skin that I could see. Even in sleep, the rings around his eyes were shockingly dark. He looked like the life-long junkie that he was.

But there were no IVs or other indications of medical care. His breathing was deep and even, and he just looked like he was taking a nap. I hated to disturb him, but we needed to hurry.

I touched his shoulder. "Evan?"

His brow creased, and he inhaled through his nose before opening his eyes.

"What are you doing here?" he asked, his voice hoarse but stronger than I remembered.

They'd definitely given him something to control his cravings or sedate him, most likely both. I gave him a brief smile before I started moving around the room, looking for some regular clothes, a jacket, and shoes. It was freezing outside, and it looked like Evan was bare-chested.

"Do you know where you are?" I asked over my shoulder. "I've come to take you home."

He let out a sharp, humorless laugh. "I don't have a home. But old Uncle Jacob is really trying to make this look like something other than a prison, isn't he?"

I found a bathrobe, some sweatpants, and a zip-up hooded sweatshirt hanging in the tiny closet, with a pair of slip-on canvas shoes on the floor below. I grabbed everything but the bathrobe and piled it on the foot of the bed. Evan had made no move to get up.

With my hands planted on my hips, I faced my brother. It was time for some tough love.

"He wants to murder you, Evan," I said bluntly. "He thinks sacrificing you will save the world by closing the rips. I think Jacob and a bunch of mages are fighting over you, and I'm pretty sure that's the only reason he hasn't already killed you. I'll leave you here if you'd like. But if you think staying alive might be a priority for you, it's time to get your ass moving. *Now.*"

His eyes widened, and he stared at me for a second. Then he pushed back the covers and swung his legs to the side of the bed. He wore only boxer shorts. I tossed him the clothes. I could tell he was trying to hurry, but my heart plummeted as I watched him. He was weaker than I'd realized. The way he fumbled, I wondered if there was some permanent nerve damage.

Once he had the pants on, I had him sit on the edge of the bed so I could bend down and slip the shoes onto his feet while he pulled on the sweatshirt. On impulse, I went and grabbed the robe and had him put it on over the sweats.

I wrapped my arm around his waist to support him, and he leaned heavily on me as we moved slowly toward the door.

I said something encouraging to him, but inside I honestly couldn't imagine how we would escape without notice. I could vanish into the *in-between*, but I couldn't take Evan there with me. The campus had to be under heavy surveillance.

But Damien had led me here. If he truly wanted me to escape with my brother, maybe there were some things in place to help us get out.

"If I disappear suddenly, just hang in there and do the best you can, okay?" I said to Evan. "I'll reappear, I promise."

He shot me a questioning look.

"I'll explain later," I said hastily. "Keep your head down."

If only I were a mage, I could disguise us both as campus personnel.

As we stood there, an alarm began to blare throughout the floor. My entire body jolted in panic. Had we set it off?

I carefully opened the door with my fingertips.

"Let's go," I said.

Hurrying Evan as fast as I could drag him along, I went for the first turn—a left just up ahead.

People in lab coats were scurrying around, and there were shouts here and there. I expected armed men to surround us at any moment, but after a few seconds, I realized people were trying to leave, not storm us. I heard someone holler something about evacuating, and I suddenly wondered if this was Damien's doing.

Regardless, it created enough chaos that no one seemed to be too concerned about me and Evan. Until they were.

"Hey," one of the labcoats said. She'd been hurrying toward us with her gaze cast down the hall but stopped short and peered at us. "You shouldn't be—"

I drew earth magic, and pain bolted through my head and down my spine. Ignoring it, I cast a ball of green energy into her midsection. She let out an *oof* sound and doubled over as my magic knocked the wind out of her.

I tried to pick up the pace, but Evan kept stumbling. We were going to have to take the elevator. Either that or I'd have to sling him over my shoulder, but I probably wouldn't be able to pick up any speed that way.

"You're bleeding," Evan grunted.

I swiped at my upper lip, and my hand came away streaked with blood. "Don't worry about it," I muttered.

The only advantage to moving so slowly was that everyone else seemed to be evacuating much more quickly than we were, and the hallways were emptying.

I somehow remembered how to get to the elevators, and when the doors opened, fortune gave us the ride all to ourselves. We got off on the ground floor and headed toward the nearest exit. I was starting to think we might actually sneak away in all the chaos when I stepped outside.

"Oh, shit," Evan and I said in unison.

The door slammed closed behind us. We'd exited into what looked like a little plaza, and apparently most of the rest of the people who'd evacuated had decided to convene here too.

"Head down," I said and started aiming us to the right, hoping to skirt the edge of the crowd and get around the corner. We made it about twenty steps.

"Stop," a male voice commanded behind us.

I kept going, and I reached out for the nearest rip spawn. Zarella had to have plenty of them lurking close by.

"Hey! You, stop right there!"

A zombie. There was a zombie heading this way. Odd, but whatever. I just wanted to command it long enough to distract the guard coming after us. I probed for the zombie's mind, but found it blocked from my control.

Actually, there were a *bunch* zombies coming.

I cringed just as they came into view. But I recognized one of them. It was the zombie Zarella had sent to talk to me on the desert highway, the same one who'd spoken to me after the underworld induction ceremony.

Evan sucked in a breath as the zombies sped over to us.

"It's okay," I whispered to him. I swallowed hard. "At least, I'm pretty sure it is. Not like we have many options at the moment."

The small horde surrounded us with a precision that was almost comical, considering.

"Come this way," the one just ahead of me said.

I looked back at the guard who'd been pursuing us. Two of his buddies had joined him, but they'd stopped where they were, obviously put off by the zombies. They were all hollering furiously into their walkie-talkies.

The horde took us around a corner and then veered sharply to the left into an open garage door.

Zarella stood there, right next to—

"Lynnette?" I blinked a few times to make sure I wasn't seeing things.

The zombies lined up against the wall as the garage door lowered.

She kept flicking glances at Zarella, and she was fiddling with her keys. She seemed thoroughly creeped out by him.

"What are you doing here?" I asked her.

"No time for that," Zarella cut in. "You all need to get out of here. As soon as you're off the grounds, you can call on the help of the authorities if you need to. Here, you're completely at Gregori's mercy."

He was gesturing urgently at a high-end SUV parked behind him. It was Lynnette's car.

I shook my head, trying to get the pieces to fit as I helped Evan into the back seat. Lynnette jumped in and started the engine, and I slid into the front passenger seat just as another door, this one at the back, began to rise.

Zarella nodded at us and then stepped off to the side. Lynnette threw the SUV into reverse and squealed out of the garage.

Lynnette seemed to know exactly where to go, and we managed to exit the grounds without anyone trying to stop us.

My pulse was still racing.

Once we were out on the highway, I turned to her. "How . . .?"

"Deb got in touch with me when she couldn't reach you." She was gripping the wheel tightly with both hands and driving about twice the speed limit. "She'd talked to that detective guy, and he told her you'd said Jacob took your brother. She asked me to help. I wasn't sure what I'd find, so I wouldn't let her come."

"And Zarella?" I asked.

"When I got here, they wouldn't let me through the gate, and they wouldn't tell me anything. I drove around the property trying to find a different way in. That's when a zombie opened one of the gates for me. Did you know Phillip Zarella was still alive?" She writhed a little in a full-body cringe.

"Yeah," I admitted. "I found out recently."

I couldn't help staring at her.

She glanced at me. "What?"

"I just can't believe you did this," I said.

She frowned as if my statement made no sense. "We may have our differences, but we're still coven sisters, Ella."

I pulled a sour face. Right. Coven sisters.

I checked behind us to make sure we weren't being pursued. Then I remembered the mages. Zarella wasn't quite right about us being safe once off Gregori property.

"Shit, we can't go back home," I said. "There are, uh, people looking for my brother."

"Come to my place," she said without hesitation.

"I'm Evan, by the way," my brother said from the back seat.

I glanced back at him. He was hunched over as if it were too much effort to hold his spine straight.

"Oh yeah, sorry," I said. "Evan, this is Lynnette, the, uh, leader of the coven Deb and I are in."

He snickered hoarsely. "You're in a coven, El?"

"Not by choice," I muttered. But I couldn't help a little spark of happiness at his comment. It was one of the few even remotely personal things he'd said since I'd found him in the vampire feeder den.

"How'd you get away from the dragon?" I asked Lynnette.

Her mouth twisted. "I had to make a sacrifice."

I looked at her in horror. "You *what*?"

"Not a blood sacrifice," she said hastily. "I had to give up one of my abilities. He let me choose. I'm . . . no longer an exorcist."

My brows rose, and I watched her face in profile. I wasn't sure if she looked more on the verge of vomiting or crying. Wow. She'd lost one of her most coveted abilities. If she hadn't been so scheming and unscrupulous up to this point, I might have felt some sympathy. But she'd made that bed.

"Bummer," I said to her, but I didn't have the energy or the desire to talk about Lynnette's problems. I had plenty of my own. "You need to know the dangers of taking us in."

I explained about Jacob and the mages, staying vague about why they all wanted my brother so badly. And I didn't go into the whole backstory about how my brother and I might have been living experiments.

Lynnette wasn't as surprised as I would have expected, but then she'd probably seen a lot of strange shit.

"We'll shore up the wards," was all she said.

We rode in silence for a couple of minutes.

"You need some major healing. I'm sure I don't have to tell you you're in bad shape," she said to me quietly. "And he needs to be in detox."

I nodded. "That obvious, huh?"

I pulled out my phone, forgetting the battery had gone dead. I swore under my breath.

"Call Deb," Lynnette said, handing me her phone as if she'd read my mind.

I scrolled to the Ds in her contacts and paused. Damien's name was in there, too. I paused. He and Lynnette knew each other through me, of course, but I wouldn't have expected that they'd exchanged phone numbers.

I nearly teared up a little when I heard Deb's voice. I quickly summarized the last few hours for her. When I got to the part about the mages, I stayed purposely vague and said I'd explain it all later. She promised to meet us at Lynnette's.

"Your magic has increased," Lynnette said to me after I ended the call.

"Yeah," I said, guarded.

"You used to be a barely-Level-I. Now you're a high Level I," she pressed.

I pushed stray strands of hair behind my ears.

"Things have been different since I got my magic back," I lied. "I guess between the reaper, the ability to access power from the *in-between*, and the spells that gave me my abilities back, something just got knocked loose. I've barely had a chance to even think about it. Pretty fricking crazy, isn't it?"

She slipped a glance at me, and I could tell she wasn't buying it. I also saw the gleam in her eye, the one that always made my stomach tighten. It was that hunger that constantly seemed to lurk just below the surface of her carefully fashioned goth-chic appearance. That ever-present yearning for power.

"It's beyond crazy," she said. "It's unheard of. You're a miracle of the supernatural world."

I let out a heavy sigh. "I wouldn't know how to repeat it, and I don't want to become news. Don't tell anyone, okay?"

I watched as the tip of her tongue slipped out to moisten her lips.

"I won't say anything to outsiders, of course," she assured me. "The others in the coven will notice, but—"

"Coven sisters wouldn't betray me," I supplied. "Right?"

"Exactly."

We'd arrived at Lynnette's, and she drove around into the alley so she could pull into the garage.

I looked over my shoulder at my brother, who appeared to be asleep with his head propped against the window.

"Hey, Evan," I said. "We're here."

We quickly helped him inside and got him settled in one of Lynnette's guest rooms. I made him drink some water, and when I went to set the glass on the nightstand, he clutched my wrist.

"They gave me something in there," he said, his voice tremoring a little. "But I can feel it starting to wear off. I'm going to need a fix. Soon."

There was a faint sheen of sweat on his face and neck, and one eye was twitching a little. My chest clenched. I'd known this was coming, but still, it hurt. He was heavily addicted to the euphoria-inducing chemical in vampire saliva. When he came off whatever the doctors at Gregori had pumped into him, he would turn into a violent, feral version of himself. Without another fix, he'd eventually go into fatal cardiac arrest.

"I'll get something for you," I said. I wasn't sure how or where, but I'd figure it out.

He leaned back, his head sinking against the pillow, and closed his eyes. I let out a slow breath, relieved to see him peaceful for a moment at least.

As I walked down the hallway back to the main living area, I heard Lynnette talking in a low voice on her phone. When she saw me, she said another word or two and then hung up.

"He's going to need a fix," I said. "Any chance you know someone who could help?"

I wasn't plugged into the drug scene, and I was afraid it would take me too long to chase down a connection.

"I've called a couple of healers," she said, all business. "One is Gina, who you know. Another has some experience with your brother's issues."

My shoulders sagged in relief. "Thank you."

She fiddled with her phone for a second. "I've been meaning to say something about what happened with the oracle."

I tried to keep my face composed. Was Lynnette Leblanc really going to apologize?

"I didn't remember that the skull ring was charmed," she said. "Honestly, it was an old spell that had almost completely worn off, and I didn't even think about it when I gave you the ring."

I narrowed my eyes. I wanted to believe her, but I didn't. Regardless, she'd saved my ass, and Evan's too. Not to mention that the dragon had already dished out a pretty stiff punishment. I was willing to let it slide.

"No worries," I said. "You're making up for it now. Let's call it even."

She gave me a smile. The doorbell rang, and I think both of us were relieved for the interruption. It was Deb. A few minutes later the healers arrived.

I'd been on guard since we'd reached Lynnette's, expecting Jacob's men or the Steins to come crashing through the door at any moment. But it had been nearly an hour since we'd made our getaway. Maybe Damien was doing something to help hold them off. I'd left my phone on Lynnette's charger, and I was tempted to go get it and send him a text. But if he was posing as an ally to the mages, I needed to let him keep his cover.

Gina had me recline on one of Lynnette's leather sofas. Before I let her begin, I reached out with my necro senses for minor demons. Finding one hanging out in a nearby attic, I took control of its mind and positioned it at the top of a power pole with a clear view of all approaches to Lynnette's house. I would have commanded more if I thought I could keep the links during the healing, but I knew I'd have to devote a good portion of my attention and energy to Gina's work.

"Don't take me too deep," I said. "I need to stay vigilant."

Her brow creased. "You've got the start of permanent damage, Ella. You need a long course of deep-healing sessions, beginning with a few days of inpatient treatment, ideally."

I waved a hand. "I know it's bad, but I can't afford that right now." If she only knew just how many ways I couldn't afford it.

She pursed her lips with disapproval but didn't press me.

I drifted a bit, allowing my body to relax while I kept my mind focused on the demon lookout.

After a while, I felt Gina starting to withdraw her magic, signaling that the healing was almost finished. At the same time, my demon minion stirred. At first I thought it was in response to the healing that caused some sort of change in my hold on its mind, but it became steadily more agitated.

I bolted upright, looking through the demon's eyes. I felt it coming a split second before it happened. Just as I retracted my connection, the creatures mind imploded. Before I lost the demon, I'd seen a flash in the sky like sheet lightning, but it was too pure white to be a storm. Magic crackled through my supernatural senses.

I rose to my feet and then reeled so hard I had to grab the edge of the sofa to keep from falling over.

"Lynnette, help me!"

She appeared in the kitchen doorway, her eyes round. "What was that?"

"Mage magic!"

I whirled around, sprinted unsteadily for Evan's room, and burst through the door. Lynnette and Deb were right on my heels. I reached for the light switch but didn't need to flip it on because the pure white glow of mage magic filled the room.

There were two people standing at the foot of the bed. One of them was my brother. The other was Damien, who was also the source of the light. My heart lifted at first, but something was wrong. The way Damien clutched at Evan's waist and arm was anything but friendly. And the blank look on Damien's face made my blood run cold.

Both of them seemed to pale, as if a black and white filter had suddenly dropped between me and them. Then the lines defining them began to smudge.

"No!" I cried, lunging for Evan.

My fingertips clutched the terrycloth sleeve of his robe, but before I could pull him to me, the fabric dissolved to nothing in my hand.

And then they were gone.

Shaking with fear and anger, I faded to the *in-between*.

Damien had used mage power to teleport himself and Evan. Up to then, I'd thought mages could only project images of themselves, not physically teleport their bodies. It was probably one of those abilities that was supposed to be kept secret from non-mages.

Well, two could play at the magical teleporting game.

If I could catch up with him, I might have a chance. That trick he'd pulled should have left him magically drained for a while.

In the realm of mist, I grabbed the glass of water on the nightstand and dipped a ghostly finger in it. I pictured the living room of Damien's loft and touched the water again.

When I returned to the living realm, I was standing next to Damien's kitchen island. I went into a defensive stance and whipped around, not sure of who or what I'd find there. But the place was empty.

I didn't have to check the other rooms. It looked like Damien hadn't been here in a while. The items we'd set on the floor around the sofa when he'd raised my magical aptitude were still there.

Turning again, slowly this time, betrayal stabbed through my fear. I'd thought he was on my side, but he'd helped me free my brother only to steal Evan himself.

"Damn it, Damien!" My voice cracked as my anger echoed briefly through the spacious, modern apartment.

As I stood there while my temples were pulsing a hard, outraged rhythm, my fists clenched and shaking at my sides, I wished he would appear right now. If he did, I swore I'd kill him or die trying.

How could he do this?

I wanted to keep searching, but I had no idea where else Damien would go. He could be anywhere, and it struck me that even before his transition to mage I hadn't really known him that well at all. I hadn't realized it at the time because Damien had always helped me. He'd always been right there, ready and willing. I'd just kept overlooking his true obsession, or assuming nothing bad would come of it.

I should have seen there was more behind his actions. He'd literally told me that the only thing he wanted in life was to not be the black sheep of the Stein family. Tagging along with me on my little adventures had been at best an amusement for him. At worst, maybe something more sinister.

But now I knew for sure—he didn't really care about anything else.

I looked out the huge windows at the twilight sky, searching it as if I'd find answers on the horizon.

Since he had what he'd always longed for, what was he going to do with my brother? What was Damien's new obsession? Did he still have something to prove to his family?

I went to the bowl of water on the floor, the one we'd placed at the traditional west position for that element, and used it to go back to Lynnette's.

I walked down the dark hallway and found Lynnette and Deb both on their phones. The healers were gone. Deb stiffened in surprise when she saw me, and she quickly ended her call.

I sat on the sofa and dropped my face into my hands. "I went to Damien's. They weren't there."

When I looked up, I saw Deb and Lynnette both staring at me with wide eyes. Lynnette licked her lips, and I could see she was dying with curiosity about the disappearing act I'd just pulled. Deb made a little gesture with her hand, and a slight frown passed over Lynnette's face. She pressed her lips together, as if holding back the questions that wanted to spill out.

I pressed my fingers over my closed eyelids, wishing I could rewind time. Wishing I could have grabbed Evan before he disappeared with Damien.

The cushion shifted as Deb sat next to me. She placed her hand on my back and moved it in small circles, trying to soothe away pain that had no cure.

"I just spoke to Chris and told him that Damien abducted Evan," she said. "He's going to use his channels to try to help."

I looked up. "Chris?"

"Lagatuda," she said with a wry twitch of one corner of her mouth.

I sighed heavily. "Thanks."

She moved again, and I could tell she had about a million questions on the tip of her tongue. She was trying to be sensitive to my feelings, but she'd probably just witnessed about half a dozen things she didn't understand.

"Go ahead, fire," I said.

"Damien is a mage? What the . . . ? And how in the world did you just disappear and then come back?"

Lynnette joined us, staring at me with open curiosity and waiting for me to respond.

I stood up and began pacing. "Yes, Damien is now a mage. He made a deal with the devil, but I don't know any more than that. As for my disappearing act, well, that's a reaper trick and what happens in the *in-between* stays in the *in-between*."

No one laughed at my weak-ass joke. Lynnette looked like a cat who'd just found a bird with a broken wing.

"Don't get any ideas," I said to her. "It's something only reapers can do."

"I'm just interested, that's all," she said, smoothing her expression.

Right. If there was a way she could siphon away my necro abilities, connection with *in-between* magic, and reaper tricks, she'd do it in a heartbeat.

I swore quietly. "What am I going to do? I don't know where Damien took Evan. Seriously, I'm open to ideas. Wide open."

Lynnette was still staring at me, her head tilted. I felt tendrils of her magic creeping around the room. What the *hell*? Was she seriously trying to manipulate me now of all times?

"Seriously, witch, don't push me," I said through clenched teeth. I started to reach for my own magic.

Deb stood and moved in between us.

"No, no," Lynnette said. "I'm not trying to do anything, I swear. There's . . . something. A spell around you. Or in you."

She squinted, concentrating.

"Yeah, I've got a couple of permanent spells on me now," I said, suddenly a little nervous. "One keeps the reaper under control. The other restricts the *in-between* magic to a manageable flow. But you already knew that."

Deb was staring at me, too. "It's not either of those."

"It's like it's hidden," Lynnette said. "Or it was, anyway."

"No longer hidden, but still locked," Deb agreed.

They were both moving closer to me, and I could feel and see their probing tendrils of magic swirling around me, lightly brushing me.

Lynnette glanced at Deb. "Do you see how to release it?"

Deb nodded.

"*What*? What is it?" I demanded.

Deb blinked several times. "I don't know how to describe it, other than a—a new capacity? A space waiting to be activated. A whole bunch of power, like more than I have, just waiting to be set free."

"Huh?" I looked to Lynnette for clarification.

Just then, the front bell rang and we all jumped.

"I invited the rest of the coven for support," Lynnette said as she hurried to get the door.

I gave Deb a frustrated, bug-eyed look. The absolute last thing I needed to deal with was a roomful of witches.

"Don't worry, she didn't tell them everything," Deb said. "Only that your brother has been kidnapped by a mage. Try to be open to their help. Who knows, they might actually come up with something useful."

I made an annoyed sound deep in my throat.

Some of my irritation dissolved when I saw Roxanne's corn silk blond head bop through the doorway. With Deb as her mentor, she'd become a sort of unofficial apprentice of the coven.

When she saw me, she ran up and wrapped her arms around my waist.

"I'm so sorry about your brother," she said. "We'll get him back. We have to, 'cause I really want to meet him."

My chest loosened a little, and her innocent sincerity made my eyes a little misty.

"I really want you to meet him, too," I said.

When she pulled back, she tipped her face up to give me a curious look. "Whoa. You've changed. Like, magically."

I gave a little laugh. "Yeah."

Her lips parted, and her eyes went distant. Her magic passed over me like a soft sigh of wind.

"You're sensing something?" I asked.

She nodded. "There's Damien magic on you."

I pulled my head back in confusion, my heart thumping uneasily at the mention of Damien's name. "What do you mean?"

"He attached a spell to you," Roxanne said. "Weird."

Deb was standing close enough to hear, and our eyes met. Roxanne had a unique ability that allowed her to identify who had touched objects, and apparently also who had cast spells.

"You're saying the spell Ella is carrying, the one that's dormant, was put there by Damien?" Deb asked her.

"Yep!" Roxanne said.

She didn't know that Damien had abducted my brother. She still thought Damien was our friend.

"Can you tell how long ago it was put there?" I asked.

Roxanne squinted at me for a few seconds.

"Couple of days, maybe?" Her face broke into a little grin. "Is Damien playing some kind of joke on you?"

"I'm not sure," I said.

But suddenly I knew what the spell was. He'd raised me from a low Level I to a high Level I, and he'd done something else, something he obviously hadn't discussed with me.

A whole bunch of power just waiting to be set free, Deb had said.

Damien had left me with the potential to raise my power even more. I'd bet anything that unlocking the spell would take me all the way to the top of the scale—a high Level III.

Why would he have done such a thing? Could he have possibly guessed that I would need more power . . . to go up against him?

No, that was too much of a stretch. Maybe he'd planted it with plans to do something with it later, but then he'd become a mage and no longer cared about the same things he had before.

Roxanne had drifted away to talk to the other witches.

"Deb," I said, my voice low. "I need to know what this is, what spell Damien planted on me."

"It's *Damien's* spell?"

I stiffened and turned to see Lynnette, who'd been standing just outside my periphery but apparently close enough to eavesdrop. She moved closer, again reminding me of a cat stalking its prey.

"That spell is Damien's work?" she asked again.

I nodded reluctantly. "Apparently."

Her eyes shone with interest, and her lips parted. "Let's see what it does."

I lifted a hand. "Wait, how do we know it's not going to make my head explode like a rotted melon, or end us all in a blast of obliteration magic?"

"Rox might be able to tell us something more about the nature of it," Deb said. She turned and called Roxanne back over.

I let out a slow breath, trying to calm my pulse.

"Can you tell us anything about the intent of the spell?" Deb asked Roxanne. "The spirit in which it was created, or anything about the emotions or mood around it?"

"I can try." The young witch cocked her head. I felt the faint brush of her magic, and a faraway look came over her face. She was silent for a full minute, and I was starting to think perhaps her abilities weren't quite up to what Deb thought they were. But then Roxanne blinked and focused on me. "It's not a trick. There's nothing mal—, malifous—"

"Malicious?" Deb supplied.

"Yeah, that," Roxanne said. "No malicious intent."

I licked my dry lips.

"Let's check it out," Lynnette said.

My eyes swept the room, taking in all the coven witches who'd gathered. "Maybe not with so many people around. In case something goes wrong."

Or in case the spell had an effect I didn't want the others to know about.

Lynnette stepped away from us and pulled herself up to her full height. "Hey ladies," she called over the backdrop of conversation. "Could you give Deb, Ella, and I just a moment? We'll meet you down in the basement."

The witches sent somber and sympathetic looks my way as they complied with Lynnette's request.

After they departed, the room seemed too quiet. My heart thumped uneasily.

"What if it's some kind of trap?" Deb asked. "Something he planted to keep Ella from going after Evan? Just because it's not malicious doesn't mean it's not something *unwanted*."

I shook my head. "I don't think it is. When he left the dormant spell, he didn't know he was going to take my brother. He didn't yet know Evan was . . . valuable. He may have had other reasons for leaving this spell, but he couldn't have known what was going to happen."

And I didn't say it, but Damien and I had left each other on more-or-less affectionate terms. We both knew that he was going to take Zarella's deal, and we knew it was going to change things. Sure, Damien had his own motives—he always had—but I didn't believe he'd meant to harm me. Not then. Now, though, was a whole different can of worms.

"Stay back, Deb. I don't want you to get caught in the blowback if something goes wacky," I said quietly. I faced Lynnette. "I want you to do it. Release the spell."

The gleam in her eyes almost made me take it back, but I wanted whatever power Damien had gifted me. I would need it if I were to have any hope at all of getting Evan back.

Lynnette's eyes became faraway as she focused on drawing magic. Then she turned her focus onto me. I saw delicate strands of elemental power weave through the air like trails of pixie dust.

"Stay still," she whispered.

Her magic suddenly cascaded over me like a bucket of cold ice water. Every muscle in my body went rigid, and it felt like an arctic tornado was sweeping out my insides. I groaned, clamping my teeth together in an effort to keep from moving. The swirling sensation grew more violent, and with it a nauseating motion sickness.

A million icy little points seemed to be speeding around inside me, darting between my cells and streaming through my blood vessels.

Then it receded, leaving me shivering and disoriented.

I blinked hard as my senses returned.

Swaying and knowing I was about to go down, my hands blindly reached for something to hold. Lynnette slung an arm around my waist and caught me with a grunt, lowering me to the floor.

I stared up at her, watching as swirling colors like rainbows on a soap bubble glowed around her. She let go of her magic, and the colors extinguished.

"How do you pull air magic?" I whispered. "I've never done it. I don't even know how."

Lynnette and Deb were both kneeling in front of me with tense looks on their faces.

"Focus on your breath," Deb said. "And think about the power of air, like in a storm. Then direct your thoughts just above your left palm, as if you're catching a vortex of wind there."

I did as she directed, focusing my full attention on the task. Nothing happened for several seconds. But then a rush of power moved the tiny hairs on my arm and a gyrating little vortex of blue magic danced in my hand.

Magic twirled through me like a breeze. The sheer movement and lightness of it were thrilling and exhilarating, so different from earth and fire.

"Ella," Lynnette said.

I looked up at her, which broke my concentration. The funnel of air magic disappeared.

"You're a Level III now," she said. "You're . . . more powerful than I am."

I breathed deeply, sensing the magnitude of the magic I could pull, but almost not believing it.

I wondered if Damien knew that I'd activated the spell, if he had any idea how readily I would use his gift against him in order to save my brother. A new determination welled up alongside my newfound power.

Jacob had said the Order of Mages had come to the same conclusion that he had about using Evan to close the rips. Before Damien had become a mage, he'd expressed disdain for the Order. But Zarella had warned that the power would change Damien, that he wouldn't be the same person afterward. I'd seen my old partner standing there with the Steins and looking quite at ease. Damien must have taken Evan as part of a ploy to get in good with the mages. To finally gain the acceptance in the Stein family.

Damien hadn't been helping me at all. He'd just wanted someone to get Evan out of Jacob's hands. Then Damien had swooped in to take the prize for himself. He might have thought he'd won, but I wouldn't let Evan slip away from me again.

About the Author

Jayne Faith writes fantasy set in the real world. She's a meditator, dog lover, TV addict, clean eater, homebody, sun baby, and Sagittarius. Her superpower is her laugh. She owns way too many colored pens and pairs of jeans. Visit her website at www.jaynefaith.com, where you can sign up for her VIP list and get free books.